It was the worst winter in London's history, and the worst dilemma in Meg's.

Fiery Lady Margaret Underwood thoroughly enjoyed being single and the toast of the *ton*. But Lady Meg also enjoyed being immensely wealthy, and by the terms of the late Earl of Barringham's will, she would soon have to marry or give up her fortune.

Then she found herself challenged by a man as stubbornly devoted to his bachelorhood as she was to her own willful ways...

Elizabeth Mansfield
The Frost Fair

BERKLEY BOOKS, NEW YORK

THE FROST FAIR

A Berkley Book / published by arrangement with
the author

PRINTING HISTORY
Berkley edition / April 1982

ISBN: 0-425-05362-8

A BERKLEY BOOK® TM 757,375

The name "BERKLEY" and the stylized "B" with design are trademarks
belonging to Berkley Publishing Corporation.

PRINTED IN THE UNITED STATES OF AMERICA

NOTE TO THE READER

The strangest part of this story is the behavior of the weather. It is also the only part which is not fiction . . .

Chapter One

For Meg Underwood, rapidly approaching the end of her twenty-fifth year, time was running out. If she didn't take herself a husband within the next five months (for in March of 1814 she would turn twenty-six), the bulk of her enormous fortune would go to a distant cousin whom she utterly loathed. *That* was the stipulation her father, the stubborn old Earl of Barringham, had added to his will when he'd begun to realize that his only child, with her proclivities to arrogance and independence, was rejecting out of hand every suitable match which was offered to her. "And *that*," Meg declared angrily to her aunt who sat watching her with amused eyes as the girl paced angrily about the drawing room of the fashionable town house they occupied in Dover Street, "is how he arranged to exert his control over me, even from the grave!"

"Margaret Underwood, be *fair!*" the diminutive, grey-haired Isabel Underwood exclaimed. Her late husband's brother had been the most indulgent of fathers to Meg. How could the girl, willful and headstrong though she sometimes was, speak so unkindly of the father she'd always adored? "He only wanted to be sure you'd have babies and carry on the line."

"Babies! The line! Really, Aunt Bel, sometimes I wish I'd been born a housemaid or the daughter of a chimney sweep so that I wouldn't have to concern myself with the *line.*"

Isabel Underwood snorted. "What utter drivel! If you're going to speak nonsense, we shall get nowhere."

"Yes, of course you're right," Meg sighed, dropping abruptly into a chair and propping her chin in her cupped hand. "If I were the sort who'd be content to be poor, there'd be no problem—I would simply remain single and permit my cousin to *have* the estate."

"If marriage is truly so repugnant to you, dearest," Aunt Isabel suggested sympathetically, "you may quite easily do just that. Let the estate go. We shan't be poor. I have my jointure, modest though it is, and you'd have a sizeable competence. Together we could contrive. We'd have to give up this house, of course, and move to a neighborhood a bit less in vogue—"

"Stop! Next you'll tell me that I'd have to turn my gowns and mend the holes in my gloves! I'm much too spoiled, I'm afraid, to become accustomed to pretty economies. Besides, marriage is *not* repugnant to me. I fully intend to enter into wedlock one day. I simply want to do it in my own time."

Isabel shook her head, unconvinced. "You've had a great deal of time already, Meg. Don't fool yourself. A woman of twenty-five, no matter how attractive, is already considered by the world to have passed her prime."

Now it was Meg who snorted. "I don't care *what* the world thinks. I've never yet lacked for suitors, have I?"

"No, you haven't, for which you can thank your father's wealth quite as much as your own charms, which I don't deny are abundant. But as you grow older, my love—and certainly as soon as it becomes known that your fortune has passed to other hands—you'll find that the number of gentlemen who come knocking at your door will drastically diminish."

"Thank you, Aunt Bel," her niece said drily. "You've cheered me up considerably."

"I had no intention of cheering you. I'm simply pointing

out that, if you are to marry at all, you're not likely to find a better field to choose from than the present one or a better time than right now."

Meg gave a rueful laugh. "The field is quite small, I'm afraid, if one eliminates the impossibles. Ferdie Sanbourne is too much the fop, Sir Alfred is a pompous ass, and Jack Kingsley, while he's the most entertaining of the lot, has too great an attachment to his mama. That leaves only—"

"Arthur Steele and Charles Isham."

"Yes. And while my enthusiasm for either one falls far short of the romantic, I can think of no major objections . . ."

"Oh good!" Aunt Isabel chirped in pleased surprise. "Now we need only decide which one."

Meg sighed in joyless acceptance of her fate. "I suppose it may as well be Charles."

"Really, Meggie?" Isabel beamed. "I hoped you would choose him. But I thought it was Steele you thought the more forceful of the two."

"Yes, perhaps. But he seems so content in his bachelorhood, one can't be sure he'd adjust to marriage with sufficient dedication. Besides, Charles is more . . . er . . ."

"Dignified?" Isabel supplied.

"Yes, dignified is the perfect word for him," Meg agreed, although her tone seemed to imply that dignity was not a quality she found exciting.

"And he's quite handsome, too, don't you think?" Isabel pressed, hoping that by her fervency she might inspire some in Meg. "The sort of distinguished features one likes to think *belong* with titles and estates."

Meg was not taken in. "Yes," she said scornfully, "the sort of looks which cry out for portraiture. I shall arrange for us to be painted together—his dignity shall soften my flamboyance, and my disreputability shall soften his pomposity."

Isabel couldn't help giggling. "That proves how well you match. Quite the perfect pairing."

Meg only grunted in disgust.

Isabel studied her with sudden misgivings. "If you're really so unwilling, love—"

"I'm not unwilling. Truly, Aunt Bel. Speaking quite seriously, I find Charles to be one of the most sensible of the men in my circle. Don't you agree?"

"Yes, he is. And quite well-read."

"And his lineage is impeccable, too," Meg added, a little twitch showing at the corners of her mouth.

Isabel, recognizing the teasing glint in her niece's eyes, tried to keep the discussion meaningful. "And he has a *kind, generous* nature," she said impressively.

"Oh, yes, very," Meg agreed, trying to keep the signs of irony from her voice. "And he has a country seat in Yorkshire—quite splendid, too, they say."

As if his property mattered, Isabel thought, frowning with annoyance. Meg had enough property of her own to suit the greediest of landowners. The girl was merely making light of a situation which Isabel felt was fraught with importance for her future. "He has a very strong *character,*" she said sternly, "and *that* is what counts."

"Yes, indeed," Meg said with exaggerated admiration, "and he's a viscount, too."

"He, at least, has a sense of *seriousness."*

"And a house in town..."

"And not the slightest touch of *vulgarity,* like some I know!" Isabel said, her mouth pursed with disapproval.

"And the most magnificent collection of carriages..."

"And a true sense of *moral rectitude...*"

"And if rumor may be believed, at least twenty thousand a year."

This was more than Isabel could stand. She uttered a shriek of laughter and soon doubled over in a paroxysm of guffaws. She was promptly joined by her niece, and the two laughed till they ached. "Oh, M-Meggie," Isabel gasped weakly when she could catch her breath, "must you be so silly? Lord Isham is a perfectly fine specimen—"

"I know, I know. I'll wed him, I promise." She jumped up from her chair. "Only please stop singing his praises, because the more you do it, the less appetizing he becomes. Come, let's go to bed before you make him seem so *worthy* I shall change my mind." Not permitting her aunt to utter another word, she pulled the older woman to her feet and, with one affectionate arm around her aunt's waist, led her from the room.

Isabel Underwood went to bed that night more relaxed in her mind than she'd been in months. She'd been more a mother than an aunt to Meg for many years, and all during that time, the girl had caused more than her share of motherly concern.

But now, *at last,* she'd agreed to marry. Isabel was certain Charles would make a satisfactory husband...if only Meg wouldn't change her mind.

The trouble with Meg was, and always had been, an excess of independence. Independence was a quality which Isabel very much admired, but an excess of it could be dangerous. An independent spirit could fool a girl into believing she could live her life alone. When young and surrounded by admirers, a girl might not realize how lonely life could become later. And Meg was twenty-five—no longer a girl at all. If she were not the dazzling, wealthy, titian-haired Lady Margaret Underwood, she might very well be called an old maid!

Of course, the epithet is ridiculous when applied to Meg, Isabel told herself as she snuggled in among the pillows. There wasn't a day that passed when the door knocker didn't sound at least half-a-dozen times to announce callers and admirers. If Meg were not so blastedly independent, she could have accepted one of those suitors years ago and had a brood of babies by this time!

In the matter of marriage, the girl's ideas were beyond Isabel's understanding. Aside from the material advantage which would come to her as soon as she signed the marriage vows, didn't Meg realize how much happiness she could gain by entering into wedlock? Didn't she want a family? Her parents were both dead, and her family was reduced to one widowed aunt—herself. Didn't the girl realize that a family circle of two was not enough?

But she was berating herself to no purpose, she remembered—the girl had agreed to *do* it. Meg would marry Lord Isham, and Isabel would have babies to dandle on her knee at last! With a final prayer that her willful niece would not change her mind, she pulled the coverlet to her neck and let herself slip into sleep.

Miraculously, Meg did not change her mind. True to her word, the very next evening she permitted Charles, Viscount Isham, to make a formal proposal of marriage, which she just as formally accepted. The news of the forthcoming nuptials, however, was withheld from the world until Lady Margaret Underwood could be presented to the Viscount's mother. The dowager Lady Isham was permanently ensconced at Isham

Manor in Yorkshire, but she promptly wrote a most cordial note inviting Meg and her aunt to the estate where, she said, a dinner would be held for members of the Isham family and a few close friends, at which the betrothal would be officially announced.

No one outside the family was to be informed of the news until the proper time, but Meg felt that it would be cruel to allow Arthur Steele, the most persistent of her admirers, to learn of the situation by reading of it in the *Times*. Therefore, late in October, a day before she was to depart for the north, she asked him to call and broke the news to him.

Arthur, a large, burly, cheerfully stoic fellow, was far less chagrined than Meg had expected. "You'll never go through with it," he said with unflappable confidence. "One week in Isham's company—and they say his place is so isolated there'll be precious little else you'll be able to do but endure his company—and you'll come flying home for good."

"If I didn't care for Charles' companionship, I wouldn't be marrying him," Meg said testily.

"The only reason you imagine you care for his companionship, my dear girl, is because you don't *know* him."

Meg, quite unsure of her decision in the first place, was scarcely reassured by Arthur's remarks. But pride, loyalty to her betrothed and a growing concern about her future made her staunchly defensive. "I know him as well as you do, Arthur. You're only saying these things because you don't want to face defeat."

Arthur shrugged, picked up his hat and stick and started for the door. "Don't want to get into a wrangle with you, my dear, especially since you seem to have made up your mind. Stubborn as a mule once you've made up your mind, and you always were. But I'd be willing to put up a hundred guineas to your *one* that you'll be back and ready for me within a fortnight."

"Done!" Meg said promptly, with a show of confidence she was far from feeling. "It's a wager."

He grinned, nodded and opened the door. "Is Isham driving you and your aunt up to Yorkshire himself?"

"Yes. We leave tomorrow."

"Then you won't have your own carriage with you?"

"No, of course not. Why?"

Arthur rubbed his chin thoughtfully with the head of his

walking stick. "I was just wondering how you'll manage to get away from him if you should decide to cut your stay short," he muttered, half to himself.

"What's this? Are you already searching for excuses to explain why I'd fail to return in time for you to win the wager?" Meg grinned in amusement. "Are you trying to hedge off your bet, Mr. Steele?"

"Not at all, my dear, not at all. If you make up your mind to escape—and you will—I'm certain you'll contrive somehow. Meg Underwood is not a girl who'd be likely to permit a little thing like the lack of a carriage to keep her imprisoned. So have yourself a very good journey, my dear."

"Thank you, sir, I shall."

"Tell you what, Meg," he said with sudden inspiration. "When you decide the time has come to make an escape—"

"*If* I decide to make an escape," she corrected.

"*If*, then. If you decide to make a run for it, send me word. I'll meet you in . . . in Harrogate and escort you back to London. How's that for gallantry?"

"It's very gallant indeed. But I shouldn't wager any more than you already have on the likelihood, if I were you."

"It's likelier than you know. Charles Isham, my dear, is a deadly bore. As soon as you realize it, get word to me. Harrogate, remember. The White Hart in Harrogate. It's a quite respectable hostelry where you and your aunt can find comfortable, safe refuge until I arrive to take you home."

"You know, Arthur," she said, suddenly serious, "even if I should send for you to escort me home, it wouldn't mean that I would necessarily agree to accept *you* in Charles' place at the altar."

He shrugged. "I know that. No obligations on either side, agreed?"

"Agreed." She smiled at him warmly. "I may not find you suitable as a husband, my dear, but I couldn't find a better friend."

He blew her a parting kiss. "We friends make the very best husbands, and so you'll learn for yourself one day. See if you don't."

Meg was to remember those words. Shockingly often, during the week that followed, they came back to haunt her, for

Charles Isham turned out to be, just as Arthur had predicted, the most crushing bore. It amazed her that she'd not recognized that quality in him earlier. She should have seen it from the first. After two days in his company, she began to wonder if she could endure a lifetime as his wife. After three days, she wondered if she could endure a *week*. After four, she was certain she couldn't endure another *hour*. She had had enough . . . enough of his prosy mother, his stuffy manor house, his overweening relatives, and the viscount himself.

That fourth day was the one before the day of the dinner at which their betrothal was to be announced. Everyone in the household was in one way or another busily preparing for it. Even Aunt Isabel had been pressed into service by Lady Isham to help arrange the flowers. Only Charles and Meg were exempted from the bustle of preparation.

Charles chose to occupy the time by giving his bride-to-be a complete tour of the portrait gallery. For Meg, the experience proved to be appalling. The gallery, a wide corridor spanning the east and west wings of the building, seemed to extend for miles into the distance, both its walls covered with paintings. Meg was made to stop and examine each and every one, while Charles identified the portrait with a brief, pompous biography. "Here, my dear," he expounded, "you see Lord Hallwell, the first Minister of the Exchequer under George the Second. In my mother's line, you know. And this is Lady Evelyn Marsdene. She married John Marsdene of the Somerset Marsdenes, quite a distinguished family, but originally, of course, she was one of the south-county Ishams."

It was all stultifyingly tiresome. As they inched along the corridor, her mind raced wildly about for a way to break through the lethargy of the atmosphere, to lighten his intense absorption in his ancestry. Such an absorption was bound to give the man too great a sense of his own consequence. It would do him good to be teased out of it.

With this in mind, she stopped before the next portrait and looked up at it carefully. "That gentleman *must* have been cleverer than he looks," she said with a wicked twinkle.

"No, he wasn't very clever at all," Charles responded without a blink. "He made a speech before the Lords, they say, but it was not greatly heeded, and I don't think he ever went back."

Meg almost gaped at him. She'd already begun to suspect

that Charles Isham did not have a well-developed sense of humor, but she doubted that he could be as mirthless as that. Perhaps he hadn't heard her properly. She would try again.

She stopped before a portrait of a particularly unprepossessing lady. "She's not a *female,* is she?" she asked sweetly.

Charles leaned forward, scrutinizing the painting carefully. "That's Lady Millicent Hallwell, born Millicent Allyn. My great uncle Joseph Hallwell's wife. He was my mother's uncle, you know."

"Yes, I surmised as much," Meg sighed, ready to admit defeat. But as the hour wore on and the names of dozens of Hallwells and Ishams were dunned into her ear, she became more and more rebellious. If she heard the stultifying biography of one more Hallwell ("My mother's side, you know") or one more Isham (either north- or south-country), she was very much afraid she would scream. It was at that point that she looked up to see the stuffed head of a huge boar protruding from the wall. "Is he a Hallwell or an Isham?" she asked with melting innocence.

He'd been studying the portrait to the stuffed boar's left, and it was with difficulty that he forced his attention away from it. "What?" he asked.

"This," she said, pointing. "Hallwell or Isham?"

He looked from her to the boar and back again with the greatest of seriousness. "That's a wild boar," he said as if to a backward child.

"A b-boar?"

"A boar."

"That's what I thought," she said, trying to stifle the gurgling in her throat. "To which side of the family does he belong?"

"I'm not sure I understand your question. It's a wild *boar.*"

"Yes, Charles, I heard you. A *boar.* That's why I took it to be *some* sort of relative." She thought he would probably hit her. Or wring her neck. It was too much to hope that he would laugh. Any sort of appropriate reaction would have pleased her.

But Charles merely shook his head mildly. "It was caught by the Isham side, if that's what you mean. My uncle Joshua Isham felled him...on a hunt in Asia. The beast is said to weigh over seventy stone—I say, where are you going?"

It had been too much for Meg. She'd clapped a hand to her

mouth to keep from guffawing into his face, lifted her skirts and fled.

After she'd shut her bedroom door behind her, thrown herself across the bed and laughed till the tears came, she lay still for a long while. Then, her mind made up, she rose and went to her dressing table. She removed her writing case from a lower drawer and swiftly penned a note. *Dear Arthur,* she wrote. *You win. Be at the White Hart, Harrogate, tomorrow evening. I shall be waiting. Meg.*

Chapter Two

While Charles Viscount Isham waited for his betrothed at the foot of the main staircase, the lady herself was stealing down the rear one.

"Really, Meg," whispered her grey-haired accessory-to-crime who was following her down the back stairs carrying a bulging hatbox awkwardly in her arms, "do you know what you're *doing?*"

"Hush, Aunt Bel. Do you want someone to hear us?"

"Yes, I think I do! Dash it all, this is the most *reprehensible* act of impropriety! There are more than twenty guests downstairs waiting to meet you!"

Meg's silvery, mocking laugh floated up to cut off her words. "I know. I wish I could see the expression on Charles' face when he has to announce to them all that I've bolted."

Her aunt Isabel rolled her eyes heavenward in hopeless

disapproval. "I wish, Margaret Underwood, that once, just *once,* you'd handle yourself like a well-reared, well-behaved creature and show a *modicum* of restraint! Why can't you be a bit conventional for a change?"

Meg, with a sloppily packed bandbox tucked under her left arm and a bulging portmanteau gripped in her right hand, managed to turn her head to grin up at her aunt. "If I were, think how dull life would be for you?"

"Not dull at all!" her aunt retorted. "Blessedly restful!"

The stairway was narrow, and their voices seemed to bounce back at them from the enclosed walls. "Hush, dear," Meg warned again.

They made a turn at a small landing. Aunt Isabel shifted the weight of the hatbox to one arm and, holding on to the bannister with her free hand, leaned over and looked down. "Goodness, there seems to be no bottom. Where does this stairway lead?"

"I haven't the foggiest idea," Meg admitted, depositing her burdens on the narrow stair and joining her aunt to peer down. "You don't think I'm so unconventional that I explore the back stairs of the houses I visit, do you?"

"Then you don't know where we're going?" Her aunt looked at her aghast. "Why, for all you know, this will lead us to the cellars!"

"What's wrong with that? Come along, Aunt Bel, we haven't time to dawdle."

"I shall not move another step! I've never entered a cellar in my life!"

"Neither have I, but I don't think we need be afraid of them. They are not necessarily dungeons, are they?"

"But, Meg, they have rats!"

Meg laughed again and picked up her baggage. "Don't be so silly. We shall reach the servants quarters or the kitchens long before we reach the cellars. Do come along."

"The kitchens? Do you plan to leave through the *kitchens?"*

"I plan to leave through the closest exit I can find. It might well be the kitchens. Why not?"

"But they'll be full of cooks and scullery maids and such, won't they, with Charles hosting a huge dinner?"

"What if they are?"

Aunt Isabel, noticing that her niece's head was already disappearing down the flight of stairs below hers, shifted the weight of her hatbox to her chest again and scurried down after her. "But how can we——? Dashing out through the kitchen, bag and baggage, like a couple of thieving housemaids! What will we *say* to them?"

"To the kitchen help?" Meg was not in the least concerned. "Don't worry about that. Just leave it to me."

The stairs did indeed lead to the kitchens. At the next turning, Meg and her aunt found themselves standing at the top of the last flight of stairs. One of the stairway's enclosing walls here was cut away, leaving them completely exposed to view from the room spread out directly below them—the wide expanse of the main kitchen. As Isabel had predicted, the area was a veritable beehive of activity. Meg could see at least a half-dozen aproned maidservants, four or five under-cooks, an equal number of scullery maids, two bakers and four liveried footman all running about between the ovens and the tables setting up foodstuffs on platters and trays.

At the center of the room, stationed behind the largest of the many workables, was the Viscount's French chef who had been distracted from directing all the activity by the presence of the butler. The butler, inordinately imposing in full, formal regalia, stood directly opposite the chef at the worktable. He was red-faced and angry as he defended himself against the Frenchman's tirade. "Is it *my* fault, you Frenchified hysteric," he was shouting, "that his lordship has ordered me to withhold the first course for another quarter hour?"

"Mais vous n'ecoutez pas!" the distracted chef railed. "I prepare *les poulard a la Perigeaux!* You *idiot Englais,* zey will be unfit for—"

But his vituperations were never to be concluded, for a footman, glancing up at the stairway, gasped loudly. "Gawd!" he squawked.

"My word!" the butler muttered, agape.

"It's 'er ladyship!" a housemaid piped.

Dead silence fell on the room as the entire company, frozen in their places, stared at the ladies on the landing.

Meg quickly surveyed the area. The wall opposite them, she noted, was an outside one, its window revealing the kitchen gardens beyond. In the far corner she could see the door which led to them. That was the exit she was seeking. Her course now clear, she turned, looked down at the faces gaping up at her and gave them a brilliant smile. "Please don't let us interrupt." she said airily. "We do not at all intend to be in your way. We are only passing through." And with a beckoning nod to her aunt, she sailed down the stairs, Isabel at her heels. While their audience remained immobilized in shock, Meg turned and, with another dazzling smile, grasped her aunt's hand and pulled her out the door.

As soon as the two ladies found themselves in the autumn-faded kitchen gardens, they burst into giggles. But in a moment Isabel's smile faded. She looked up at the darkening sky, became aware of the icy air that nipped at her neck and shivered. "Meg, this is absurd!" she said worriedly. "I have the strongest feeling that it'll come on to *snow!*"

"Snow? In October? It's you who's absurd, love. Do come along. I think the stables must be this way."

Isabel had no choice but to follow. "It's been known to snow in October, you know," she muttered as she dutifully trotted behind her purposeful niece, "and this *is* north country. Besides, it's almost November. I tell you, I can smell snow in the air just as surely as I can sense that we're heading for trouble."

Meg only tossed her head in disdain and strode on. Another moment brought them to the stables. There they found the groom, a short, muscular, almost completely bald fellow who, wrapped in his work-apron, was on his knees examining the hoof of one of the horses. At the sight of two ladies from the house, he jumped to his feet and snatched off his apron. Meg carefully explained that she and her aunt wished to be taken to the nearest inn.

"Now, yer ladyship?" the fellow asked in surprise.

"Yes, right now." She put down her bags, opened the reticule which had hung from the crook of her elbow, and took out a gold sovereign.

The man backed away from the proffered coin and frowned. "Lord Isham didn't order no carriage tonight," he said suspiciously.

"His lordship doesn't know anything about it," Meg admitted frankly.

The groom scratched at his chin. "Are ye sayin' that ye don't *wish* 'im to know? I don't think it'd be right fer me to—"

"Don't be silly, man," she cut in with asperity. "The trip can't be a very long one. Where is the nearest inn?"

"In Masham. On'y half-an-hour down the road, but—"

"Then why the to-do? I intend to hire a carriage there, and you'll be able to return here with yours so promptly that his lordship will never know you'd gone."

The groom rubbed his bald head. "I don't know, yer ladyship. I'd like t'oblige ye, surely, but there'd be a terrible do if Lord Isham found out. I ain't even the coachman, y' see. On'y a groom, I be. An' Lord Isham'd surely take it as stealin', even if you an' me call it borrowin'."

"The man's right, Meg," Isabel put in. "Isn't it bad enough to ruin your *own* reputation—and mine? Must you make trouble even for the servants?"

"I tell you there'll be no trouble. He says he can be back in an hour."

"Less 'n that, if *I* wuz drivin'," the groom admitted. "I kin 'andle these 'orses better'n anyone in Yorkshire."

"Well, then—?" Meg offered him the coin again.

He shook his head. "I wouldn't need that t' do it, m'lady, if I tho't it wuz right."

"Can it be so very wrong to borrow a carriage and a couple of horses for less than an hour?"

"Less'n an hour if the weather 'olds," the groom said, weakening. "It feels like snow, if y'ask me."

"What? You, too? I promise you, my man, that it will not snow. What is your name, by the way?"

"Roodle, yer ladyship. 'Enry Roodle."

"Well, Roodle, are you going to take us, or do we have to *walk* the distance in this chill?"

With the question put that way, Roodle had no choice but to acquiesce. Quickly, he saddled his most dependable horses—two matched chestnut mares—to the phaeton, the smallest closed carriage in the Viscount's collection. Then he borrowed the coachman's caped coat and high hat from the alcove where it was stored ("In fer a penny, in fer a pound," he told himself with a shrug), and they set out.

Once settled into the carriage and on their way, the two women lapsed into silence. Isabel, leaning back against the cushions, permitted herself to sink into gloom. Meg had changed her mind about marriage after all! It was her blasted independence. Isabel was at her wit's end about what to do to marry the girl off!

The trouble was that Meg didn't realize that her life was far from full. She had a large circle of friends and admirers, a great deal of money and many entertaining activities with which to fill her days. And in addition, the girl had, for the past few years, managed her estates and made all the decisions necessary in keeping control of a large fortune. She was accustomed to running her own life. While Isabel could understand her reluctance to give up that independence, she was nevertheless convinced that Meg's life would be more complete with a proper family. Not with Charles, necessarily, if Meg really didn't care for him, but with someone. Even if the problem of the inheritance were not looming up on the horizon to complicate matters, she would still wish for Meg to find a husband.

Isabel turned and studied her niece surreptitiously. If one were entirely objective, the aunt supposed, one might not be able to claim that the girl was a beauty. She was too tall and built on lines that were too statuesque to suit current fashion. And her chin was too strong. But no one would deny that her eyes—a warm dark brown—sparkled with humor, and that her skin—though quite liberally sprinkled with freckles—was smooth and glowing. Of course her hair was a problem, and not unlike the girl herself; while its red-gold color and thick texture were magnificent, it was completely unruly and would go where it willed. Meg refused to cut it, yet no restraints, no binding, no combs or broaches could keep it from following its independent will. Yes, that's where the trouble was—excessive independence.

The girl's voice cut into her reverie. "Stop sighing, Aunt Bel. You've done so three times in the last two minutes. I know you're worrying over me, and I won't have it."

"How can I help it? You're destroying your future."

"By running away from Charles Isham? Really, Isabel—"

"By running away from a promise. By running away from a proper life!"

Meg made a face. "Do you think I would have had a 'proper life' with Charles?"

"Yes, I do. He's a fine, respectable, worthy man. And you found him so, too, for you accepted him."

"Yes, I did. But I don't know *what* made me do it."

"You did it because of his worthiness." She fixed her eyes on her niece in frowning disapproval. "Why did you change your mind about him?"

"I didn't change it, exactly. I just realized that I couldn't bear to spend my life with his respectable worthiness."

"See here, Meg, I've had enough of your disdain for the qualities which everyone else finds admirable! What's wrong with respectability?"

"Oh, Aunt Bel, it's so dull! I found myself bored after only four days in that house. What would I have felt after four years?"

Isabel frowned. "I was there with you during those four days, and I didn't find it dull. Am I to conclude that I'm dull, too?"

Meg looked contrite. "You know I didn't mean that," she said, throwing her arm about her aunt's shoulder and hugging her. "You're the sweetest and best aunt in the world. And the only reason you didn't find Charles a stifling bore was because you didn't spend as much time with him as I did. Do you remember when he asked me to go with him to see the portrait gallery?"

"Yes. Yesterday afternoon, wasn't it?"

"To you it may have been an afternoon. To me it was a month! Whatever I said to him didn't make an impression at all. I might as well have been conversing with a mushroom! I even tried to be provoking. I said the rudest things—"

"Oh, Meg, you didn't!"

"Yes, I did. And that's the whole point. He should have shouted, taken offense, wrung my neck. But he did nothing! I'm really quite convinced that the man hears only what he wants to hear. I couldn't go through with it, Aunt Bel. I'd rather end up an old maid without a penny. So . . . I decided to bolt." She turned her aunt's face up to hers and added with appealing earnestness, "Please say you're not angry with me, dearest. You wouldn't wish me to spend my life with someone so . . . stodgy, so dull, so utterly devoid of humor."

Isabel squeezed her niece's hand in conciliation. "Of course I'm not angry, my love. I only wish . . . Ah, well, never mind. In any case, was it necessary for us to run off this way and leave poor Charles so completely unprepared? He'll have to face a roomful of dinner guests without knowing *what* to say to them. Wasn't that a bit cruel?"

Meg tried to look contrite. "I tried to tell him, really I did. 'I don't think we'll suit,' I said over and over again. Charles is simply incapable of hearing what he doesn't want to hear. I did leave a note, you know." A heartless giggle escaped her. "I wonder how long he'll keep those poor people sitting at the table before he realizes we've gone?"

Isabel, while disapproving of her niece's irresponsible behavior, nevertheless had to bite her lip to keep from smiling at the vision of the disastrous scene probably taking place at that moment in the Isham dining room. "It was quite dreadful of you to end the betrothal in this way, Meg. It would serve you right if he followed us and demanded your return to help him face the dinner guests and to make proper explanations to them and to him."

"I hate explanations. And I hate dull dinner parties. That's why I bolted." She could detect the twitch at the corners of her aunt's mouth. "He'll never catch us, you know. By the time he realizes we've flown, we'll have arrived at the inn at Masham. And by the time he decided to follow us—if he's foolish enough to do so—we shall be at Harrogate. He'll have no idea which route we've chosen or where we shall be stopping. So I haven't a worry in the—"

"Good Lord!" her aunt cried suddenly, staring out the window behind Meg. "What's that?"

Meg jumped, startled. "What, Aunt Bel?" she asked, whirling around to see if Charles had indeed decided to follow her and bring her to heel. "Is it—?"

"Look! Didn't I warn you?"

Aunt Isabel had been right. Through the dimness of the October twilight they could discern a number of thick, white flakes floating by the carriage window. It was snowing.

Chapter Three

"It's only a flurry," Meg assured her aunt with firm optimism.
"I wouldn't give it another thought."

But by the time the groom had turned the carriage into the
yard of the Horse With Three Tails Inn, the ground around
them was buried under a thin cover of white. Meg, pretending
that she was still unperturbed, let Roodle help her down. "Wait
here in the carriage, love," she said to Isabel, "until I hire
another equipage. I mean to get us to Harrogate before we stop
for the night."

"Why Harrogate? It's already become dark," her aunt said
worriedly.

"Harrogate isn't more than an hour's ride. And the White
Hart there will provide us with more comfortable lodgings than
this forsaken place. Besides, I shall feel more at ease when
I've put some distance between ourselves and Charles Isham."

She walked quickly through the snow to the inn. One look

at its tiny taproom convinced her that she would not find sleeping accommodations to her satisfaction in this modest, out-of-the-way hostelry. There were only two patrons in the room; a few more and the place would have been crowded. If there were bedrooms upstairs, they would probably be completely unsuitable, and Meg was certain there was not a private parlor to be had on these unimposing premises. She took off her bonnet and shook it out, brushed back a heavy lock of damp red hair from her forehead and looked around her.

A woman of florid complexion and wide girth was filling a tumbler with ale from a cask set on a shelf behind the bar near the door. There was no one else in the room who seemed to be in charge of the establishment, so Meg approached the woman. "I wish to hire a carriage to take me to Harrogate," she said.

The woman threw her a quick glance and shook her head. "Not t'night, ma'am. It's comin' down snow." And without another glance at Meg, she turned off the tap and carried the brimming glass to a gentleman seated at a table near the front window. "'Ere y'are, sir, just the way ye like it," she said with obvious deference as she placed the glass before him. Then she lit an oil lamp on the table, made a clumsy curtsey and returned to the bar.

Meg, annoyed at the cavalier treatment accorded to her, especially when compared to the polite service the man at the window had received, smoldered. "My good woman," she said in any icy undervoice, "I don't think you understood me. I have urgent need of a carriage. I will pay whatever price you require, but have your ostler harness the horses at once!"

The woman leaned her heavy arms on the bar and gave Meg a sneering smile. "I don't think ye understood *me!* I ain't hirin' out my rig to no one tonight. Do y' think I'll chance my only carriage on a snowy road? Where'd I be if it overturned, eh? Where'd I be?"

"If your driver is so ham-handed as to overturn the equipage on what is a mere *film* of snow, then I'll drive it myself!"

"You?" The woman gave a screeching laugh. "That's a good one, that is!"

An old man sitting nearby, dressed in rough farmer's garb, hooted. "Don't know wut the worl's comin' to, I don't. Ladies, *drivin'!*"

Meg felt the color rise to her cheeks. Chagrined, she turned to look at the gentleman at the window, hoping for some support. But the man had spread a newspaper on the table before him and was absorbed in reading and swilling his ale. Curling her fingers into angry fists, she turned back to the woman. "Ladies do drive carriages, and quite well, too. I, myself, have bested several gentlemen in races we've run in London. So let's have no further discussion on matters you know nothing about. Your driver may sit alongside me and watch as I drive. He'll learn something. And I'll pay for his lodging at Harrogate so that he needn't return with the carriage until the snow has disappeared. Will that suit you?"

"No, it won't. I ain't hirin' out my carriage tonight, and that's that!"

Meg wanted to stamp her foot in irritation. She'd never been spoken to in such a manner. These country bumpkins had not the least idea of how to behave toward their betters. What made matters worse was her awareness of a growing feeling of helplessness. She did not wish to remain in this inadequate, rustic hovel for the night, especially after being so irritatingly humiliated; she couldn't go back to face Charles and his houseful of guests; and unless she could procure a carriage, she couldn't move on to Harrogate, where Arthur Steele might already be awaiting her arrival. Then where was she to go? For the first time in her life she felt the beginnings of real panic. "Then I'll *buy* the carriage outright!" she said, inspired by desperation.

The woman blinked. "Buy it? And the 'orses, too? Ye must be daft."

"Not at all," Meg said grandly, her panic disappearing. At such times it was quite satisfying to feel the power of wealth. "Shall we say three hundred pounds?"

The old farmer choked. He'd always known that city folk were extravagant, but this one was beyond all. "Yer cracked in yer noggin," he croaked gleefully.

"Three 'undred?" the woman asked in disbelief. "Y'ain't even seen it!"

"Is it a closed carriage? If it is, then I care about nothing else. I will, of course, look over the horses. Have we a bargain?"

The woman hesitated. She would be making a substantial profit if she accepted the offer, but she would have to be without a carriage for some time. "Let's see the color o' yer cash," she said, her eyes narrowed.

"Well, of course, I don't carry such an amount with me," Meg explained cheerfully as she opened her reticule, "but I can give you twenty sovereigns and my vowels for the remainder—"

"Vowels?" asked the woman, frowning suspiciously.

"My note, you know. I'll send my man of business to redeem it as soon as I return to London."

"Note?" The woman laughed scornfully. "You must think I'm daft as you! I ain't givin' up my carriage fer a *note!*"

Meg looked up with renewed alarm. "But you must—"

"Cracked in 'er noggin," the old farmer repeated, nodding to himself.

"You don't understand!" Meg gritted her teeth in impatience. "I'm Margaret Underwood. My note is my *bond.*"

"Ye don't say!" the woman sneered. "Yer bond, eh?"

The old man uttered a hiccoughing laugh. "'Er bond!"

"Yes, my bond! My note is as good as gold, I promise you," Meg assured her urgently.

"Nuthin's as good as gold," the woman said bluntly. "Gold is gold, and promises is promises. I ain't givin' up my carriage fer no promises." She turned her back on Meg. "Want another pint, gaffer?" she asked the old man.

"Don't mind. Listenin' to city folk do make un' chuckle so, it brings on a bit o' thirst." The old man grinned.

Meg pressed her lips together to keep herself from bursting out with an angry, unladylike retort. Instead, she took a few impatient strides about the room, wondering anxiously what on earth she would do next. Her eye fell upon the man seated near the window. There was something about him—the quality of his coat, the deferential way the woman had treated him—that proclaimed the gentleman. Perhaps he might help her.

But something made her hesitate. Although the man was impressively tall and strongly built and had a face of decided character, he had so saturnine an air that she was momentarily put off. She continued her pacing while she regarded him surreptitiously. *What sort of man was this?* she wondered. He looked out of place drinking ale in so unpretentious and sequestered an establishment. With his short-cropped hair (which, although shot with grey, was thick and vigorous—the man couldn't be much beyond thirty-five years of age) and well-cut sporting coat, he'd have looked more at home in a hunting lodge with a glass of port in his hand.

In normal circumstances, she would have been completely indifferent to his presence. He was obviously country gentry—quite beneath her touch; in other circumstances she would have cut him completely if he'd attempted to speak to her. It went quite against the grain to approach him, but she was desperate for some assistance. If only the man were not so resolutely absorbed in his paper and ignoring everything else . . .

However, she had no time for leisurely contemplation and maidenly shyness. Aunt Isabel was probably beside herself with impatience by this time. Squaring her shoulders, she approached the man's table. "I beg your pardon, sir—" she began.

A pair of cold, dark eyes lifted from the page. The man's mouth seemed to tighten, and his breath expelled with what was unmistakably a sigh of resignation as he reluctantly pulled himself to his feet. "Yes?"

His obvious displeasure did nothing to make the situation easier for her. She felt herself flush. "I . . . er . . . know this is rather awkward, but I find myself in some difficulty. My name is Margaret Underwood . . ."

"Yes?"

The cool monosyllable was like a dash of cold water to the face. It took all her courage to proceed. "Well, you see . . . Dash it all, you *must* have overheard what passed between barmaid and me."

"You mean Mrs. Perkins. No, I did not overhear. I don't pay attention to women's wranglings."

Meg was completely taken aback. The man was positively icy. Almost any gentleman she'd ever encountered would have jumped at the chance to act the gallant for her. What was the matter with this one? But she had gone too far into the conversation to withdraw now. "It is *not* women's wranglings," she said, trying to keep the signs of annoyance from her voice. "It's a matter of business. I don't think Mrs. Perkins understands about monetary notes. Since you seem to be a gentleman of some substance, and since you and Mrs. Perkins are acquainted, I wonder if you would be so good as to explain to her that it is perfectly safe to accept a note from me in the amount of—"

"No, ma'am, I shall not be so good," the gentleman cut in flatly.

Meg couldn't believe her ears. "Wh-what?" she stammered.

"I don't care to involve myself, ma'am."

"But . . . it's only the smallest sort of involvement, I assure you," she explained, feeling as if she'd stumbled into what was either a nightmare or an asylum for the insane. "You see, I am Margaret Underwood—"

"Yes, you said that."

"*Lady* Margaret Underwood—"

Behind her, Meg heard the barely muffled snickers of Mrs. Perkins and her "gaffer." The old man sneered, "Lady indeed!"

Meg ignored them. "Of the Underwoods of Suffolk—"

"Yes?" the gentleman queried with a barely masked lack of interest.

"My father was Edward Underwood. Surely you've heard of him? The fifth Earl of Barringham?"

"It would make no difference if I had."

She would have liked to hit him! The man was completely unreachable. "Are you just going to stand there and do nothing to help me?" she exploded in disgust. "Surely you must see that the vowels of the daughter of the Earl of Barringham are good anywhere in England!"

"Yes, they may well be," he said, quite unimpressed.

"Then won't you *please* tell Mrs. Perkins so?"

"I've already told you that I don't care to interfere in the bickerings of females. Please excuse me." And with a curt nod, he sat himself down and immediately absorbed himself in his newspaper.

Meg stood rooted to the spot. The impudent fellow had actually had the temerity to seat himself while she remained standing! Had she been a man, his behavior would have given sufficient cause to call him out!

The other two in the room were snickering behind her back. Meg felt her face redden in humiliation and chagrin. She glared at the seated man with venom. Never had she met anyone so lacking in gallantry. No, *worse*—the fellow was completely lacking in human *feeling!* He deserved to be horsewhipped . . . flayed till he bled! She would have liked to strike him down and stamp him into the ground with her heel! Her glare was so smoldering it should have burned the back of his head, but the maddening creature paid no heed. He merely turned a page with deliberate care and continued to read.

She let out an explosive, hissing breath, put up her chin and stalked out of the taproom, out of the inn and out of the sight of them all. Never, she swore to herself, would she step into the Horse With Three Tails Inn again—not as long as she lived! Not even if she had to sleep in the snow and freeze to death!

The sight of the snow-covered innyard gave her a momentary shock. The layer of white on the ground had perceptibly thickened, and the snowflakes were falling densely, with a steady purposefulness that was much more alarming than the flurries had been. Roodle was walking the horses in circles to keep them warm, and their steamy breath was visible in the icy dark. If it were not for the fact that under their covering of snow the leaves were still visible on the branches of the nearby trees, Meg would have imagined she'd emerged from the inn right into the heart of January.

At the sight of her, Aunt Isabel lowered the carriage window. "What kept you, my love? I hope you haven't asked them to harness the horses. It's much too dark and snowy to proceed further, isn't it? Shall we stop here for the night?"

"I'd rather die!" her niece exclaimed through clenched teeth. Without a word of explanation, she turned to Roodle, who had ceased leading the horses and was waiting for her instructions. "Are you married, Roodle?" she asked.

"What, m'lady?" The groom was clearly astounded by the irrelevancy.

"I asked if you are a married man. Do you have family residing in this district?"

"No, ma'am, I ain't an' I don't."

"Then there's nothing or no one here to make you desire to remain in this particular region, is there?"

He squinted at her as if she'd lost her mind. "Well, yes, ma'am, there is. I *live* here, y' see."

"Yes, but there's nothing to prevent you from living elsewhere, is there?"

He shook his head as if he were trying to clear his brain, sending a flurry of snowflakes whirling from the brim of his high-crowned hat. "I don't know as I follow yer meanin', m'lady. I can't live nowheres else if I'm in the 'ire of Lord Isham. An' if ye'll pardon me sayin' so, if I don't get 'is carriage back t' the stable soon, I mayn't 'ave a place t' live a-tall."

"But," she persisted, "would you consider *living* somewhere else if you were *employed* by someone else? For a higher wage, of course."

"Lord Isham pays me forty quid per," the groom responded proudly.

"Per annum? Miserly. I'll double it."

The sturdy little fellow gaped, visibly shaken. "Double?" he croaked. He pushed his hat back from his forehead and rubbed at his bald pate with nervous fingers which protruded from the holes of a thick glove. "Ye wish me t' work fer *you?*" he asked, his brow knitted in confusion. "Fer *eighty quid?*"

"Yes, I do. For eighty quid per. What do you say?"

"Well . . ." He furrowed his brow and thoughtfully resumed walking the horses. "I dunno why I shouldn't . . . if you ain't diddlin' me . . ."

"I'm not diddling. I'm deadly earnest. There is, however, one condition."

Roodle stopped his walk, cocked his head to one side and looked at her through suddenly narrowed eyes. "I might've figured on that. There's some bobbery y' want o' me."

"Yes. I want you to make off with his lordship's carriage and horses."

"Make off with 'em? Ye mean steal—?"

"We'll return them eventually. But yes, I suppose it *is* stealing. I want you to steal them and take Mrs. Underwood and me back to London, where you will find employment as *my* coachman in *my* stables for as long as it suits you to stay."

"London!" the groom breathed, wide-eyed. "Gawd!"

"And one thing more—"

He winced. "I know'd it. Yer goin' t' ask me t' murder someone."

For the first time since she'd arrived at this insufferable place, she broke into a laugh. "No, not quite as bad as that. It's only that I have to tell you that there won't be time for you to go back to Isham Manor to get your things."

"Do y' mean—? You ain't thinkin' o' startin' out this very night!"

She laughed again, a laugh of triumph, of relief, and of careless disregard of any consequences. She reached for a riding crop that lay resting on the coachman's seat. "I'm thinking, Roodle," she grinned, thrusting the crop into his hand and springing upon the carriage steps, "of starting *right now.*"

Chapter Four

Aunt Isabel pressed her nose against the window of the carriage, nervously peering out into the night, but her niece leaned back against the cushions and grinned. She'd managed to escape from Charles Isham and from the confines of the Horse With Three Tails Inn, and even the danger of a drive through the snowy blackness couldn't dampen her high spirits.

She could hear Roodle whistling to himself in the coachman's seat as he guided the horses along the road, but whether the tune expressed a gleeful exuberance over his new prospects or a tense anxiety over the condition of the roads she couldn't say. She rather expected it was the former, for once he'd decided to throw his lot with her rather than return to face Lord Isham's wrath, he'd been as optimistic and helpful as she could have wished. By the simple expedient of hanging a lantern at the end of a pole suspended out from the horses' harness, he had made it possible to see the road ahead. With a coachman of his ingenuity, Meg was certain that they would manage to reach Harrogate without mishap.

But she could see that her aunt's hands were tightly clenched, the knuckles showing white. She could hardly blame the poor woman for losing her usual spirit—this had been a dreadful day for her. Ever since Meg had first told her, that morning, that they were to steal out of Lord Isham's house by late afternoon, the poor dear had been on edge. They'd had to endure all the activities which the Ishams had planned for them, while at the same time finding opportunities to pack as many of their belongings as they could carry. Isabel had been as brave as Meg could have wished, but this ride through the ever-deepening snow was more than her aunt could stand.

Perhaps it was cruel to push on to Harrogate. In the best of weather—and in broad daylight—the ride would take an hour. But under the circumstances, with the coach barely inching along the road, the trip might last well into the night. It might even be possible that Arthur Steele, too, was being delayed by the storm. She looked out of the window at the steadily mounting snow. Should she stop at the nearest inn and leave Harrogate for the morrow? She had never before believed it, but perhaps discretion *was* the better part of valor.

One more look at her aunt's tense face decided her. "Don't look so frightened, Aunt Bel," she said soothingly. "I've changed my mind about attempting to reach Harrogate tonight. I'll instruct Roodle to stop at the very next inn."

While Meg did so, Isabel brightened. As soon as Meg leaned back against the seat, her aunt grasped her arm. "Oh, I *am* glad, dearest. My nerves wouldn't have withstood another hour of this ride. Do you think we shall come upon an inn quite soon?"

"At any moment, I'm certain. And I shall demand that they provide my adorable, loving, long-suffering aunt the very best room in the house."

The prospect of enjoying the warmth of a fireplace, a bed and a comforter to cover her was enough to ease the worried lines from Isabel's forehead. She leaned back against the cushions and let herself relax. When the carriage drew to a sudden halt, she uttered a glad cry and leaned toward the window to see what sort of place the coachman had found. But she saw nothing but blackness. "Meg, where are we? Why—?"

Roodle's face appeared at Meg's window. He explained that a lowhanging branch had brushed against the lantern and that some of the load of snow it bore had fallen inside, dousing the flame. That problem, combined with the fact that the thick snow was obscuring the light from the two small brass lanterns on the corners of the carriage, had cut his visibility entirely. He would have to spend a few minutes in rectifying the situation.

Isabel's anxiety immediately returned. Meg took her hands and tried to reassure her. "It's only a momentary delay, love. We shall be setting off in another—"

A strange sound assaulted her ears, and it was a moment or two before she grasped that she was hearing hoofbeats of approaching horses, their clatter muffled by the snow. The sound was very close. She realized, with horror, that if Roodle had not yet managed to light the lantern, the oncoming vehicle would not see them until almost upon them. She had just time enough to gasp before she heard Roodle shout hoarsely, "'Ey there! Look out!"

There followed an alarmed cry from a voice just ahead of them in the road. Then, in swift succession, came the neighing of rearing horses, the sound of her aunt's piercing scream and the terrifying crunch of the wheels of the oncoming vehicle brushing against theirs. The coach bodies scraped together with a blood-chilling cracking of wood. Meg felt her carriage wobble, sway crazily to the right, waver hideously on its right wheels and topple over. She felt herself being thrown from her seat to the top of the coach which was now at a ridiculous angle *below* her. She felt the weight of her aunt's body against hers as they both tumbled through the air. Her head struck something solid and then . . . an enveloping blackness.

Outside, Roodle stood for a moment immobilized. The second carriage had come upon them so quietly through the snow that he'd become aware of them only at the last moment. He'd seen the horses rear up in surprise, the carriage crunch against his own and topple over on its side, pushing his phaeton over and into the ditch. He'd seen the terrified horses of the other carriage break loose from their damaged harness and gallop off into the night. It was only then that he realized he'd been clinging to the reins of his own horses which were still rearing and neighing in fright.

He shook off his momentary paralysis and quickly calmed the beasts. They were as fine a pair of chestnuts as he'd ever seen, and they knew him well. His pats and murmurs were reassuring to them. When they quieted down, he was able to find the lantern and, with trembling fingers, managed to light it. As soon as the light flooded the scene, he heard a lady scream, "Hackett, is that you? Help me!"

There was an immediate stirring in a pile of snow at the side of the road, and a head emerged from the drift. Before Roodle could reach him, an elderly man scrambled to his feet and limped toward the wreckage. "Miss Trixie?" he croaked tremblingly, brushing the snow from a head of thin, white hair.

"Get me out!" the female voice shrieked. "Hackett, you cod's head, get me out of here!"

"I'll save ye, Miss Trixie, I'll save ye," the old man uttered without conviction, hobbling about the wreck aimlessly, unable to reach up to the door of the tilted vehicle.

Roodle, suddenly aware that he'd not heard a sound from *his* ladies, held the lantern aloft. "Are ye hurt, Miss?" he asked.

The window in the door above him (now more like a skylight than a door) was lowered and a gloved hand waved. "I'm not much hurt," a voice said from within, "but I want to get out!"

"I'll get ye out in a moment," Roodle promised, but, worried about *his* passengers, he ran quickly round to the other side. There he found the phaeton almost completely upside-down in the ditch. His heart hammered in terror, for there was no sign of life within. "You, 'Ackett!" he shouted. "Come 'ere an' 'old this lantern fer me."

The white-haired old man limped over and did as he was bid. Roodle, using the narrow overhang of the phaeton roof as a foothold, climbed up the side of the carriage and managed to reach the door handle. Awkwardly, with great effort, he pulled it open. "'Ere. Shine the light in 'ere," he ordered the old man below. "Yer ladyship, are ye 'urt?"

There was a blessed stir of movement, and Mrs. Underwood's face appeared in a beam of light. "Is that you, Roodle? I'm afraid s-something dreadful's happened to my M-Meggie. I c-can't seem to rouse her."

"Are *you* all right, ma'am?" Roodle asked.

"Yes, I think so."

"Then give me yer 'ands. We'll get ye down."

"But, Meg..."

"Don't ye worry none. We'll get 'er out o' there an' bring 'er round."

But it proved so difficult to lower the shaken Mrs. Underwood to the ground (for the weak old Hackett was not able to assist in any way but to hold the lantern) that Roodle didn't see how he could lift out a comatose female. He took the lantern from Hackett, climbed up into the carriage again and looked carefully at his unconscious mistress. She lay wedged in the corner between the carriage roof and the far side. He could see no blood or bruises. He took one of her hands and chaffed it timidly, but she didn't react. With a discouraged sigh, he picked up a fallen lap-robe, threw it over his shoulder and climbed out. He wrapped the shivering Mrs. Underwood in the robe, mounded some snow in a pile near the horses, where the wreckage offered some slight shelter from the wind, and made her sit down.

"Meggie—" the distraught woman asked pathetically.

"We'll 'ave 'er out in a shake," he answered with more conviction than he felt.

"Hackett!" shouted the female from within the other carriage. "Where are you? Have you forgotten me?"

Roodle picked up the lantern again and walked round to the rear of the wreck. The timid Hackett followed him. "Please help Miss Trixie out," the old man implored. "She'll have one of her tantrums if you don't."

"I don't give a tinker's damn fer 'er tantrums," Roodle muttered shortly. "My lady's layin' in there with maybe a broken neck and—Wait! What's that?"

"I don't hear any—"

"Sssh! It's a 'orse, it is, or my name ain't—"

Before he finished, the horse galloped into view. Roodle almost crowed with relief when he caught sight of the rider. The man was tall and sturdily built. Here, at last, was someone who could offer valuable help.

Hackett, however, was considerably disturbed by the sight of him. "S-Sir G-Geoffrey!" he stammered.

The rider, startled by the sight that greeted his eyes, pulled his horse to and leapt to the ground. "Hackett? What on earth—? Good Lord, what a crack-up!" He turned to Roodle. "Is anyone hurt?"

Before he could answer, there was a sharp cry from the impatient female within the second coach. "Geoffrey! Is that you? *Please* help me out of here!" Her voice had changed from impatient command to a nasal whine.

Sir Geoffrey's brows lifted in surprise. "What's Trixie doing out at this—?" He suddenly tensed. "Is she hurt?" he asked Hackett.

"No, sir," the old man assured him. "She says she's quite all right."

"Is there anyone else in the carriage?"

"Oh, no, sir," the old coachman said hastily.

Sir Geoffrey expelled a relieved breath, but almost immediately his expression became a sneer. "You took her to the Lazenbys, I suppose."

"Y-Yes, sir," Hackett said, lowering his eyes guiltily.

"Against my express orders?"

"W-Well, y' see, sir—"

At that moment, a dazed Mrs. Underwood appeared in the circle of light, the lap-robe trailing pitifully behind her. "Where *is* she?" she whispered tearfully. "Where's my Meg? Please tell me she's not . . . *dead!*"

Sir Geoffrey stared at her, and then turned a pair of alarmed, questioning eyes to Roodle. "Is there someone *else*—?"

"Yes, sir," Roodle said urgently. "I been tryin' t' tell ye. She's layin' in t'other carriage, out cold."

"Then, quick, man, lead the way."

"Geoffrey!" the impatient female shrieked from within the wreck. "You're not going to *leave* me here! I'm freezing!"

"Serves you right!" Sir Geoffrey barked and followed Roodle without a backward look.

The first sensation Meg became aware of was of cold. There was a cold wetness on her eyes and cheeks, and cold air seemed to be blowing all around her. Then she was aware of water dripping on her hand. Like tears. Then sounds began to filter into her consciousness—the wind, voices, the neighing of horses . . .

Then she remembered. The accident! She'd hit her head. She could still feel the throbbing pain of the blow. She realized she was lying outside, on the snow . . . and, slowly, through the pain, the sound came to her of someone crying. It was her aunt, murmuring in her ear and weeping on her hand. "Aunt Bel . . . ?" she murmured.

She heard her aunt gasp joyfully. "She spoke! Oh, Meggie, my dearest, *do* open your eyes."

With an effort, she forced her lids open, expecting to see Isabel's tearful face gazing down at her. Instead, she found herself blinking up at the saturnine visage of the man from the Horse With Three Tails Inn!

Quickly she shut her eyes again. It was probably some sort of hallucination, a trick of her injury. Surely it had been Isabel's voice she'd heard a moment ago. Very carefully, she opened her eyes again. The hallucination was still there. "You!" she said with loathing.

The man gave her a mocking smile, and then turned to look at someone on Meg's right. "I think your niece has recovered her wits," he said drily.

She turned her head. "Aunt Bel! Are you all right?"

Isabel beamed joyfully and leaned down to hug her. "I'm fine, dearest, now that I know you're alive. You've given us the most dreadful fright."

"Do you think you could try standing, ma'am?" the repulsive gentleman suggested. "I think it's time that we seek shelter from this storm."

Meg assured them that, except for a small lump at the back of her head, she was really quite well, and they helped her to her feet. As soon as she stood erect, however, she knew that all was *not* well with her—a wrenching pain in her ankle warned her that she'd either sprained or broken it—but she didn't wish to alarm her aunt and so said nothing.

She was startled at the number of people who stood watching her. In addition to her aunt and the ungallant gentleman, there was Roodle, beaming at her in relief, and a stranger with white hair who wore the livery of a coachman. "Ain't we goin' to help Miss Trixie *now,* Sir Geoffrey?" the stranger pleaded.

The ungallant gentleman scowled, turned on his heel and walked round the wreckage. The others followed, Meg gritting her teeth to keep from limping and revealing to the entire company that she was the only one who'd been hurt.

Sir Geoffrey gave Roodle a leg up, and the groom scrambled over the upturned side of the coach and disappeared into the open window of the door. In a moment the head of a pretty young lady appeared, her bonnet askew, her hair in disarray, and her face streaked with tears. Roodle, lifting her from below, assisted her to climb out on the coach. From there she was able to jump down into Sir Geoffrey's waiting arms.

No sooner did the young lady's feet touch the ground than she fell on Sir Geoffrey's neck, weeping. "Oh, Geoffrey," she sobbed, "it's been so d-dreadful! Thank goodness you came along to rescue m-me."

Meg watched while the gentleman, frowning irritably, removed the young woman's arms from round his neck. "Are you sure you're not hurt?" he asked coldly.

"Yes." She hung her head pitifully, her shoulders shaking with sobs. "I was only . . . th-thrown about a bit."

"Then stop crying and gather your wits about you. We'll have to help these people make their way to Knight's Haven with us."

Meg would have liked to slap him. The coldness of his treatment of the poor young woman who was obviously his wife was just another indication that the fellow was a heartless, inhuman beast. And now she would have to take shelter in their home! The prospect filled her with distaste, but there was nothing she could do but accept the man's hospitality. Her head throbbed, her ankle was excruciatingly painful, the carriage was obviously useless, and she was in no condition even to think of making alternate plans.

Sir Geoffrey, after a brief discussion with Roodle, organized the group into action. He explained that his estate, Knight's Haven, was fortunately situated only a short distance from where they now stood. There were three horses available to them: the two chestnut mares still harnessed to Lady Margaret's equipage, and his own stallion. The ladies would ride them, with each of the men leading the horses on foot. Whatever baggage the ladies Underwood carried in their coach would undoubtedly be safe where it was. One of the servants would come for it first thing in the morning.

Sir Geoffrey didn't wait to hear if there were any objections to his plan, and no one offered any. He tossed Trixie upon his stallion, handed Hackett the lantern and bade him lead the way. Then he and Roodle unharnessed the other two horses, he lifted Isabel carefully on one of them, and Roodle led the mare off behind Hackett.

As soon as he saw the others on their way, Sir Geoffrey

lifted Meg upon the third horse and, grasping the bridle near the bit, began to follow the procession. But the horse's gait was unsteady. With a muttered curse he stopped, knelt down and examined the chestnut's left foreleg. "Damnation, there's a wound!"

"Oh, dear," Meg said in concern. "Is it very bad?"

"I can't tell in the dark." He looked ahead to where the rest of the procession was disappearing beyond a rise of land. "It doesn't pay to call them back just to take a look. We shouldn't do the mare too much harm if we walk her the rest of the way, but perhaps she shouldn't be made to bear a burden. Are you up to walking? We haven't very far to go."

Wincing, Meg slipped down from the chestnut's back. Whatever it cost her, she would not let this arrogant man see that she was in pain. "Go on," she said, tight-lipped. "I'm following right behind you."

They hadn't progressed three steps before she realized that the task she'd set herself was impossible. Her ankle couldn't stand the pressure. The pain was unbearable—she had all she could do to keep from screaming. Uncertain as to what to do, she paused, shifted all her weight to the uninjured leg and shut her eyes, letting the waves of pain subside. Suddenly she was seized by two powerful arms and lifted off her feet. "Broken your ankle, eh?" Sir Geoffrey muttered. "Jingle-brained female!"

She sputtered in fury. "How *dare* you touch me! Put me down at once!"

"Put your arms about my neck and be still!" he ordered. "This is going to be difficult enough without your making it worse. Why couldn't you tell me you'd been injured, like a sensible creature? I could have made proper provision for your transport if I'd known—"

"I was under no obligation to tell you anything!"

"What has obligation to do with it? We are speaking of plain good sense. Even a simple-minded ninnyhammer would have better sense than to try to walk on a broken ankle."

"I didn't expect to walk on it. I was going to ride, remember?"

He shifted her weight so that she rested higher on his chest, bringing her face on a level with his. "I told you to put your arms round my neck. Please do so at once! It will help the balance. You're no featherweight, you know."

She could feel the muscles in his arms tense with the strain of her weight. Reluctantly, she did as he bid her. Her face was close to his, and his arms—one supporting her back and the other her legs—pressed her closely against his chest. The position placed her in such intimate proximity to the man that she felt deucedly uncomfortable. To mask her embarrassment, she said with a conscious lack of gratitude, "I think, sir, that you're quite the *rudest* man I've ever come across."

He completely ignored the remark. "Can you reach the horse's reins? I don't think I can hold on to you and the horse as well."

She reached back over his shoulder and managed to grasp them. They started forward, Sir Geoffrey slogging awkwardly through the deepening snow, Meg feeling clumsily heavy and burdensome in his arms, and the horse limping behind them. "Back at the inn," she reminded him nastily, "you said that you didn't care to involve yourself with me. Now you're carrying me to your own home. That, sir, is involvement with a vengeance. I'm surprised that you didn't decide to leave me back there to freeze to death in the snow."

"If you're going to talk rubbish, ma'am, I may yet do it. I'd be obliged if you'd hold your tongue until we reach home. There, of course, you can talk nonsense with the females in my household to your heart's content."

"And you, sir, had better change your tone when you speak to me!" The man was truly infuriating, and Meg had no intention of putting herself at the mercy of his barbs, no matter how dependent she was on him at this moment. "I don't intend to permit you to berate *me* with the sort of verbal abuse you seem to enjoy inflicting on females, even your wife."

"My wife? What are you talking about?"

Meg was nonplussed. "I'm talking about your cruelty to the poor creature after Roodle helped her from the wreckage."

"Do you mean Trixie? In the first place, ma'am, that was my sister, Beatrix. I have no wife, thank heaven. In the second place, I was not in the least cruel to her."

"Wife or sister, your attitude was abominable. If I were she, I would have struck you."

She could feel, rather than see, his scowl. "I would like to suggest, ma'am, that since you know nothing about my sister or myself, your comments are quite meaningless. And since I've more than enough plaguey irritations to deal with at the moment, I'd appreciate it enormously if you'd cease your maggoty bibble-babble."

"Would you, indeed!" she retorted through gritted teeth. "Let me see if I understand you. In the past few minutes you've called me a jinglebrained female, a simple-minded ninnyhammer, a fat cow and a plaguey irritation. But *I* am not to be permitted to say a word! Is that the way you wish to establish the rules?"

She thought she felt a rumble of laughter in his chest, but there was no sound of amusement in his voice when he responded, "I did not call you a fat cow."

"Well, you said I was no featherweight, which is much the same thing."

He stopped in his tracks, turned his head and glared at her. "I've asked you repeatedly not to talk rubbish, but evidently you are neither capable of uttering a sensible remark nor remaining silent. Therefore, I'm going to carry you in such a way that will make the burden easier for *me* to bear and will prevent *you* from being able to murmur idiocies into my ear." With that said, he shifted his hold on her and, with one heave, slung her over his shoulder as if she were a heavy sack of grain.

The reins fell from her grasp, and the breath was pressed out of her. "Put me...*down,* you...beast!" she gasped. She found herself hanging from her waist, her head and arms dangling down behind him. The position was not only humiliatingly ridiculous, it was completely uncomfortable. Her head throbbed, her breath came in gasps, and when she tried to kick her legs, the pain in her ankle made her groan.

Paying no heed to her grunts and her evident discomfort, he squatted down, picked up the reins and walked on. Meg, dizzy and bereft of breath, could only pummel his legs with her fists. After a while, realizing that her exertions were doing no good at all, she subsided. Thus, powerless, breathless and limp, like a slain doe or a sack of sawdust, she was carried over the threshold of Knight's Haven.

Chapter Five

Her first glimpse of the house was of the stone floor of the hallway. It was of polished slate and covered with a faded Persian carpet that must, a long time ago, have been quite magnificent. Dangling helplessly from his shoulder as she was, she could see nothing else but a number of booted or slippered feet. The hallway was evidently full of people shocked into silence by the sight of Sir Geoffrey looking like a hunter returned from a kill, with a woman slung over his shoulder instead of a stag.

"Geoffrey!" a female voice cried, appalled.

"Meggie!" That was Aunt Bel. "Sir Geoffrey, what—?"

Her shocked voice was drowned by a great hubbub of voices, all of them evincing horrified disapproval. Feet came closer, and Meg could detect that she and her tormenter were being surrounded. "Geoffrey, put the poor creature down at once!" the first voice ordered.

"I will, Mama, as soon as you step aside and let me take her to the sitting room. She's broken her ankle and can't stand on her own."

There were cries of sympathy and a chorus of alarums, suggestions and commands. Meg could feel Sir Geoffrey's huge sigh of impatience. "Will you all stop this useless babble?" he demanded. "Mama, take Mrs. Underwood into the sitting room. You, Trixie, take off your bonnet and cloak at once. Keating, see that the fire is built up in the sitting room, will you? And then do something about all the wet garments. Mrs. Rhys, will you tell Cook we'd like some hot soup and whatever else she can put together for a light supper? We'll have it served in the sitting room. You, Hackett, take Lady Margaret's man— what's your name, fellow? Roodle? Take Roodle downstairs and see that he's fed and given a room. And as for you, Sybil, if you dare to indulge in one of your fainting spells, I shall wring your neck! It would be a great deal more helpful if you'd pour a glass of brandy for our invalid."

The feet turned away, and Meg watched as the floor moved beneath her again. Stone became parquet, and when she could see another Persian rug below—this one brighter and less shabby —she was deposited full-length on a faded, gold velvet sofa. Isabel immediately bent over her. "Is the pain very bad, dearest?" she asked, her eyes cloudy with alarm.

"I'm all right. Just a bit . . . breathless," Meg answered, taking a moment to glare up at Sir Geoffrey before she permitted herself to close her eyes and surrender to the luxury of reclining against the cushions.

"But your ankle!" her aunt wailed. "Why didn't you tell me?"

If there was anything Meg disliked (next to being carried over a man's shoulder like a trussed-up side of venison), it was being fussed over. She opened her eyes and pulled herself to a sitting position. "Perhaps it's only a sprain," she told her aunt reassuringly, trying valiantly not to indicate to her worried aunt or her odious host that she was quite dizzy, uncomfortably damp, chilled and ready to shriek with pain. She gritted her teeth, clenched her fists and struggled to regain her self-possession. Forcing her head erect, she blinked her eyes and looked around her.

She was startled to discover the number of people standing before her and watching her with what she could only describe as fascination. *Good heavens,* she thought with embarrassment, *what must I look like!* She became aware that a number of dripping strands of hair had fallen over her forehead. She lifted a hand to her head and found that her bonnet was gone— probably lost in the snow during her hideous, upside-down journey from the wreck—and her hair completely disheveled. She must look a fright.

With her hand uselessly trying to tuck up her hair, she was suddenly and irritably aware of Sir Geoffrey's eyes on her, his expression one of barely masked contempt. He'd taken note of her attempt to improve her appearance and had obviously interpreted her behavior as that of a woman of excessive vanity. The man was revoltingly toplofty and arrogant; she was again smitten with a powerful urge to slap his face. But at the same time she had to admit to herself that her concern for the appearance of her hair was quite out of place under the circumstances. Perhaps he was right to think her vain.

But the contemptuous expression she thought she'd detected on his face disappeared. With a small, rather ironic bow, he said, "Welcome to Knight's Haven, your ladyship. And you, too, Mrs. Underwood. May I present my family? This is my mother, Lady Carrier."

A large-bosomed woman with a head of artificially colored russet hair stepped forward, smiling broadly. "How delightful to meet you, Lady Margaret, although I suppose I shouldn't say delightful when the circumstance has been brought about by dreadful accident—and you injured, too!—but it *is* delightful otherwise. I've already met your aunt, you know, out there in the hallway, and as I told her, you may be quite surprised to learn that I was acquainted with your dear mother. In London, you know. We had a house quite near to yours—"

"Yes, Mama, but there will be plenty of time for reminiscences later," her son cut in coldly. "I must introduce our guests to my sisters before they become hopelessly confused. Lady Margaret has already mistook Trixie for my wife. *This,* your ladyship, is my sister Beatrix Carrier, whom you've already encountered to your sorrow. Trixie, come and give her ladyship your apologies."

The young woman, now divested of her cloak and bonnet, gave her brother a frightened glance and came forward. "I am very s-sorry, your ladyship, about the accident. I'm sure I d-don't know what to say to—"

Miss Carrier was much younger than her brother, looking

no more than twenty. She had dark brown hair, tied up tightly on each side of her forehead and falling over her ears in curls, eyes modestly lowered, and a pair of full lips which looked as if they were overly accustomed to pouting. "You needn't say anything, Miss Carrier," Meg said kindly. "The accident was not your fault, you know."

Trixie threw her brother another quick glance before answering. "Thank you, your ladyship. And I wish you will call me Trixie. Everyone does."

"And now, ma'am," Geoffrey said, "you must meet the youngest of our family. Here she is, bearing a warming drink for you. My sister, Sybil Carrier. Give Lady Margaret the brandy, Sybil."

The girl looked to be barely seventeen, with light brown hair neatly braided round her head, pale cheeks and light eyes now wide in interested admiration of the London ladies. She dropped a bobbing curtsey and approached the sofa. "Will you take the brandy, my lady?" she asked shyly, offering the glass.

Meg smiled at her warmly. "How do you do? Shall I call you Sybil? Thank you for troubling yourself, but I don't wish to drink anything."

"Take it," Sir Geoffrey ordered. "It will do you good."

Meg's smile faded. She met his eye, her own darkening angrily, and put up her chin. "Thank you, sir, but I don't *wish* for any brandy." She wanted him to know from the outset that she would not take orders from him. She was quite ready, despite her weakened condition and the presence of his family, to demonstrate to him that her spirit had not been cowed by his high-handed treatment of her.

But he didn't challenge her. He merely shrugged, took the drink from his sister and drank it himself. "And now," he said after the brandy had been neatly downed, "you must meet Mrs. Rhys in whose care you shall be until you're restored to health." He led forward the last observer in the room, a robust, neatly aproned, white-capped woman who curtseyed and smiled at Meg pleasantly.

"Oh, yes, Mrs. Rhys will have you well in no time," Lady Carrier agreed, sitting down beside Meg on the sofa. "She's our housekeeper, you know, but in addition to her ability in running this great old monstrosity of a house, she has great skill with herbs and medicines. You'll do very well if you leave yourself in her hands."

The housekeeper accepted the compliments with merely a

matter-of-fact nod of her head. "I think yer ladyship's lookin'
a bit peaked, which ain't no surprise," she observed. "Do y'
wish t' wait fer supper, or would ye prefer yer bed?"

Meg was about to ask for bed when the butler entered with
a large tray. Even from across the room, Meg could smell the
well-seasoned barley soup. Its aroma was so tantalizing that
she realized at once how hungry she was. She and Aunt Isabel
hadn't had a morsel to eat since noon. Poor Aunt Bel must be
famished. "I do think a bowl of soup . . ." she murmured.

"Oh, good!" Lady Carrier said eagerly. "I am so glad you
aren't going to retire just yet. Set up the table here, Keating,
and we shall all join in the repast. I positively long to have an
opportunity to chat with you both. It's been so long since we've
visited London that I quite yearn to hear the latest *on-dits.*"

Sir Geoffrey cleared his throat. "I hope, Mama, that you'll
be good enough to excuse me from this female *tête-à-tête.* I
have a few matters which must be attended to. And if you can
spare Trixie as well, I'd like to take her with me for a few
minutes."

Meg caught sight of an exchange of alarmed glances between Trixie and her mother. But Lady Carrier only sighed and
said, "Of course, Geoffrey," and Trixie, her hands clenched
nervously, followed her brother from the room.

Meg felt a stab of misgiving. Perhaps she should have ignored her hunger and gone up to bed when she'd had the
chance. Sir Geoffrey obviously found his guests an unwelcome
intrusion, and there was an underlying feeling of tension in this
house. Besides, she didn't think she could endure making idle
conversation while her head pounded and her ankle pained.
But the housekeeper wordlessly piled some cushions under her
foot, which eased the pain a little. And the late supper, served
with meticulous deftness by Keating, the butler, was hot and
soothing, tasting quite delicious to the hungry guests. Even the
conversation proved to be less of a strain than Meg had feared,
for Lady Carrier barely stopped chattering long enough to permit proper answers to the many questions with which she in-
terlarded her monologue about the luxury and excitement of
her London days.

Lady Carrier interrupted her prattle only once—when
Trixie, her eyes looking suspiciously red-rimmed and her underlip more pouting than before, returned to the room. The
mother watched with concern as Trixie took a place at the

table, but Trixie kept her eyes lowered and said nothing. After a moment of awkward silence, Lady Carrier resumed her chatter as if nothing at all was amiss.

In spite of her pain and weariness, Meg studied with interest the faces of the women of Sir Geoffrey's household. It was evident that the forbidding, saturnine gentleman did not inherit his looks from his mother. Her watery blue eyes and weak chin were completely unlike his dark, craggy countenance. Neither did his sisters closely resemble him, although Trixie had his dark coloring and Sybil his high cheekbones. Trixie, in spite of her petulant mouth, was close to being a beauty, Meg thought. With her large, speaking eyes and dark curls, she probably attracted every man in her vicinity. Sybil, on the other hand, was pale, sallow and too unformed and immature to be ready to compete with her sister in feminine attractiveness.

The meal had ended, and the ladies were sipping the last of their tea, when Geoffrey returned to tell them that Mrs. Rhys had readied the bedrooms for his guests. "Your man Roodle tells me that the mare's foreleg is only slightly bruised and should be good as new in a few days," he informed Meg, "and the fellow asked me to assure you that he is pleased with the room we've given him over the stables. I'm afraid, however, that I've some *bad* news regarding the doctor. The groom I sent to fetch him was unable to get very far. The drifts are becoming too deep. We shall have to wait for morning to have your ankle examined. I'm sorry."

Aunt Isabel, her spirits much revived by the warming effects of the fire and the good meal, had become less anxious about her niece's condition and hastened to reassure her host. "There's no need to apologize, Sir Geoffrey," she said cheerfully. "Neither the storm nor the accident was any fault of yours."

That's all very well for you to say, Aunt Bel, Meg thought irritably. *You don't have a bruised head and a swollen ankle!* Meg found it quite impossible to be well-disposed toward her host, and she resented her aunt's noticeable approval of him. In a way, everything that had happened this evening was his fault. If he'd been a bit more gallant in the taproom of the Horse With Three Tails Inn, this entire calamity might never have occurred, and she might now be happily asleep in the best bedroom of the White Hart at Harrogate, with Arthur Steele near at hand and ready to see her home. But none of the others around the table knew anything of the occurrence at the tap-room, and it would be paltry on her part to throw the matter up to him while she was a guest in his home—a guest whom circumstance had forced on him. Therefore, although *he* was not acting the compleat gentleman, *she* would show that she could act the compleat lady. "My aunt is quite right, sir," she said grandly. "Even without the ministrations of a doctor, I shall survive the night."

"I was quite certain you would, ma'am," he replied, un-impressed.

They all rose to say their goodnights, Isabel helping Meg to get to her feet. The action set off a chain of reactions Meg did not expect: a spear of pain shot from her ankle through her entire being, while at the same time her head throbbed dizzily. She swayed, her eyelids drooped and a frightening lassitude almost instantly seemed to overcome her. *Good Lord*, she thought with horror, *I'm going to swoon.*

But before she could surrender to the enveloping blackness, she felt herself being scooped up again in a familiar pair of arms, and she was suddenly fully awake. "I'll take her up-stairs," Sir Geoffrey was saying to Isabel.

"Put me down," she murmured irritably. "It isn't at all necessary for you to carry me. It was only a momentary diz-ziness. With my aunt's support under my arm, I'm sure I can manage on my own." She still felt dizzy, but she was not so lightheaded that she could ignore her feelings of embarrassment and distaste at being in his arms again.

"Don't be a fool," he said curtly. His mouth was tight, as if he were trying to keep grip on his patience. "You may as well grow accustomed to this, ma'am. I suspect that this method of transport may be your only recourse, during the next few days, for getting from place to place. Now be a good girl and put your—"

"I know. Put my arms about your neck and be still."

The corners of his mouth turned up in a sardonic smile. "I'm glad you've learned your lesson so well."

He carried her to the stairs, the rest of the assemblage trailing behind. With her hands clasped round her neck, she found herself staring at his profile. His forehead was creased with frown lines, his nose rather prominent and his chin almost forbiddingly strong. The closeness of that face to hers made her exceedingly uncomfortable, and she forced herself to turn away from him. Instead, she looked with interest at the house, the view being much better from this angle than it had been on her entrance. The house was very old, with high ceilings, wide corridors and grandly scaled rooms. There was something medieval about the front hall, with its stone floors and walls, high, narrow windows and faded tapestried hangings. The stairway was very wide and seemed to carry the eye upward with its graceful curves. At first glance one had to be impressed.

But on closer examination, it became plain that the days of this mansion's grandeur had long since passed. Everything was faded, worn and shabby. The carpets showed patches of wear, the massive pieces of furniture were nicked and scratched, and the window hangings should have been replaced years ago. Was the family impoverished, she wondered, or merely negligent?

The ceilings of the second floor were not quite so high, and the room to which Geoffrey carried her was cozily scaled. There was a charming old four-posted bed between two casement windows, its hangings light and clean. A fire was burning in a small, tiled fireplace, and candles had been lit in an adjoining dressing room which she could see through the door in the far corner. Mrs. Rhys had evidently been busily occupied while the rest of them had supped.

Sir Geoffrey placed Meg gingerly upon the bed. "Mrs. Rhys will be right up to help you undress," he said and turned to go.

"Thank you, sir, for all your trouble," Isabel said from the doorway, "but we needn't bother Mrs. Rhys any further. I shall take care of Meg."

"It's no bother, Mrs. Underwood, I assure you," Sir Geoffrey said, surprising Meg with the note of kindness in his voice.

"Do go along to bed, Aunt Bel," Meg urged. "You look done in. Mrs. Rhys and I shall deal well enough."

"Yes, Mrs. Underwood," Lady Carrier argued from the corridor, "our Mrs. Rhys likes nothing better than taking charge of a sickroom. Let me show you the way to your bedroom. Did you decide to give her the Marlborough Room, Geoffrey, my dear?"

"Yes, indeed. You must forgive Mama, Mrs. Underwood, for her inordinate pride in what is really a quite ordinary bedroom. The one thing that prevents her from completely despising this house is the fact that the memorable Duke once spent a night under this roof."

Mrs. Rhys bustled in at this moment, bearing a small tray on which were a number of glasses and jars filled with mysterious liquids and creams, and she firmly ordered them all to go about their business. Isabel, succumbing to Sir Geoffrey's and Lady Carrier's persuasion, bid her niece a reluctant goodnight and permitted herself to be led away.

As soon as Mrs. Rhys closed the door on them, Meg allowed herself to groan wearily. The pain in her ankle and the hammering in her head were bringing her close to the point of tears.

"There now, my lady, don't you fret. We'll 'ave ye comfortable in no time," Mrs. Rhys murmured sympathetically. She bent over her patient, examining her carefully. With knowing fingers, she probed at the lump on the back of Meg's head. "Don't think anything's broke in there," she said with brisk authority, "but it wouldn't surprise me none if ye 'ad the headache fer quite a while. Now let's 'ave a look at that ankle."

She sat down on the bed and lifted Meg's leg to her lap. Carefully unlacing the modish short-boot, she slowly eased the shoe from the foot, causing Meg to gasp with pain. The ankle was swollen to more than twice its size, and the discoloration of the skin could be seen right through her white silk stocking. "Poor lass," the housekeeper sighed. "You'll 'ave a troublesome night. But when the doctor binds it t'morra, it'll feel much better, you'll see."

Keeping up a stream of optimistic promises about the speedy way a youthful body heals itself, the kind, quick-fingered woman cut off her stocking, stripped off her clothing, washed her with a sweet-smelling, lotion-like liquid and slipped a clean muslin night-dress trimmed with lace over her head. "It belongs to Miss Trixie. She says she hopes ye'll find it comfortable."

"Do thank her for me, Mrs. Rhys. You've all been very kind."

Mrs. Rhys was gently brushing the tangles from Meg's thick hair when there was a knock at the door. "It must be my aunt," Meg said, her brow knitted in pain and her mouth tense. "Be a dear, Mrs. Rhys, and tell her I've fallen asleep. She won't sleep a wink either if she becomes worried about me."

But it was not Isabel at the door. Meg heard Sir Geoffrey's voice in murmured conversation with the housekeeper. After a moment, Mrs. Rhys returned to her side and pulled a comforter over her. "It's Sir Geoffrey, my lady, come to bandage yer ankle. Just let me cover you up a bit, an' we can 'ave 'im in."

"But I don't *want*—" The sentence died on her lips, for Sir Geoffrey at that moment stepped into the circle of light thrown by the branch of candles on her night table. For a brief moment, he stood stock still and stared at her, a strange, arrested look in his eyes . . . almost as if he'd wandered into the wrong room. Instinctively, without realizing she was doing it, she pulled the comforter up to her neck. "Sir Geoffrey, what—?"

He recovered himself at once. "I don't mean to intrude, ma'am, but it occurred to me—and Mrs. Rhys concurs—that you're not likely to get a wink of sleep with your ankle unbound. I've brought some bandages which we'll be able to tie into a passable support which will do until the doctor gets here. And this drink I have here will help even more to put you to sleep."

"That was very kind in you, sir, and I don't wish you to think me ungrateful, but I scarcely think—"

"A common affliction of females," he interrupted caustically. "They 'scarcely think' at all."

"Come now, Sir Geoff, let's 'ave none o' yer sharp tongue," Mrs. Rhys scolded. "Ye mustn't mind, 'im, my lady. 'E's always makin' wicked remarks about our sex."

"Yes, I've noticed that," Meg muttered drily.

"Did you hear, that, Mrs. Rhys?" he asked as he came up to the patient's side. "I'm not the only one with a sharp tongue. Here, ma'am, drink this down."

"No, it looks dreadful. I don't want to drink *anything*."

"Do what the lad tells ye," Mrs. Rhys urged. "It's only a bit o' laudanum, I expect."

"I've been doing what 'the lad' tells me all *night*," she said sourly. Then, looking at him questioningly, she asked, "*Is* it laudanum?"

"Yes, merely enough for a mild, sedative effect. Try, just once, to do as I ask without argumentation. The night will be very long and painful for you if you don't."

With ill grace, she accepted the glass from his hand and began to sip. He and Mrs. Rhys immediately turned their attention to her ankle. Mrs. Rhys turned back the comforter just enough to reveal the injury and lifted the leg to her lap again. Sir Geoffrey, with remarkable gentleness, began to wind the bandages around the bruise.

By the time the job was done, the glass was empty and Meg was becoming pleasantly drowsy. The sharpness of the pain seemed considerably diminished, her vision was fuzzy, and her thoughts seemed unfocused and disjointed. The goodnight she uttered in response to theirs sounded drunkenly indistinct to her ears, and when the door closed behind them, she snuggled down into the pillows feeling whoozily content.

Just before slipping into sleep, she found herself puzzling over the enigma of the strange females in the household and her even stranger host. Sir Geoffrey Carrier. He was completely odious—even in her present stupor, she was sure of that. He'd proven himself to be arrogant, disdainful, insolent and ungenerous. Yet during these last few minutes, he'd seemed quite different. Was it only the effect of the laudanum on her brain . . . or was the fellow, somewhere deep beneath the surface, actually *kind? No*, she thought before sleep enveloped her. *No. Sir Geoffrey the Ungallant, kind? Impossible!*

Chapter Six

By the next afternoon she'd decided it must have been the laudanum—there was nothing kind about the man at all. The evidence had piled up by that time to prove that Sir Geoffrey Carrier was indeed the blackguard he'd seemed from the first. And this time the evidence came from his own family.

The day had begun with the discouraging news (from a housemaid who'd come in to open the draperies) that the snow was still falling. There would be no visit from the doctor today, for the snow had considerably deepened during the night and the wind had whipped it into sizeable drifts. So much for Meg's expectation that the mild autumn weather they'd experienced a day earlier would soon reassert itself. Winter had evidently decided to come early and to settle in to stay.

Before she'd shaken herself fully awake, her aunt had tiptoed in. "Are you awake, dearest?" she'd asked timidly.

"Yes, love, do come in," Meg greeted her, sitting up in stiff painfulness and trying to smile with sincerity.

Isabel didn't look much refreshed from her night's sleep. Her wiry grey hair had been neatly brushed into a tight bun at the back of her head, and her traveling dress had been freshly pressed, but the color had not returned to her cheeks and her eyes were still underlined with weariness. Nevertheless, she perched on the bed beside her niece cheerily and examined her closely. "I hope I didn't waken you. Are you feeling any better this morning?"

"Much better, Aunt Bel, and full of contrition for having embroiled you in so disastrous an adventure."

"Oh, pooh, don't trouble yourself about that, my dear. If it weren't for the fact that you've suffered an injury, I would be quite enjoying myself."

"Enjoying yourself? You can't mean it! Marooned by an intense and unseasonal snowstorm in this great barn of a castle with only a crippled niece and a most peculiar family for company, and you call that *enjoyment?*"

"I can't say I'm enjoying the fact that my niece is *crippled,* you wet-goose, but as for the family and this rather eccentric old castle they've chosen to live in, I'm finding them all rather interesting."

"Are you really?" Meg asked in surprise. "Why?"

"Well, it's something like living in a novel by Mrs. Radcliffe. I was observing the family at breakfast this morning and—"

"Have you already breakfasted? What *time* is it?"

"It's after eleven, my love."

"After eleven? Good heavens, how could I have been permitted to sleep for so long? Why didn't you—? What must they think of me?"

"Don't worry, Meg. Sir Geoffrey explained that he'd given you a sleeping draught. He expected that you wouldn't rise very early."

"Oh, he did, did he? He told me he'd given me only a mild sedative—but now it appears I've been positively drugged!"

"I shouldn't get on my high ropes over it, Meggie, if I were you. You're looking ever so much better than you were last night, so the sedative seems to have done you no damage. And since Sir Geoffrey feels that you would do well to rest in bed today anyway, there was no harm in your sleeping a bit late this morning."

Meg's eyebrows rose in annoyance. "Sir *Geoffrey* says . . . Sir *Geoffrey* feels . . . You're quite full of Sir Geoffrey this morning, aren't you? Suppose I tell you that I don't *wish* to rest in bed today—what then?"

"Sir Geoffrey says he'd be happy to carry you downstairs if you'd prefer, so you needn't take that tone," Isabel responded placidly.

"Hmmmph!" Meg leaned back against her pillows and frowned. "Very kind of him, I'm sure! I'd rather stay here in bed for a *week* than have him carry me."

Her aunt studied her quizzically. "What's gotten into you, Meg? It's not like you to behave ungraciously. We *are* intruders here, after all."

"Yes, but if he hadn't—" She cut herself short. She'd decided last night not to say anything about the scene in the taproom, yet now, with very little provocation, she was about to reveal the story. She clamped her lips shut.

"Hadn't what, Meg?" her aunt asked, cocking her head curiously.

"Nothing. What was it you began to say earlier—about observing the family at breakfast?"

"Oh, yes. It seems that the entire family consists of the four of them—Sir Geoffrey, his two sisters, and their mother. The girls were born in London, and they all lived there except Sir Geoffrey who was in military service. Then, when his father died, he sold out and moved the family here. I learned that much from Lady Carrier. She seems very much to resent his having uprooted them, and all the ladies seem to be abnormally afraid of him. I can't help but wonder why. *I* find him a perfectly affable, sensible sort of person."

"Perhaps they know him better than you do," Meg uttered under her breath.

"What did you say, love?"

"I said that affable is the last word I should choose to describe him."

"Really?" Isabel peered at her niece with shrewd interest. "What word would you—"

But their conversation was cut short by the arrival of Mrs. Rhys, who bustled in with a cheery smile and a breakfast tray.

With her aunt's urging and the housekeeper's assistance, Meg breakfasted and performed her ablutions, all of which caused her considerable discomfort. But Isabel and Mrs. Rhys agreed that her traveling clothes were too bedraggled to be worn, and they both left her to find some more suitable attire for her to wear before the stream of visitors (who were certain to knock at her door before very long) should begin to appear.

They had barely closed the door behind them when the first visitor presented himself. It was Roodle, come to pay his respects and to see for himself how his new mistress had survived the night. He was full of apologies for his part in getting her into this fix, but when she assured him that she didn't blame him and pointed out that they were no worse off snowed in here at Knight's Haven than they would have been at the inn at Harrogate, he sighed with relief. He then was able to ease *her* mind about the condition of the injured horse. "I been treatin' 'is leg with a poultice o' me own devisin'. 'E'll be good as new. Wish I could say the same about the carriage." He shook his head worriedly. "Don' know as *that* kin be repaired good as new."

"As soon as the storm blows over, we shall see how matters stand," Meg said.

"I ain't waitin' fer the storm to blow over. I'm goin' out there now and take a peep at the wreck."

"You'll do no such thing," Meg ordered. "If Sir Geoffrey's man was unable to get through to the doctor last night, surely you won't be able to get through today, when conditions must even be worse out there."

"But, yer ladyship, we can't leave the phaeton just a-layin' there in the ditch! Are ye forgettin' it's stole?"

"I'm not forgetting anything. The snow has made the road as inaccessible to everyone else as it is to us. There's not the least need for you to alarm yourself, Roodle."

"That's all very well fer you, ma'am. But it'll be me what'll 'ave to 'ang if Lord Isham catches up with us."

"I promise you that *no one* will hang. If we're discovered, I shall merely pay his lordship for his loss and that will be that."

Roodle shifted his weight from one booted foot to the other, keeping his eyes on the ground in obstinate disagreement. "It's on'y a bit o' snow, ma'am. There ain't nothin' goin' to 'appen t' me if I plow through it fer a bit, is there?"

"I don't know what may happen. It's not a 'bit o' snow' you know—it's a severe storm. I see no reason for you to endanger your life and safety by going out in this dreadful blow just to—"

"Who's thinking of going out?" a voice asked from the open doorway. It was Sir Geoffrey, dressed in a caped greatcoat and heavy boots and carrying on his shoulders Meg's portmanteau. Behind him stood a footman bearing the rest of the baggage Meg and Isabel had stowed in the carriage. *"You,* Roodle?"

"Yes, sir. I wanted to take a peep at the wreck, to see if—"

"To see if the carriage can be salvaged? There's no need for that. We've just taken a look at it. I think your phaeton can be restored to full usefulness. I've arranged to have it hauled to Masham for repair as soon as the roads have been cleared."

"To Masham?" Roodle echoed hollowly, casting a horrified glance at Meg. "But . . . that's near Isham Manor!"

Sir Geoffrey looked from Roodle to Meg with uplifted brows. "Have I done something amiss? I'm well acquainted with the wheelwright at Masham and can assure you of his competence."

Meg cast a quelling look at her new coachman. "You've done nothing amiss, Sir Geoffrey. Nothing at all. Roodle is merely a bit . . . overzealous. We both are very grateful to you, aren't we, Roodle?"

"Yes, ma'am," Roodle muttered, his eyes on his shoes.

Sir Geoffrey turned to signal his footman to follow him, and the two went to deposit the baggage in the dressing room. Roodle looked up and gave his mistress a shrug which said as clearly as words that they were in a fine fix and that whatever happened next would be no fault of his, and he bowed himself out.

Sir Geoffrey, having disposed of the baggage, dismissed the footman. "Mrs. Rhys or one of the housemaids will unpack your things, ma'am," he said, turning to the door.

"Is that why you ventured out? Just to fetch our *baggage?"* Meg asked in surprised ingratitude.

He threw her a quizzical glance over his shoulder. "I know how unhappy you ladies can be when separated from your combs, your silks, your lotions and your laces," he said disdainfully.

"We ladies," she retorted with asperity, "are not such frippery creatures as you suppose. I, for one, could have managed perfectly well without——"

"Oh, Meg, dearest, just look at what Mrs. Rhys has found for you!" Isabel clarioned from the corridor, prancing in eagerly and holding aloft a colorful Chinese kimono of rustling silk. "Oh, Sir Geoffrey . . . I didn't see you there."

"I was just leaving, Mrs. Underwood," he said, giving Meg a leer of scornful triumph. "I know you ladies would like to be private to deal with your fripperies." And with a last mocking look at Meg, he sauntered from the room.

"I hope I didn't drive him away," Isabel murmured, looking from Meg to the corridor where Geoffrey was disappearing down the hall.

"If you did, I'm quite delighted. The odious man cannot open his mouth without giving offense."

Isabel blinked. "Offense? What offense?"

"The wretch didn't even ask how my ankle did. Blasted rudesby!"

Isabel peered at her niece, perplexed, but tactfully decided not to probe the matter further. "Here, put this on. I think Lady Carrier is on her way to call on you."

In another moment, Lady Carrier knocked at the door and entered with a great rustle of skirts. She was followed in by her two daughters who took places at each of the two bedposts at the foot of the bed while their mother settled herself into the bedside chair. "You *do* look better this morning, your ladyship," Lady Carrier said effusively, "although I shall not feel easy in my mind about your condition until Dr. Fraser had looked at you."

"Will you ask Dr. Fraser to look at me, too, Mama, when he comes?" Sybil asked plaintively. "I'm feeling quite queasy today."

"You always feel queasy," Trixie said to her sister unkindly.

"Of course, Sybil, dear. The doctor shall certainly have a look at you," their mother said, ignoring Trixie's comment. "My poor Sybil has a very delicate constitution," she confided to her two guests.

"That's not what Geoffrey and Dr. Fraser think," Trixie said maliciously.

"Be still, Beatrix," her mother scolded. "Robust gentlemen like Geoffrey and Dr. Fraser don't always recognize the problems of delicate natures such as Sybil's. Not that you need have any qualms, Lady Margaret, about Dr. Fraser's qualifications. He is very knowing and efficient. Of course, he hasn't the manners or the subtlety of the best London medical men—for he can be unbelievably brusque and churlish at times—but he's a sound practitioner. Very sound. Geoffrey believes his talents are as great an any doctor he's met, and though I can't go *that* far, I can assure you that you'll come to no harm in his hands."

"Thank you, Lady Carrier. I find your recommendation most...er...reassuring. But I wish, ma'am, that you'd call me Meg. Lady Margaret is much too distant and formal a manner of address from someone who has so generously welcomed into her home a pair of troublesome intruders."

"Oh, my dear, not troublesome at all! Not at all! In truth, Lady Meg (which is what I will call you to honor your request for informality, but we must use our titles, you know, for I wish the girls always to have respect for one's position in the world), but to return to what I was saying, in truth I couldn't be happier about having your company. We very seldom have visitors, you know, this place being so far from London or from any really *proper* society..." She sighed and pulled a handkerchief from the bosom of her dress. "It can be so very dreadfully lonely sometimes," she said, dabbing at her eyes, "that I think I shall go quite mad."

"Oh, Mama, don't exaggerate," Trixie muttered in disgust. "The Garrelsons come for dinner nearly every week, and so do Lady Habish and her girls—"

"To say nothing of Sir Edmund and Lady Lazenby and their son *Mortimer*," Sybil added pointedly, making a face at her sister.

Trixie colored to her ears. "Sybil!" she hissed warningly.

"Really, girls," Lady Carrier remonstrated, turning to glare at her daughters, "you will have her ladyship and Mrs. Underwood believing that you have no manners at all!" She turned back to Meg with an indulgent smile. "It's quite true that I offer my table to the local gentry from time to time—one can't live completely cut off from the world, you know—but one can't even *compare* such company with the circle of friends we had in London. Oh, dear, I do miss them so!" And she dabbed at her eyes again.

"Mama, you know perfectly well that you find this Yorkshire society very pleasant," Trixie insisted. "I've heard you say many times that you never had a better friend than Lady Habish."

Lady Carrier was more discomfitted than irritated by her daughter's contrariety. "That is because Lady Habish is the sort who would fit in anywhere," she said defensively, "even with the *haut ton* of London."

"Which is more than you can say of the Lazenbys—and their so-dashing son," Sybil said to her sister with a taunting smirk. "One could hardly picture *them* fitting into the tonnish circles of London."

"They most certainly *would*," Trixie fired up angrily. "Besides, what do *you* know of the tonnish circles of London?"

"Girls, please!" their mother cautioned with ineffectual embarrassment.

Isabel, in an attempt to avert a quarrel between the girls, smiled at Trixie understandingly. "I take it that the Lazenbys' dashing son is a particular friend of yours?"

Trixie blushed, but Sybil hooted mockingly. *"Very* particular, I'd say. She positively *dotes* on him."

"Sybil, you prattle-box, hold your tongue!" Trixie muttered in a threatening undervoice. "You're setting up my bristles, and I warn you—"

"There's no need to ruffle your feathers on our account, Trixie," Meg said in some amusement. "My aunt and I find it perfectly natural for a lovely young lady of your age to dote on a dashing neighbor. We would account it strange if you did not."

Trixie cast Meg a look of surprised gratitude. "Would you really? How kind of you to say so."

"Geoffrey wouldn't agree with you," Sybil said, continuing to taunt her sister. "Geoffrey says Mortimer Lazenby's a popinjay and that Trixie's an indiscriminate—"

"Sybil!" her mother cried, appalled.

"Dash it, Sybil, I'll—" Trixie took a threatening step toward her sister.

"Stop it, both of you!" Lady Carrier ordered with a real attempt at firmness. "What will our guests *think* of you?" She turned back to Meg, her face collapsing into tearful self-pity. "It's all Geoffrey's fault, you know. He's put us all on edge, just because . . . because . . . well, I may as well admit it to you, I permitted Trixie to attend a perfectly unobjectionable little party last night . . ." She sniffed pitifully into her handkerchief.

"It was objectionable to Geoffrey," Sybil said. "He guessed it was at the Lazenbys, even though you tried to make him think—"

"As far as I'm concerned," Lady Carrier said petulantly, "there's nothing wrong with her going to the Lazenbys. There's nothing at all objectionable about Mortimer, either."

"He's really quite up to snuff, Lady Meg," Trixie said, coloring again. "His family is completely respectable, and he's very handsome and neat as a trencher—"

"A veritable jack-a-dandy," Sybil said scornfully.

"There's nothing wrong with dressing in the latest mode," Trixie flashed back. "Just because one lives in the country, one needn't look like a bumpkin, isn't that so, Lady Meg?"

"But one needn't look like a twiddle-poop, either!" Sybil shot back.

"Girls, that will do! Do you see, ladies, how discomposed we all are? You must forgive us. If only Hackett had had his wits about him and hadn't driven into your carriage, we would never have fallen into this fix, for Geoffrey would never have learned that I permitted Trix to go. You can imagine how chagrined he is, having discovered our little secret in such a *dreadful* way—just coming upon the scene of the accident and discovering his sister buried in the wreckage. He's read us the riot act in no uncertain terms, you can be sure of that!"

Trixie's mouth took on a pouty look, but she said nothing. Sybil looked from her sister to her mother in disgust. "Must we be forever talking about nothing but Trixie's *affaire-de-coeur?* The entire subject has given me the megrims."

Trixie lowered her eyes in shame. "Sybil is right, for once, though she *always* gets migraines. You must think us dreadfully vulgar to be washing our dirty linen in front of you."

"Not at all," Isabel murmured comfortingly.

"Besides, we suspected something of the sort from remarks we overheard last night," Meg admitted.

Lady Carrier began to sniffle again. "You are very kind, my dears, to be so forgiving of our overwrought state, especially when you have troubles of your own. But when the storm has passed and your leg has been properly treated, you will both be able to return to your exciting lives in London, while *we* remain imprisoned in this horrid backwater—"

"Now, Mama—" Trixie remonstrated.

"It's true! Don't you *see* what our exile here has wrought?" She dabbed at her eyes again and drew in a trembling, mournful breath. "If we had been living in London, Trixie would have had a proper come-out and would have been able to choose from among *dozens* of beaux, and—"

"I'm sure she will have dozens of beaux in any case, Lady Carrier," Isabel said soothingly. "She is so very pretty, and so is Sybil . . . and they both have plenty of time to find all the beaux they—"

"Not here in Yorkshire. We are so thin of company here, you see," Lady Carrier sniffed into her handkerchief.

"Then why don't you return to town for a time?" Isabel suggested. "You could rent a house for the season . . . or even visit one of your friends for a short period. Even a fortnight would be enough to permit the girls to meet a number of eligible gentlemen."

"Oh, yes, a fortnight would be like heaven!" Lady Carrier sighed, lifting her head, her eyes brightening at the vision. "How I would love it . . . to visit my old friends . . . Lady Dewsbury, Countess Lieven . . ."

"And to go to all the shops and bazaars . . . and the *balls* . . ." Trixie breathed.

"And to have one's lungs checked by the famous physicians," Sybil murmured yearningly.

"And to play a card game more exciting than copper-loo," Lady Carrier said dreamily.

"And to hear an opera at Covent Garden . . ."

"And to know that one could find an apothecary just down the street . . ."

"Do you mean to say," Meg asked in disbelief, "that the idea of a trip to London has never occurred to you before?"

"Oh, yes," Lady Carrier said, the dreamy expression fading from her eyes. "But of course we try not to dwell on it, because we know that Geoffrey would never permit it."

"No, he wouldn't," Trixie agreed.

"Not in a thousand years," Sybil added decisively.

"But why not?" Meg asked, her irritation with the tyrannical Geoffrey growing by leaps and bounds. "Surely your son cannot dictate—"

"Hush, Meg," Isabel interrupted tactfully. "You have no

right to make comments on the Carriers' intimate family matters."

"Oh, don't say that, Mrs. Underwood," Lady Carrier urged. "We've revealed the intimate matters of our family quite freely to *you*, so why should we take offense if you speak freely to us?"

"But there may be many good reasons why your son has objections to a London trip—reasons of health or finance or personal situations which Meg and I know nothing of. It is quite beyond our province to make suggestions," Isabel said firmly.

"My aunt is right, of course," Meg said, chastened, "but I would be happy to offer you the hospitality of my home, in return for your hospitality to us, if ever you should decide to come down to London for a visit."

"Oh, Lady Meg, how generous!" Lady Carrier pressed her hands to her bosom, rendered speechless by Meg's offer.

But Trixie sighed and shook her head. "My brother wouldn't hear of it. He thinks that London is a breeding ground of dissipation and corruption and that we're well out of it."

"Does he indeed?" Isabel asked in surprise. "I didn't receive such an impression of him. Is your brother an Evangelical, Trixie?"

"An Evangelical?" Trixie giggled at the idea. "Oh, no, nothing like that. It's only . . . he feels that, if one has any weakness of character, to be living in London would only make it worse."

"Or weakness of constitution as well," Sybil interjected.

"Are you saying that your brother finds *your* characters too weak to withstand living in town?" Meg couldn't help asking.

"He thinks *all* females' characters are too weak."

"Oh, I see! But not *male* characters, of course." Meg's disdain was not noticeable to her visitors, but her aunt recognized it and threw her a look of rebuke.

"Perhaps *some* males," Trixie responded thoughtfully, as if considering the question for the first time.

"But certainly not Sir Geoffrey himself?" Meg asked in a voice that now was heavy with irony. "He didn't leave London to keep *himself* from corruption, did he?"

"Geoffrey?" Lady Carrier exclaimed, shocked.

Trixie giggled again. "Oh, Lady Meg, you must be joking! My brother is completely *in*corruptible."

"That's quite true," Geoffrey's mother nodded in grave assent.

"He's the most incorruptible person in the world," young Sybil agreed, sighing deeply. And then, as if their assessment of Geoffrey's character was the most depressing of realizations, they all three lapsed into glum silence.

Meg looked from one to the other of the three Carrier women with profound sympathy. While she'd found their characters far from admirable (she'd felt twinges of distaste on several occasions during their conversation), she nevertheless couldn't help feeling pity for their situations. Their problems and their weaknesses had undoubtedly been greatly exacerbated by the despotic high-handedness of Geoffrey Carrier, the man who dominated their lives. She understood quite well why they'd turned so glum. Incorruptibility was usually a characteristic one could greatly admire, but to be incorruptible in one's *tyranny* was a very different matter.

She'd had a passing perception, last night, that the man might have a streak of kindness in him, but the perception was undoubtedly false. She was now certain that it had been a mental lapse resulting from a laudanum-induced fuzzyheadedness. But fuzzyheadedness was not her usual condition. She would not lapse again! From now on she would deal with Sir Geoffrey in the way that he deserved. The women of his family might bend to his will, but he would find in Meg Underwood a very different sort of female!

Chapter Seven

"Don't you see, Aunt Bel, that the man must be a complete tyrant?" Meg asked her aunt later that afternoon when they found themselves at last without visitors.

"No, I don't see that at all. Sir Geoffrey seems to me to be a perfectly sensible, polite and thoughtful man."

"But look at the evidence," Meg persisted. "He uprooted his family from London, despite their deep desire to remain there, and forced them to live in this drafty old castle far from normal society just because it suits *him*. And he rules every aspect of their lives, even decreeing that his sister's natural need for parties and beaux be stifled. Isn't that tyranny?"

"I don't know, Meg. Perhaps it is. But perhaps he has good reason for his behavior."

"What sort of reason *could* he have."

Isabel shrugged. "How can I answer that? I'm not privvy

to the family secrets. But it does seem to me that neither his mother nor his sisters are endowed with much good sense. Perhaps he's been forced, by their lack of competence, to make decisions *for* them."

"That is always the excuse of tyrants!" Meg bent forward and rearranged the pillows under her ankle, poking at them irritably. "Wait until he begins to tyrannize over you. Then we shall see if you're still so eager to defend him."

"Don't be silly. Why should he tyrannize over me?"

"Because he believes all females are incompetent. That's what I find most irritating about the man."

Isabel studied her niece curiously. "Has he treated *you* as an incompetent, Meg? Is that why you've developed this un-reasoning prejudice against him?"

"Unreasoning prejudice! The fellow has made no secret about *his* prejudice against *me*. He's already called me a sim-pleton, a jinglebrained ninnyhammer and a plaguey irritation. What have you to say to *that,* eh?"

Isabel gaped. "Meg! You can't mean it. He wouldn't—!"

"He would and he did. And what's more, he implied that I was fat!"

Isabel snorted derisively and got to her feet. "Now I know you're making all this up. Isn't this a story made out of whole cloth?"

"It is not a story. It's completely true—and there's a great deal more I could tell you that's every bit as reprehensible."

"I'm not sure I want to hear it," Isabel retorted. "Besides, it's time I went to change for dinner. Since Sir Geoffrey was so tyrannical as to go out in the storm and retrieve our baggage from the wreckage, I may as well shed this travel dress and adorn myself in something more appropriate for the evening."

Meg grunted. "I suppose you find him heroic! He retrieved our baggage because of gallantry, I suppose. Hah! I assure you, Aunt Bel, that the only reason he went out in the storm was to see the condition of his own carriage."

"You may be right," Isabel conceded, going to the door, "but I sincerely hope, my dear, that *you* will not be so tyrannical as to desire me to accept *your* evaluation of the characters of the people we meet above my *own*. I did so in the case of Charles Isham because you know him better than I do. But in this case, I prefer to make my own judgment."

"Really, Isabel," Meg said coldly, feeling a bit offended,

"I've never tried to influence your judgment. You may feel quite free to think as you please . . . about Sir Geoffrey or anyone else."

"Thank you. I'm very much obliged, your ladyship, I'm sure. Now if you'll come down off your high ropes long enough to bid me adieu, I'll take my leave. Are you certain that you don't want the tyrant to carry you down to the dinner table?"

"Quite certain," Meg muttered sulkily. "I don't want him to carry me *anywhere*. I hope you have a delightful evening without me."

Isabel, recognizing the petulant self-pity of the suffering invalid in her niece's tone, merely blew her a kiss and took her leave. It would do the girl good to be left in peaceful solitude.

The solitude was not as beneficial to Meg's spirits as her aunt had hoped, for she lay back against the pillows, her eyes shut, and permitted herself to become more consciously aware of the ache in her ankle and the inconvenience of her situation. She had hoped that she would be well on her way to London by this time. She'd left Isham Manor in eager anticipation of a return to her own abode with Arthur Steele as escort. By tomorrow, she'd expected to be sleeping in her own bed, following her usual pursuits and surrounding herself with her own intimates. Instead, she was imprisoned in this draughty old mansion for an indefinite period, prevented from keeping her appointment with Arthur and unable, this time, to steal away down the back stairs or even to free herself from this alien bed. She was in worse case than she'd ever been at Isham Manor. Her thoughts were dolefully depressing, and the sound of the wind howling outside her windows made a completely appropriate accompaniment to the gloom of her mood.

The sound of a tap on the door only irked her more. Would she never be given a moment's peace? "Come in," she muttered.

"Have I disturbed you?" Sir Geoffrey asked from the doorway. "I've only come to ask if you wish Mrs. Rhys to bring your dinner here, or if you'd prefer to be carried downstairs?"

"I wouldn't dream of asking you to carry me downstairs," she said sullenly. "Not being a lightweight, I would be too great a burden on you."

"As to that," he responded coolly (although she thought there was a tiny hint of amusement in his eyes—the light was too dim to be certain), "I would not let that problem weigh too heavily. I've impressed into your service the footman who is standing here behind me, and he, as you can see, is considerably younger and no doubt much stronger than I."

Meg ground her teeth in fury. The man had never yet said a word to her that was anything but insulting. "Thank you, sir, but a supper tray here in bed is all I require. And do thank your footman, too," she added with icy sarcasm. "It was very brave of him to volunteer to perform so *prodigiously burdensome* a task."

"As you wish, ma'am," he said and turned to dismiss the footman. But not before Meg caught a glimpse of the slightest twitch at the corners of his mouth. This wasn't the first time she'd suspected that he'd enjoyed a secret laugh at her expense.

He remained in the doorway after the servant had left, studying her through narrowed eyes. "Are you in much pain?" he inquired.

"Why do you ask?" she responded sullenly. "Are you trying to convince me that you're suddenly willing to become 'involved' in my problems?"

He came in and sat down beside her on the bed. "Are you still smoldering over our little altercation at the inn? I think it's time you stopped dwelling on that bit of nonsense."

"That 'nonsense' was directly responsible for everything that's happened to me since. If you'd *helped* me with Mrs. What's-her-name—"

"Perkins."

"Yes, Perkins. If you'd given me some assistance with her, I might well be on my way home by this time, without this broken ankle and the lump on my head."

"Or you might still be lying in a ditch somewhere in Mrs. Perkins' rickety equipage, dead as a doornail and buried, unnoticed, under two feet of snow."

"I would *not* be—"

"Don't act the fool. It was not a night to be out traveling. I'd hoped, by putting a damper on your plans, to force you to spend the night at the inn, which is what anybody with a grain of sense would have done. Instead of which you managed to procure a carriage somewhere else. Where did you get that phaeton, by the way?"

"That, sir, is none of your affair."

He shrugged. "Yes, I'm aware of that. I'm also aware that there's something havey-cavey about your acquisition of that rig. I don't care whether or not you choose to confide the circumstances to me, but when the snow melts—as it surely will within the next few days—and the magistrates make their way to my door, I shan't be able to fob them off if my information is inadequate."

"You needn't trouble yourself about the magistrates. I can take care of them myself . . . quite well. I've managed for many years to deal with my own problems, and all without help from you."

"Very well, ma'am, please yourself. Although I don't think my behavior at the Horse With Three Tails warrants quite such vehement antagonism. Your ankle must be paining you quite severely."

She drew herself up in disgust. "That is just the sort of arrogant interpretation of my mood which I might have expected from you, Sir Geoffrey. If I show antagonism, the cause, of course, cannot be *your* fault—oh, no! It must be something else . . . like my injury!"

His eyebrows lifted again. "Is there something else that I've done which angered you?" he asked in what seemed to be sincere surprise. A look of unmistakable amusement shot into his eyes. "It can't be that I complained about your not being a featherweight, can it? Surely you must have received enough compliments about the perfection of your form to withstand a little teasing. I imagine that half the men in London must have told you—"

"*All* the men in London have told me about the 'perfection of my form'!" she declared grandly. "And for you to believe that I'd fall into the sulks over your slights is the *greatest* of the insults you've yet heaped on me."

"I was not aware of heaping any insults—"

"No, of course you were not! You think so little of the members of my sex that you're not even conscious, I suppose, of how you disparage us."

"Come now, your ladyship," he remonstrated patiently, "you mustn't let a small injury cast you so deeply into the dismals that your reason and your sense of humor are affected."

Her eyebrows lifted superciliously. "It quite amazes me, sir, how you condemn yourself with every word you utter. If

I dare to find any faults in you, I must be either mentally deranged, lacking in humor or suffering from my injury!"

"Not at all," he said, his patiently pleasant expression darkening with a puzzled frown. "I don't claim to be without faults, I assure you. But my faults had not, before this, kept me from maintaining cordial relations with the guests of this house."

"They must all have been men," she retorted.

He gave a little snort of laughter and, with a shrug, as if to say that it was quite hopeless to reason with a female, made one last attempt to placate her. "I'm sorry, my dear, that you feel in some way offended, but is it quite fair to assume that *all* your sex would find me similarly offensive?"

"It is not an assumption but an almost proven fact."

"That all females find me offensive?" He stood up and stared down at her, one eyebrow raised in sardonic disbelief.

"If you hold my sex in low esteem, they *must* find you so. I've listened all afternoon to your own mother and sisters, and I've learned from them the extent to which you use your position of responsibility to disparage them, control them and tyrannize over them." She could see him stiffen, but she went heedlessly on. "From the first moment I saw you, I found you arrogant and unfeeling. And everything I've learned since only reinforces that impression. If I am showing 'vehement antagonism,' it is not my 'small injury' which causes it—or even my irrationality or my lack of humor. It is nothing but you yourself!"

Every muscle in his face seemed to have hardened, and his eyes glinted like steel. "I had hoped we could brush through this enforced proximity with a minimum of tension," he said icily, "but I see that the difficulties are not to be avoided. Well, then, ma'am, since my family has seen fit to pour out our intimate secrets into your ears, I may as well be equally frank. Yes, my dear, I *do* hold your sex in low esteem. I have to deal daily with a mother whose propensity for gaming is quite out of control, with one sister whose attraction toward fops and coxcombs is completely indiscriminate, and with another who imagines she suffers from every disease listed in the *Encyclopaedia Medica*. It is my onerous duty—without a bit of compensatory satisfaction, I assure you—to keep their various idiosyncratic proclivities under some sort of restraint. If this duty (necessitated by these *felicitous* examples of feminine virtue) has failed to endear your sex to me, I plead guilty.

But I warn you, ma'am, that my esteem for womankind will not be a bit enhanced by the addition under my roof of still another female to harass my peace—one who is so foolishly self-admiring that she reads into every one of my casual remarks a personal affront! You would be well advised, if you wish this period of our enforced association to pass with a minimum of friction, to keep your hostility to your host from showing too blatantly, to refrain from encouraging his family in their excesses, and to behave with some modicum of the sense you claim to possess. And now, goodnight to you, ma'am. I will see that Mrs. Rhys brings you a supper tray within the hour." And with that, he stalked from the room, shutting the door firmly behind him.

She gaped at the door openmouthed. His cold disdain had left her speechless and shaken. Never in her life had she been spoken to in such a way! How dare he treat her as if she were just another burdensome female he was forced to endure?

She found herself seething. She was quite unaccustomed to being belittled by the gentlemen she met. Wherever she went—in the most fashionable circles of London society—the gentlemen all danced attendance on her, eager to do her least bidding, exerting themselves to earn her slightest smile, vying with each other to win her favor. Why, even the Regent himself, during a dinner at Carleton House, had stumbled over his tongue trying to make a favorable impression on her. Yet this impertinent rudesby presumed to treat her with such contempt! If he'd approached her in a London drawing room—a mere country baronet—it would have been she who disdained him!

That was the problem, of course—she was in his realm, his castle, his kingdom. Here she was forced into situations where their confrontations had not been favorable to her. She'd always been in some way a supplicant. Everywhere she'd encountered him, she'd had to beg for his assistance—in the taproom, at the scene of the wreckage, and here at Knight's Haven. She had needed his help, his support, his indulgence. He'd never seen her in situations where *she* could be in control ... and where *he* might have to play the supplicant. Oh, how she would love to see their roles reversed! How she would love to drive him to his knees before her so that she could have the exquisite pleasure of laughing at him—of declaring to him that she found him beneath contempt, that she was not at all interested in "masculine fripperies," or that she found him nothing more than a "plaguey irritation."

She sat up in bed, a smile suddenly lighting her face. To reverse their roles might not be a very difficult task to accomplish, she realized suddenly. Not at all difficult. She need only remember who she was. She was Lady Margaret Underwood, the toast of the *ton!* All she need do is make him aware of it, too.

Yes, even here in his realm she could manage it. There in the dressing room were several of her London gowns and all the accessories and accoutrements she would need. With only a few of her very effective mysterious smiles, a glance or two from under her lowered lashes, the merest brush of her hand against his cheek, and he, like so many others, would be hers for the asking.

His mother and sisters had said he was incorruptible. Perhaps that had been true before, but he had not yet met Lady Margaret Underwood at her best. Geoffrey Carrier, the incorruptible knight, hiding from the world in his remote Haven and surrounded by women who were too blindly admiring or too fearful to challenge his authority, was about to face his first *real* female adversary.

She could almost feel sorry for him. If ever a man was ripe for corrupting, it was he. And if anyone could corrupt the incorruptible—well, by heaven, that one was she!

Chapter Eight

That evening, with the help of Mrs. Rhys, Meg unpacked her belongings and selected the various gowns and accessories she would need for her devious purpose. Leaving her ball gowns, her walking suit and several other costumes which were unsuitable for an invalid packed away, she looked over the remaining garments with a critical eye. The only costumes appropriate for her present circumstances were her morning dresses and the most casual of her afternoon attire. Fortunately, even the most insignificant garments in her wardrobe were made by the same talented, expensive *modiste* who'd made the ball gowns—it was not for nothing that Lady Margaret Underwood was considered by the *ton* to be all the crack.

The green jaconet, she decided, would be the dress to wear the next day. It was the softest of muslin weaves, its green the color of glowing jade, and while it seemed to have been styled to please a lady of puritannical propriety, it became wickedly flattering when buttoned up on a lady of admirable form. The *modiste* had designed the bodice to reach high up to the neck, but she'd countered its severity with artful little tucks which emphasized the curves of the wearer's bosom. The sleeves were charmingly puffed at the shoulders and then narrowed to fit tightly over the rest of the arms, ending at the wrist with narrow little white cuffs. A matching white collar trimmed the neckline, making the wearer look deceptively demure. The waist was high, flatteringly gathered beneath the bust, and the skirt billowed out below with generous fullness. Meg could spread its width out on the bed in a graceful swirl as she leaned back against the pillows. With her hair vigorously brushed and spilling over her shoulders, with the slightest touch of rouge on her cheeks and the merest brush of blacking on her lashes, she had no doubt her appearance would be breathtaking. *Geoffrey Carrier,* she murmured to herself as she slid down under the comforter and settled herself as comfortably as possible for a night's sleep, *is a doomed man*.

But without having taken a sleeping draught, she was able to sleep only fitfully. Her ankle pained, the wind howled outside her windows, and the impressions of the past day kept her mind in a state of unease. When she did manage to doze off, she was troubled by strange, disquieting dreams. In one of them she was imprisoned in a medieval castle, held shackled to the wall by a chain and manacled at the ankle, her cell door guarded by a black-armored knight whose face was hidden by the visor of his helmet. But she didn't have to see his face—his identity and the cold antipathy he felt for his prisoner were chillingly clear.

By morning, however, the mood inspired by the dreams dissipated, and her self-confidence of the night before reasserted itself. The storm had ended in the night, and the still-cloudy sky was lightening perceptibly. That fact alone was cheering; with the storm over, traffic would soon be able to move on the roads, the doctor would arrive to speed her recovery, and the end of this enforced confinement would soon be in sight.

Mrs. Rhys bustled in early, as Meg had requested her to do, the freshly pressed, jade-colored jaconet over her arm. Meg, determined that Sir Geoffrey should not lay eyes on her again until she was ready for him, lost no time in preparing herself for the encounter. After being assisted to dress and (with considerable awkwardness and distress) arranging herself on top of the neatly spread bedclothes, she requested that Mrs. Rhys bring her a hand-mirror and her ormolu case which contained her creams, powders and cosmetics. These provided, she released Mrs. Rhys to her other duties and set about repairing, with whatever artificial means she had on hand, the ravages that storm, pain and sleeplessness had stamped on her complexion.

She had barely begun when a knock sounded at the door. Quickly she returned the paints and creams to the box and thrust everything under her pillows. Then she hurriedly spread out her skirt, leaned back against the pillows, arranged her hair to fall in billows over each shoulder and called, "Come in," in her most mellow voice.

But it was only Isabel. "Oh, I say," her aunt exclaimed in approval, "you *are* looking better."

Swallowing her disappointment, Meg smiled at her aunt. "Good morning, my dear. I see that the sky is clearing at last."

"Yes," Isabel said, perching on the bedside chair, "but you mustn't expect our situation to change at once. The entire world seems to be buried in whiteness."

Meg, about to present a more optimistic forecast, was suddenly brought up sharply by the sight of her aunt's face. Isabel did not look well. The shadows beneath her eyes were even more pronounced than they'd been the day before, and her eyes themselves were red and watery. "Dash it, Aunt Bel, haven't you been sleeping?" she asked bluntly.

"Do I look hagged?" Isabel put a hand up to her cheek. "I was afraid so. I think the accident, the storm and the strain of the escape from Isham Manor are having their effect on me. I find myself feeling too fitful to sleep well."

Meg was conscience-stricken. "It's all my fault. If only I'd recognized the faults in Charles Isham's character sooner, we might have avoided this trip and still be comfortable and cozy at home."

"Nonsense," Isabel said with spirit. "This has been an invigorating adventure. One good night's sleep, and I shall be quite myself again. Perhaps tonight, without the sound of the wind rattling the panes, I shall be able to sleep without these disconcerting dreams that have been troubling me."

"Have you had unpleasant dreams, Aunt Bel? So have I.

I blame mine on my blasted ankle, but what is the reason for *yours?*"

"The late hours I've been keeping, I suspect. But I shan't let that happen again," Isabel said firmly. "Tonight I shall not permit Lady Carrier to keep me up so late. She's positively *addicted* to card games, you know—we played copper-loo until the wee hours. I shall have to admit to her that late hours do not suit the constitutions of elderly ladies like me."

"Elderly, pooh!" Meg said affectionately. "You have the figure and the brisk movements of a mere girl. If only you'd take my advice and put a bit of dye on that grey hair, no one would guess you were over thirty."

Isabel hooted. "Over thirty, indeed! I'm well over fifty, and not in the least ashamed to admit it. I'll tell you a little secret, my love. I *like* my grey hair. All my life, because of my lack of height and the drab color of my hair, I'd been such an undistinguished little mouse. Now, at last, I feel that there's some dignity in my appearance."

"Very well, Aunt Bel," Meg grinned, "If it's *dignity* you prefer to youth, you'll not hear another word from me about dye. I shall find you lovely whatever your hair color."

"Thank you, dearest." She pressed her niece's hand and rose. "And now I'd best take myself downstairs, or our hosts will think me a typical London slugabed."

Alone again, Meg resumed her attentions to her face. She carefully applied a touch of rouge to her cheekbones and was just brushing a coating of charcoal dust to her lashes when another tapping sounded at the door. Hastily, she again hid her things under the pillows, again spread her skirt and arranged her hair, again leaned back languidly against the pillows and again invited the caller to come in.

Again she was disappointed. It was Trixie who stood in the doorway, a tray in her hands. "I told Mrs. Rhys that *I* wanted to bring your breakfast, Lady Meg. Shall I come in?"

Trixie helped Meg to settle the tray and then sat down on the bedside chair. She watched with admiring eyes as Meg buttered her biscuit and sipped her tea. It was obvious that Meg's every gesture, every look, every word inspired the younger girl with awe. "What a very lovely dress," Trixie sighed. "Is it Parisian? And your hair! I wish I could arrange *mine* to fall so, but mine's too badly frizzled by the crimping I've done. Is crimping still the fashion in London?"

A long conversation about London fashion followed, despite Meg's efforts to shorten its duration. But even when neither of the ladies had a thing left to say and an awkward silence fell on them both, Trixie didn't rise to leave. Instead, she suddenly leaned toward Meg and, with an unexpected burst of emotion, exclaimed, "Oh, Lady Meg, I'm so miserable! I must talk to somebody who knows the way of the world as you do."

There followed a long and detailed account of her passion for her latest swain, Mr. Mortimer Lazenby. It had been love at first sight at an assembly ball at Masham, and Trixie was convinced that there never had been or would be a more felicitous romance. "He's the most dashing man I've ever known," the girl confided, "and he's declared his feelings for me in the most *flattering* way. He is truly worldly, Lady Meg, and always makes me giggle with his witticisms. And one can see just by looking at him that his taste is impeccable. His waistcoats never show more than two colors, his shirt-points are always stiffly starched, and he revealed to me in the greatest secrecy—although I know it will be no secret to *you,* so I have no compunction about revealing it—that his man polishes his topboots with champagne, a trick which, you are undoubtedly aware, was devised by Mr. Brummell himself."

"The young man sounds like a paragon," Meg said with a smile. "I'm sure it won't be long before the world will be wishing you happy."

"But that's just *it,* ma'am. I shall *never* be happy. Geoffrey won't allow it."

Meg studied the girl's lowered head with sympathy. "But if the young man is all you say, than why—"

"I have no idea why Geoffrey opposed him," Trixie said glumly.

"Is the fellow impoverished? Is that the problem? Will he not be able to support a wife in the proper style?"

"No, it can't be that. The Lazenbys are a very substantial family, and Mortimer is the oldest son."

"Do the Lazenbys object to the match for some reason?"

"No, I don't think so. His mother has always been most cordial, and I am invited to *all* their parties."

"Then I must admit, Trixie, that I don't understand your brother's objection."

Trixie's omnipresent pout became more pronounced. "I don't understand it either. Geoffrey can be the most *stubborn—!*

I know I shouldn't have kicked up a dust the other day when he said I couldn't go to the party, but *anyone* would have cried and carried on as I did! But Geoffrey said it proved that I was too childish to know my own mind. I know I've changed my mind often about beaux in the past, but *this* time I'm absolutely certain! And Geoffrey has taken a dislike to almost every man who's ever called on me. I think he really wants me to remain on the shelf for the rest of my days!"

"Oh, I'm sure that can't be true. Was there no one he approved of?"

"Only one fellow whom he brought round himself. It was one of his friends from the regiment. Geoffrey insisted that Captain Brownleigh was the best of good fellows, but I found him a bore. He was not nearly tall enough to make an impression, he wore nothing but hunting jackets or regimentals, he didn't know how to dance, and he could speak of nothing but his experiences on the peninsula. Does that sound to *you*, Lady Meg, like the sort of man to make a proper husband?"

"Well, I suppose—"

"Of course not. *You* would never consider marrying a man who couldn't cut a figure in a ballroom or with whom you couldn't converse at the breakfast table, would you, even if your brother insisted that he was the salt of the earth?"

Meg, remembering how she'd run away from Lord Isham in spite of the recommendation of her beloved aunt, had to admit that she wouldn't.

"You see? I knew it!" Trixie exclaimed, delighted to have found support from a lady of Meg's quality. "But Geoffrey would not understand my feelings. He was quite furious with me for what he called my inability to see beyond the surface. And then, when Captain Brownleigh became engaged to Lady Caroline Pettibone, Geoffrey didn't speak to me for a week! Now, really, could *I* help it if Lady Caroline could see beyond the surface better than I could?"

Meg couldn't help smiling, but she turned away so that the girl shouldn't see. For a moment she felt an unwilling spark of symphathy for poor Sir Geoffrey. She had a vague recollection of having heard that the Pettibones' daughter had married a blunt but reputable army man. If he was the Captain Brownleigh of whom Trixie spoke, he was said to be well-to-do, honest, upright and thoroughly likeable, and Caroline Pettibone was believed to be the happiest of brides. It was no wonder that Geoffrey had been irritated that his sister had thrown aside such a prize.

On the other hand, it was cruel of Geoffrey to expect a girl to marry against her will. Trixie may have misjudged the Captain's character, but there were other men in the world. Couldn't the opinionated Sir Geoffrey have considered a candidate who was of Trixie's liking rather than his own? What right had he to make himself the sole judge? It was typical of the arrogance and tyranny of his character that he wished to exercise such complete control over the lives of the women in his care. "And this Captain Brownleigh was the only suitor of whom your brother approved?" she asked.

"The only one. And, really, Lady Meg, I am at my wit's end about what to do. Geoffrey refuses even to permit Mr. Lazenby to *call* on me!"

"That is most unkind of him," Meg murmured.

Trixie, her underlip trembling in sincere anguish, turned her large eyes pleadingly up at Meg. "Oh, Lady Meg, *tell* me what to do!"

Meg stared down at her, nonplussed. As much as she would enjoy finding a way to block Geoffrey's absolute rule, it was not proper for her to interfere in matters which were not her concern. But the girl was in dire straits and seemed quite unable, by herself, to do battle with the overweening Sir Geoffrey. She needed help from *someone*. "Let me think about it, Trixie," she said gently. "Perhaps I *can* think of something if I try."

With a glad cry, Trixie jumped up, smothered Meg in a quick embrace and, happy tears flowing, ran from the room.

Absently, her mind still on Trixie's problem, Meg took out her mirror and resumed her efforts with her lashes. This completed, she studied her face in the hand-mirror to make sure that her appearance was suitably attractive for her purposes. *Yes,* she decided, *I will do.* It was the best one could expect within the limitations of the raw material. Her chin was far too prominent for real beauty, and her skin was irritatingly disfigured by freckles, but there was nothing she could do about those shortcomings. As for the rest, she would do well enough. *Very well, Geoffrey,* she said to herself, *I am quite ready for you.*

But no one knocked for hours.

By the time a tapping was again heard at her door, Meg had slumped down on the pillows and fallen into a doze. With a start, she sat erect and reached hurriedly for her mirror. Her hair was tousled and her mouth slack with sleep. Nervously, she smoothed her hair, adjusted her posture and her skirts, and bit some color and life back into her lips. "Come in," she called sweetly when all was readied.

But this time it was Lady Carrier. The dowager sat down beside Meg and whiled away an hour of the afternoon with a detailed account of last night's card game in which she'd won from "dearest Isabel" the sum of two guineas. "It would have been a much more significant win if Geoffrey had permitted us to play *silver*-loo, but he won't hear of it. He says this is a private home, not a gaming hall. As if they don't play silver-loo in the very best houses in London, as I've told him more than once. But there's no use saying anything to Geoffrey once his mind's made up."

It was twilight before the next knock sounded. Before inviting the visitor to enter, Meg hastily lit the candle on the table near the bed, for what was the good of fussing over her appearance if Geoffrey wouldn't be able to see her? But the visitor was only Sybil, who hung about in the doorway sniffing into a handkerchief. "I won't come in, Lady Meg," she explained in a listless whine, "for I'm certain that I'm coming down with a putrid infection of the sinuses, and I don't wish to endanger your health, especially when you are already infirm. I've only come to pay my respects."

"Thank you for coming, Sybil. Do go along and rest yourself. Perhaps by tomorrow we shall both be feeling more the thing," Meg responded.

"You'll be feeling more the thing, very likely, but *I* shall be worse. Of that I'm quite certain," the girl said and wandered off down the hall.

That visit was followed by one from her aunt. Then Mrs. Rhys brought her supper tray and, as the evening wore endlessly on, each of the previous callers returned to say their goodnights. By the time the hall clock had struck ten, Meg was convinced that the irritating Sir Geoffrey did not intend to call on her at all. All the trouble she'd taken with her appearance, all the plans she'd hatched in the dull stretches of the day, had been for naught. For this day at least, her quarry had eluded her.

Mrs. Rhys and Isabel helped her to undress, bid her a fond goodnight and shut the door. Meg sat awake, staring at the dying fire in glum chagrin for a long while, but then, with a sigh, she comforted herself with the thought that all was not lost. Tomorrow was another day. She would try again. If he still hadn't come by dinner time tomorrow, she would send for him. She would simply admit that she was tired of sitting in her bedroom and wished to be carried downstairs. If she could manage to convince him that employing the footman for that purpose was improper, he would have to take her up in his arms again. Her skirts would fall gracefully over his arms, her perfume would tantalize his senses, and her cheek would—quite accidentally, of course—brush against his. The poor fellow would be quite lost. She could wait until tomorrow.

To insure her coming success, she opened up her ormolu box and withdrew a tightly stoppered glass bottle. It contained a lotion which she'd purchased at the Pantheon bazaar but had never used—a lotion purported to do wonders for the skin. Made of cucumber water, extract of white flowers, green grape juice and a secret ingredient (which she'd learned by persistent questioning was oil extracted from the flesh of white pigeons), it was said to make the skin soft, supple, freckle-free and fragrant. The very thing needed by a lady who had—what was Aunt Bel's phrase?—passed her prime. She put on a nightcap, tucked her hair into it so that the lotion would not soil her shiny locks, and began to smear the stuff on her cheeks.

Just after she'd carefully covered every inch of her face with the thick greenish cream and had begun to rub it in, a knock sounded at the door. She froze in horror. It couldn't be! Not now! "Yes? Wh-who is it?" she asked quaveringly. But she knew the answer.

"You weren't asleep, were you?" Sir Geoffrey asked. "I saw the light under your door. I've brought you a sleeping draught. May I come in?"

"No! I don't *want* a sleeping draught," she told him sullenly. "Go away!"

"Don't be childish. Your aunt told me that you suffered from bad dreams last night. She's just taken some herself. There's no good reason not to—"

She sighed helplessly. She couldn't refuse him admittance without seeming to be a petulant fool. Quickly, in the hope that the dying firelight would be enough illumination for him to make his way, she blew out the candles at her bedside and lowered her head so that the ruffle of her nightcap would shade her face. "Oh, very well," she muttered, "come in if you must."

He came in and approached the bed warily. "Why on earth did you blow out the candles?"

"I can see you well enough," she said shortly, keeping her head turned away and thrusting out her hand for the glass.

But he didn't give it to her. "Can't you turn round and sit up properly?" he asked, puzzled. "You don't want to spill this stuff all over the sheets."

Wincing in frustration, she sat up and, keeping her head lowered, took the glass from his hand. As she began to drink she was painfully conscious of his knit-browed stare at her averted face. It was quite typical of the man's irritating behavior that he'd waited until *this* moment to call on her. If he managed to get a good look at her face she might never be able to overcome the aversion he'd be bound to feel!

"Do you always wear a nightcap?" he asked companiably as he waited for her to drain the glass. "My sisters have led me to believe that only elderly frumps and housemaids would indulge in so antiquated a custom."

"Since I am obviously neither a frump nor a housemaid," she snapped (spoiling the effect of her haughty tone by her averted head), "your sisters must be mistaken."

She put her full attention to swallowing the vile-tasting liquid in the glass. If she could gulp it down quickly, she might rid herself of her visitor before he noticed anything more damaging than a nightcap. But the taste was too strong to allow hasty ingestion, and she was forced to sip it slowly. As the level of the liquid in the glass declined, her head lifted in almost-imperceptible degrees, and before she realized that her position had changed, she heard him gasp. "Good Lord! What's the matter with your face?"

"Nothing! Nothing at all." She turned away and held out the half-filled glass to him. "Here, take it. I don't want any more."

"But . . . there's something green on your—"

"Oh, be still!" she ordered in disgust. "It's only a . . . a lotion."

"Oh, is that all," he said in relief. "I was afraid you'd contracted some dread disease."

"Disease?" She couldn't refrain from throwing him a look of scorn. "What sort of disease did you imagine it was? Leprosy?"

He uttered a snorting laugh. "Yes, something like that.

Whatever did you wish to accomplish with that dreadful stuff?"
he asked, leaning down and peering at her face with amused
interest.

Embarrassed and humiliated, she tried nevertheless to brazen it out. "It's for...for...removing freckles," she said,
putting up her chin and facing him courageously.

"Removing freckles? Why? What's wrong with freckles?"

"Surely even you, sir, must realize that freckles are disfiguring, and not at all in style."

"Disfiguring?" he echoed in disgust. "You must be mad.
And you wonder why I hold your sex in disrespect! Who with
a grain of sense would care if freckles were in style? Who but
a complete idiot would tell you they were disfiguring? I hope
you don't discover to your sorrow that your precious lotion
takes away your *skin* with the freckles it purports to remove!"
He stalked to the door. "Women!" he intoned in disgust before
he shut the door behind him.

Meg stared at the closed door nonplussed. Her encounters
with her host were becoming a source of intense frustration.
Would she *never* be able to bring the fellow under control? The
rudesby had, for the second time, neglected to ask how she
felt and hadn't even taken the trouble to bid her goodnight!

She touched with inquiring fingers the thick film of lotion
on her cheeks. *I must look a sight!* she thought ruefully. She'd
probably ruined any chance she had of making a mark on him.
He'd as good as called her an idiot!

Of course, if one examined his words carefully, one might
find a nugget of hope—it was certainly clear that he didn't
consider her freckles disfiguring. This didn't necessarily mean
that he liked them, exactly, but there'd been something in his
tone that suggested he'd been appalled to think she wanted to
remove them. It wasn't much—especially when one compared
his speech to words of men like Arthur who'd declared that
her freckles were adorable—but it was the only bright spot she
could discern in the otherwise abortive encounter. Even with
the laudanum beginning to take effect, she couldn't feel
cheered. But she didn't feel completely defeated either.

Chapter Nine

The next morning the sun came out in unexpected splendor, as if trying to make up in brilliance for its days of absence. It set to work at once on the snow blanketing the fields and trees, and the welcome tinkle of dripping water added a musical accompaniment to the sparkling day. Even the reflected light that danced in shimmering prismatic shapes on the walls of Meg's bedroom seemed to give off a diamond-like twinkle. If it weren't for the pain in her ankle, the boredom of her enforced confinement and the frustration of her lack of success with Sir Geoffrey, she would almost feel glad to be alive.

Sir Geoffrey sent word through Mrs. Rhys that a groom had made it on foot to Dr. Fraser's abode, and that the good doctor would make his way to Knight's Haven by that afternoon. In the meantime, to everyone's surprise, Lady Carrier's crony, the tall, angular Lady Habish, accompanied by her elder daugh-

ter Harriet (who was as tall and angular as her mother), appeared at the door. They had decided to slog on foot through
the snow for the entire mile-and-a-half between their abode and
the Carriers' to pay a call, having found the past two days of
enforced solitude too confining for their sociable natures.

To their delight, they learned that there was more society
at Knight's Haven than they'd expected. "The walk through
the snow will certainly have been worth your while," Lady
Carrier told them excitedly, "for although you will hardly credit
it, you are going to meet our *guests*. Yes, guests! The storm
has brought us *two* distinguished ladies from London!"

After a lengthy explanation of the occurrences which had
brought the visitors to her doorstep, Lady Carrier insisted that
they all immediately repair to Meg's bedroom and become
acquainted. Nothing less would do.

Chairs were brought by the footman and two maids and
placed in a circle round Meg's bed, and all the females of the
household, with the two visiting neighbors, seated themselves
for a morning of excited chatter. After the introductions, everyone spoke at once, for Lady Habish turned out to be as loqua-
cious as her friend, and neither of them would remain silent
long enough to permit the other to complete a sentence. Meanwhile, Trixie and the young Miss Harriet Habish put their heads
together, whispering and giggling over their girlish confidences
without the least concern for the presence of the others. And
Sybil, ignoring all the noise, leaned back in her chair with her
eyes closed, opening them only when she remembered—every
half-minute or so—to blow her nose with delicate nicety into
her lace handkerchief.

Meg and Isabel exchanged smiles of fond indulgence, for
the group gathered round them seemed to characterize the naive
charm of country society. The older ladies were so thoroughly
engrossed in and excited by the trivialities of their restricted
lives, the younger ones were so innocently mischievous about
their secret flirtations, and even Sybil was so determinedly
dramatic in her desire to be mysteriously ill that the London
ladies found them all beguilingly bucolic.

But after half-an-hour of the noise, after having to listen to
their babble about people and incidents she knew nothing of,
after being forced to nod and smile in response to Lady Habish's
platitudinous and unctuous compliments, Meg found them losing their charm. She began to wish that they'd leave her to

herself. She began to feel horribly bored. She began—good God, was it possible?—to watch the door in the vain hope that Sir Geoffrey would make an appearance. She hated to admit it to herself, but she did wish he would come. He might be overbearing, insulting and arrogant, but at least he wasn't dull.

Besides, she'd made the same preparations to catch his eye that she had the day before: the skirts of the green jaconet were spread out gracefully upon the bedclothes, her hair was brushed, her lashes were artfully darkened. She was quite ready for him again. Why didn't he come?

The ladies remained in Meg's bedroom almost two hours, during which time neither Meg nor Isabel uttered more than half-a-dozen sentences. As a result, Lady Habish, when rising to take her leave, declared loudly that she'd never in her life met *anyone* of such eloquence, charm and wit. "I shall hold a party in your honor two nights hence," she announced, "so that all our neighbors will have the good fortune to make your acquaintance."

Isabel looked at Meg dubiously. "Thank you, Lady Habish," she said, "but it's unlikely that Meg's ankle will have mended sufficiently to—"

"That is not a problem of any consequence," Lady Habish insisted, unwilling to brook a refusal. She regarded herself as the most important personage in the entire region and had long ago convinced herself that her parties were the most desirable of any of the entertainments the surrounding gentry enjoyed. It was inconceivable to her that anyone would refuse an invitation to her table by choice. "I shall see to it that her ladyship is carried to and from our carriage (which I shall send at seven to fetch you all) in the greatest comfort. I've no doubt you will both be refreshed by the change of scene."

Lady Carrier was not in the least put out by what some hostesses might have considered a slur. "*Do* say yes, Lady Meg," she urged. "It will do all of us good to get out a bit."

A chorus of voices joined in pressing them to accept. Trixie, in particular, seemed breathlessly eager for Meg to agree. Meg immediately perceived the reason for her urgent look—her Mortimer would undoubtedly be invited. Unsure of what to do, Meg glanced at her aunt inquiringly. Isabel answered with an almost imperceptible shrug, as if to say that she was quite willing to do as Meg wished. With that feeble encouragement,

Meg smiled good-naturedly at Lady Habish and gave a tentative assent.

After her visitors had all left her, Meg sighed in relief. She was convinced that she would truly enjoy some moments of solitude. But when that solitude extended to an hour, and then to two, she began to feel oppressed. Lying in bed in this helpless fashion was beginning to pall. She was restless and strangely dissatisfied. If only someone had been thoughtful enough to provide her with a book . . .

She began to wonder idly what sort of library a man like Sir Geoffrey might have assembled to keep himself content in this remote place. If the boor didn't bother to call on her soon, she would send for him and ask to be carried to the library to select some reading matter for herself. That would be a way to—

But a knock at the door interrupted her scheming thoughts. Giving a quick fluff to her hair (but without conviction that the action would have any purpose; the visitor was probably not he), she invited the caller to enter. Her heart leaped to her throat when she saw it was Geoffrey at last. For the first time in two long days, he'd made an appearance when she was completely ready for him. She looked up eagerly at his face to take note of his reaction to her improved appearance.

If he did show a reaction, however, she didn't see it. Her attention was distracted by the appearance of another man who followed Geoffrey into the room. "I've brought Dr. Fraser to see you, ma'am," Geoffrey said without preamble. "I've been telling him that I expect him to put his best arts in your service . . . to make up with his skill for what my coachman did to you with his lack of it."

Dr. Fraser said a brisk "Good day, ma'am," and set his bag down on a chair. He was a wiry, compactly built man of indeterminate age who seemed to crackle with suppressed energy. There was a bounce in his stride and a bracing, no-nonsense air about him which gave Meg confidence. She was quite ready to believe that he knew what he was about.

The doctor peered at her briefly through narrowed eyes. Then he took a *pince-nez* from his coat pocket and snapped it on the bridge of his nose. He looked at her over it, under it and through it. He examined her eyes, the back of her head where the remains of the lump could still be felt and, finally, the ankle. With Geoffrey's assistance, he bent over her leg and began to unwrap the bandages. Before the task was completed—her tense posture made them realize how painful the handling was to her, and they proceeded very slowly—the door opened and Isabel came tiptoeing in. "May I come in to hear what the doctor has to say?" she asked timidly.

Dr. Fraser didn't lift his head, but Geoffrey smiled up at her. "Of course, Isabel," he said, surprising Meg with the tone of familiarity in his voice. "I should have sent for you myself, if this impatient fellow here had not demanded my whole attention."

Isabel took a place at the foot of the bed and watched with troubled eyes as the bandages were unwound. Before the task was quite completed, the door opened again. This time it was Lady Carrier, with Sybil in tow. "I want you to look at Sybil, Dr. Fraser," she ordered, seating herself in the bedside chair, "when you've finished with her ladyship, of course. Sybil has not been at all well these last few days. We're very much afraid she's contracted an infection in her sinuses."

"Yes, a putrid infection," Sybil echoed dramatically.

Geoffrey and the doctor exchanged looks of mild vexation, though neither gentleman said a word. Ordinarily, Meg would have been irritated with the attitude of superciliousness that the look implied, but this time she could not help but sympathize with Geoffrey. His mother had shown a want of sensitivity to have intruded so familiarly upon Meg's examination. Meg was vexed with the woman herself.

The bandages removed, the doctor moved Meg's foot back and forth, causing her to gasp. He leaned down and examined the discoloration intently, grunted, and straightened. Then, without a word, he bounded over to Sybil, pushed her down so that she was seated on the bed and looked down her throat. He also looked carefully at her eyes and into each of her ears. Again he grunted and again said nothing.

While everyone in the room watched him with silent suspense, the doctor took a stance, with legs slightly apart and hands clasped behind his back, in the center of the room. Slowly with intent deliberation, he studied the faces of everyone present, peering at each one in turn over the top of—and then through—his *pince-nez*. Finally he grunted again, cleared his throat and began to speak in a voice which surprised Meg by its strong Scottish burr. "Verra well, then, I've goamed the hale jingbang of ye. You, Lady Margaret, are nae so badly off. Yer ankle's had an unco' terrible sprain, but it's na broke. I've a salve that'll soothe ye a thocht, an' I'll re-bandage it tightly afore I leave. Ye'll na put any weight on it fer a week or so, ye ken. Stay off yer feet an' keep the leg elevated.

"An' as fer *you,* Miss Sybil Carrier, yer sinuses are fair bonnie. Noo, harken t' me, lass. I'm nae fer hearin' anythin' more concernin' yer nose or throat, do ye ken? I'm a wee weary o' lookin' at 'em. May I suggest ye find *anither* part o' yer body in which t' lodge yer next complaint?"

"But as fer *you,* ma'am," and here the doctor wheeled about and bounded across the room to confront Isabel, "I cain't say I like the look o' *you.*"

Isabel gave a jump and a startled gasp. "What? Whatever do you mean?"

"Yer eyes, ma'am. I dinna like yer eyes."

"Well! Of all the—!" Isabel drew herself up in offended dignity. "I can't say I like yours, either, if it comes to that!"

"Dr. Fraser means, Isabel," Geoffrey interjected quickly, "that he thinks you may not be quite well."

"Not well? Sick, you mean?" Isabel asked, bemused. "Is *that* why he doesn't like my eyes?"

Dr. Fraser clicked his tongue. "I've naught to say aboot yer eyes *personally,* woman. It's just the *look* of 'em, ye ken. They're too red an' watery. Ye've somethin' brewin' inside ye, if I know anythin' aboot m' business. Ha'e ye been feelin' as ye should?"

"I've been feeling perfectly fine," Isabel said with asperity, frowning at the doctor with instant dislike, "and I'll thank you to keep your feelings about my eyes to yourself."

"Wheesht, woman, hold yer clack and let me examine yer throat! Sit yersel' doon on the bed and open yer mouth."

"I'll do nothing of the sort," she responded angrily. "I am not your patient, and I haven't the slightest need of your services."

The Scotsman glared at her for a moment and then shrugged. "Suit yersel', woman, suit yersel'. Ye'll be changin'yer tune afore lang."

"I shouldn't count on that, doctor, if I were you. I wouldn't want your services even if I *were* sick. Don't like my eyes, indeed!"

"But, Aunt Bel, perhaps—" Meg said worriedly.

"Your aunt is quite right, Lady Meg," Lady Carrier cut in, throwing a reproachful glance at the doctor. "The man's impossible! I don't care if he *is* a brilliant diagnostician, as Geoffrey claims, he has the manners of a stablehand. Really, Dr. Fraser, it's bad enough that you belittle my Sybil in that unkind way, but *she,* at least, is *accustomed* to your manners. But to have you come here and insult our *guests* is the outside of enough!"

"And *I* don't believe," Sybil muttered sullenly, "that he's at *all* a good diagnostician. There *is* something wrong with my sinuses."

"Be quiet, Sybil," Geoffrey ordered sharply. "And you, too, Mama, if you please. Dr. Fraser has come through the drifts on foot just to listen to what have turned out to be a series of petty complaints—"

"Well, really!" Meg gasped, affronted.

"They are *not* petty!" Sybil cried at the same time.

"Geoffrey, you go *too far!*" his mother said above the others.

"I repeat, *petty* complaints," Geoffrey insisted in disgust, "and I won't have Fraser abused. As for you, Isabel, if you'll take the suggestion of a well-wisher, please permit the doctor to examine you. You mustn't be fooled by his manner; the pressure of time and the many demands on him have forced him to become somewhat brusque, but he knows—"

"Never!" Isabel said firmly. "I have the greatest respect for you, Geoffrey, but in this case I shall follow my own instincts. I'm quite well, whatever he chooses to think, and I don't wish to subject myself to his scrutiny."

"Let the woman be, laddie," the doctor muttered, already busily bandaging Meg's ankle. "She'll be biddable eno' in a day or two. Didna ye say ye'll ha'e a dram waitin' fer us afore I go?"

"By all means," Geoffrey said heartily, packing the doctor's bag for him while the Scotsman finished his bandaging. "Keating will have brought your favorite drink to the library by this time. Shall we go?"

By the time the irate ladies had relieved their tempers by abusing the doctor behind his back and had gone off to their various bedrooms to rest and brood, the pain in Meg's ankle caused by the examination and treatment given her by Dr. Fraser had subsided. In fact, she had to admit that it felt better than it had since the accident. Perhaps the doctor was as knowing as Geoffrey claimed. In that case, her aunt should have permitted the man to examine her. Was Isabel really on the verge of illness? What was it that the Scotsman suspected?

The problem was so worrisome that she barely paid attention to the next tapping at her door. She muttered an absent "Come in," her mind occupied with alarming suspicions of her aunt's condition. It was only when Sir Geoffrey opened the door that she realized she'd forgotten to brush her hair or check her appearance.

"Dr. Fraser told me to tell you that he'd return to change your bandages in a couple of days," he said from the threshold, his hand on the knob of the door.

"Oh, good," she said in some relief. "Perhaps by that time you can persuade my aunt to let him examine her."

"*I* persuade her?" Geoffrey asked in some surprise. "Why not you yourself?"

Meg shrugged. "I shall try, of course, but she seems to hold you in high regard, though I cannot imagine why."

"Can't you?" He flashed a sudden, completely disconcerting grin at her. "The reason, my dear, is that your aunt is a woman of extraordinary good sense and keen perception."

"For a female?" Meg asked sourly.

"Yes. Extraordinary. That's why I can't understand why she took such an irrational dislike to Fraser. He's really a fine man and a fine doctor. You thought so, too, didn't you?"

"I suppose so. How can I be sure on such short acquaintance? But I admit that I'd feel much relieved to have him examine her and tell me that he was mistaken and that the red, watery eyes only mean that Isabel is overtired. *Will* you try to persuade her to consult him?"

"Certainly, ma'am. I shall do my best."

He made a little bow and began to pull the door shut behind him. With her mind set somewhat at ease by his promise, her attention flew to her determination to make a mark on him. If she was to succeed, she couldn't afford to let this opportunity go by. "Sir Geoffrey?" she called quickly.

He opened the door again. "Yes, ma'am?"

"I was thinking . . . I say, you don't have to hang about on the threshold like that, do you? Please come in for a moment."

He looked at her somewhat warily and then came in, stopping at the foot of the bed and looking at her with one eyebrow upraised. "What can I do for you, ma'am?"

"In the first place," she said with some asperity, "you can stop calling me ma'am in that condescending way. My friends call me Meg."

"I'm sure they do. But I wasn't aware that you considered me a friend. If my recollection of a recent conversation between us is accurate, you consider me arrogant, unfeeling and offensive. There's not much sign of friendship in those adjectives."

"Perhaps not, although I suppose one might make friends even with *such* a person. And you have been scrupulously considerate at a host—I grant you that."

"Thank you. Am I to take it from these surprisingly temperate remarks that you wish to call a truce?"

"Yes, I do. And I wish you to call me Meg."

"Very well, Meg. Now, what is it you wish me to do for you?"

She turned her eyes up to his and blinked at him flirtatiously, hoping that the blacking she'd applied to her lashes earlier that day had not smudged. (*Oh, why,* she asked herself, *didn't I look in the mirror before I let him in?*) "I was wondering, Geoffrey," she murmured in her most demure, dulcet tones, "if it would be at all possible to be carried down to your library for a while. It's so dull to be cooped up in this room all day without even a book to read. If I were brought down and permitted to select some books for myself, I'd—"

"Say no more, ma'am. If I were a truly considerate host, I would have seen to it before." There was a distinct gleam of malicious laughter at the back of his eyes. "I'll get the footman to carry you down at once."

"The . . . footman?" she echoed, disappointed.

"Yes, the footman." He turned to the door, but not before she noted, to her chagrin, that his mocking gleam had extended itself to the corners of his mouth.

"Yes, of course," she said furiously, "I'd forgotten that you'd found me too heavy a burden for you."

"Quite," he agreed irritatingly. Before taking himself out of the room, he looked back at her for a moment, his taunting smile now very pronounced. "For such a tiny favor, my dear, there was not the slightest need for you to go to the trouble of trying to turn me up sweet. With a mother and two sisters forever asking favors of me, I've become completely immune to demure smiles and fluttering lashes."

"Ooooh!" She picked up one of the pillows and threw it at him wrathfully. But he pulled the door closed behind him in plenty of time to keep the fluffy missile from meeting its intended mark.

Seething, she glared at the door which, to her surprise, promptly opened again. Sir Geoffrey stuck his head in. "Oh, by the way, *Meg*," he said with an innocently pleasant smile, "I just want to say that the green thing you're wearing suits you. Very fetching."

And he was gone. She made a face at the closed door. "How fetching can it be," she muttered irritably, "if the best thing it fetches is the blasted footman?"

Chapter Ten

Isabel bustled into Meg's room carrying two gowns, one over each arm. "Which shall I wear to Lady Habish's tonight?" she asked. "I'm afraid the purple may be too grand for a country *soirée*, but the burgundy is too young for me, is it not?"

Meg put down the book she was reading and glanced at her aunt with a worried frown. Isabel was certainly running about with her usual energy and spirit, but Meg was not reassured about the state of her health. "Why are you dressing yourself so early, Aunt Bel? It's only mid-afternoon."

"I know. It's the height of foolishness, is it not, to begin to prepare oneself at such an hour? But the Carrier ladies are already closeted in their rooms dressing their hair, and I haven't anything better to do."

"You could lie down and rest for an hour or two," Meg suggested.

Isabel threw her niece a look of suspicion. It was two days since that annoying doctor had paid his call, yet both Geoffrey and Meg continued to watch her for symptoms and to nag at her to let the man examine her. "I don't need any rest. I feel perfectly fit," she said with a touch of irritation.

But Meg was not at all convinced. Her aunt's cheeks were frighteningly pale and her eyes bleary. "Are you certain you wish to go through with this, Aunt Bel? I don't expect it will be an entertaining evening, what with having to endure the stares and effusive compliments of a crowd of bumpkins. We can quite easily claim ill health and stay behind."

"It's not at all becoming in you, Meg, to treat these people with such disdain. Living in the country doesn't make one a fool, you know. You should not be so quick to pass disparaging judgments on them."

Meg felt a twinge of shame. "I'm sorry, love. You're quite right. Nevertheless, we needn't go to the party if we are not feeling well enough."

"*We* are quite well enough for anything, if it is *my* health to which you refer. If you *yourself* are in pain and feel unequal to the exertion, that is quite another story."

Meg hesitated. Would it be better for her aunt if she pretended to be feeling ill? "Well, I—"

"But it would be most unkind of us not to make the effort, you know. Lady Habish has undoubtedly made all sorts of preparations . . . and in our honor. She would feel the keenest disappointment if her honored guests failed to attend. And even here, you know, tonight's festivities have been causing the greatest stir imaginable . . . the maids running about with laces to sew and sashes to press, the footmen racing down the halls with slippers to polish, Mrs. Rhys doing double duty as hairdresser . . . one would think they were preparing for a royal coronation! It would be cruel of us to put a damper on the excitement—which is what would happen if we were to refuse to attend."

Meg sighed. "But are you certain, love, that you're up to it? I think this entire adventure—from the moment when we stole from Isham Manor—has been very tiring for you."

Isabel raised her eyebrows haughtily. "You are thinking of what that dreadful doctor said, aren't you? You may put that incident entirely out of your mind, my dear. The man is an odious fool. I assure you, Meg, that I'm as well as I've ever been in my life. You and Geoffrey give Dr. Fraser's impertinent remarks too much credence. The only thing that tires me is your constant nagging."

"Very well, Aunt Bel, I'll stop nagging. If you're sure . . ."

The two women 'turned their attention to the selection of their gowns, Meg persuading her aunt that the burgundy was not too youthful, and Isabel assuring Meg that her Bordeaux-brown silk crape would not be judged too rakish by the country-bred society. With these important decisions made, Isabel departed to begin her preparations.

Meg was brushing her hair and waiting for Mrs. Rhys to come and help her put on her gown when Trixie hammered at her door. The girl burst in wrapped in her robe. Although not yet dressed, her hair had already been coiffed and curled for the evening. Meg noted that it was arranged in a most attractive style, pulled back from her forehead and held in place over each ear with ornamented combs, below which her curls fell in free profusion over her ears. Her face would have looked lovely except for the redness of her eyes. "Good heavens, Trixie, you've been crying!" Meg exclaimed.

"Oh, Lady M-Meg, you m-must help me! I'm in the most d-dire straits," the girl blubbered, dropping into a chair and dabbing helplessly at her eyes. "Geoffrey has just told me that h-he intends to escort us to the Habish's tonight!"

"Escort us?" Meg found the news surprising, but not at all dismaying. "Why should *that* bring on this flood of tears? I should think you'd find it very kind of your brother. I suspects he dislikes affairs of this sort."

"Kind? Kind?" Trixie looked at Meg appalled. "It's the very w-worst thing that could possibly have happened! Don't you see?"

"No, I'm afraid I don't."

"He's doing it on p-purpose! To k-keep me from having anything to do with M-M-Mortimer!"

Meg blinked. "Do you mean that he's discovered that Mortimer will be there?"

"He guesses. Oh, I d-denied knowing anything about it. I even suggested that Lady Habish didn't intend to invite the Lazenbys at all (which is an outright fabrication, for I know from Harriet that they'll all be there), but Geoffrey said that his own p-presence at the affair will be his assurance that I will n-not be having anything to do with Mortimer."

"So . . . that's why he'd decided to escort us," Meg muttered, beginning to smolder. She'd permitted herself, at first, to believe that Geoffrey had decided to attend the party because of *her*. In the two days since they'd declared their "truce," they'd spent some very pleasant hours together; only the day before he'd taken her down to the library (laughingly explaining that the footman was "indisposed"), and they'd spent the afternoon talking of novels, of Byron's new verse-romance, *The Giaour* (which they both agreed was too melodramatically lurid), and of the Regent's apparent swing toward intractable Toryism (which they both felt was a troublesome development). She'd been impressed by signs of her host's extensive erudition, and he had apparently found her conversation to be both sensible and engaging. She'd been quite pleased with herself. Her scheme, she'd believed, was working very well. When she and Isabel would be ready to leave (certainly within a week's time), she would have his heart in her pocket.

But he was not attending the Habish party because of a wish to be in her company. He was only reverting to his tyrannical behavior and trying to maintain his iron control over his sister. That realization made her furious, and her fury was made all the more intense by her awareness of her own sense of disappointment. Why did this small evidence that she'd not yet conquered him cause her such a twinge of pain? She was only playing a game with him, after all.

"Don't redden your pretty eyes with crying, Trixie," she said with sudden resolve. "Tears, you know, never do a bit of good. We must come up with a scheme to outwit him, that's all."

Trixie's head came up eagerly. "A scheme? Oh, Lady Meg! Do you think we could?"

They could . . . and they did. It took Meg only twenty minutes to concoct a very promising plan. By the time Mrs. Rhys arrived to help Meg dress, Trixie's eyes were shining and the plot was already in motion.

When Geoffrey arrived at Meg's door promptly at seven to say that Lady Habish's carriage had arrived and that he was ready to take her downstairs, he stopped in the doorway, astounded. Meg was standing up, her weight on her good leg and leaning for support on a bedpost. She was looking ravishing in a gown of lustrous brown silky crape cut scandalously low over the bosom. Her thick, red hair had been pulled back into a tight knot at the back of her head, but enticing little tendrils had already escaped and were framing her face with a soft halo of glowing color. The word glowing described her perfectly. Even her skin seemed to give off a warm incandescence. He found himself, for a moment, completely unable to do anything but stare.

Meg, too, found herself staring. Geoffrey in his evening clothes seemed a very different man from the saturnine fellow in hunting togs she'd seen in the taproom of the Horse With Three Tails. The cut of his coat would have done justice to any London tailor, his shirt-points reached a height of perfect style without rising to the extremes that a dandy might have preferred, his neckcloth was impeccably tied in the admirable but not overly intricate *Waterfall,* and the leg revealed by the skintight breeches was as shapely as a tailor (or a lady) could desire. Even the expression of his face seemed changed—it was warmer and more . . . accessible. If he'd approached her in a London drawing room looking like *this* she was not at all certain, as she'd been earlier, that she would have cut him.

She was the first to recover. "Look, Geoffrey, what Mrs. Rhys and I have concocted!" she said, pointing to the bed. On the spread lay a broom from which the straw had been cut away. A thick padding, made of several strips of folded flannel, had been sewn over the stump.

Geoffrey stared at it in complete puzzlement. "What is it?"

"Don't you see? It's a crutch. With the padded end under my arm, I can manage to hobble about on my own, without requiring anyone to assist me."

Geoffrey looked dubious. "I don't see why you should have found this necessary. We have a household full of people ready to give you an arm—"

"But requiring the assistance of others every time one wishes to move about is so galling you know. With this, I can move about quite well. Watch."

She spoke with more assurance than she felt, for she had not had time to practice. However, she did manage, albeit clumsily, to hobble out of the room and down the hall, Geoffrey following anxiously behind. At the top of the stairs, however, she paused. The stairway, curving down below her, seemed horridly formidable. Before she could dredge up the courage to attempt it, she was swept up into his arms. "That was a plucky exhibition, my dear, and I'm all admiration, but I draw the line at permitting you to maneuver the *stairs* with that contrivance," he told her as he started down the stairs.

He's going to ruin the plot, she thought worriedly as she clutched him round the neck with one hand and held on to the crutch with the other. Everything hinged on her being able to use the device when they arrived downstairs. But the awareness of his arms about her, the closeness of his face to hers, and the perceptible beating of his heart distracted her from her plotting. The sensations she felt when he carried her were becoming disconcertingly exciting. She could feel her pulse begin to race. Could he hear her heart as she could his? Was he aware that the rhythm of its beat had decidedly accelerated since he'd lifted her up against his chest?

All too quickly they reached the bottom, and he set her on her feet, keeping a hold on her so that she would not have to put her weight on her injured ankle. But standing there with his arm about her was not the way Meg could catch her breath or concentrate on the execution of her little plot. She had to distance herself from the distraction of his closeness. Gently, she disengaged herself from his hold and leaned back against the newel post of the stairway. While she regained her breath, she cast a surreptitious look at him through lowered lashes and noticed, with annoyance, that he was not in the least discomposed by having held her in his arms.

Her equilibrium regained, she looked up to find the ladies standing about all ready and waiting for her. Lady Carrier was resplendent in a velvet cloak and feathered turban, in the center of which gleamed a diamond brooch; Sybil was appropriately and modestly gowned in a girlish blue lustring covered with a warm pelisse; the butler, Keating, was helping Trixie—luminously lovely in silvery-white—to put on her cloak; and Isabel, as she fastened the buttons of a warm, wool spencer over her burgundy gown, was eyeing her niece in approval. "How lovely and festive you all look," Meg told them warmly.

"Oh, but *you*, Lady Meg," Trixie exclaimed, "will *truly* take everyone's breath away!"

"Yes, indeed," Lady Carrier agreed admiringly, "our dressmakers will undoubtedly be asked to make copies of your gown for every lady who sees you tonight. Oh, here's Mrs. Rhys with your cloak, my dear. Look, Trix, it's of brown velvet lined with the fabric of the gown. Do you see what it means to have a London *modiste?* But put your own cloak on, my love, for we're all ready to go. It won't do for us to stand about here in the hall when we're dressed for outdoors. Geoffrey, take her ladyship to the coach right now, if you please."

"No, thank you," Meg said firmly, putting her crutch into place under her arm. "I shall manage it all by myself." And she began to hobble toward the door.

"Don't be a ninny," Geoffrey said, pulling on his greatcoat before hurrying after her. "You may not be aware of it, but there are nine steps leading down from the doorway to the—"

He was interrupted by a loud gasp. Meg had stumbled. Her crutch fell to the floor with a clatter, and uttering a piercing scream, she tumbled down in a heap and lay still.

All the ladies shrieked in horror and clustered around her, but Geoffrey pushed through and dropped to his knees beside her. "Meg, what—"

Her eyelids fluttered open. "Oh . . . my *ankle*," she moaned weakly. "I'm such a . . . fool!"

He stared at her a moment through narrowed eyes and then lifted her to a sitting position, supporting her against his shoulder. "Have you hurt anything else?"

"No . . . I don't think so . . ."

"Oh, dear," Trixie said in concern, "what a dreadful pass. Do you think you can still go to Lady Habish's?"

"How can you even think of such a thing when her ladyship is obviously suffering?" Lady Carrier muttered, but the tone of her voice clearly indicated that Lady Habish's *soirée* was as much her concern as her daughter's.

"Oh, but you *must* think of it," Meg insisted weakly. "You must all go at once, of course. I shall be quite all right by myself. Mrs. Rhys . . . and Keating . . . shall be able to help me . . ."

"Nonsense, my love," Isabel said firmly, "I shall stay with you. I'm sure Lady Habish will understand."

Trixie and Meg exchanged looks of secret alarm. "No, no, Aunt Bel, you mustn't," Meg put in quickly. "Didn't you say yourself that, since the party is in our honor, our absence would be terribly cruel? At least *one* of us must make an appearance. *Do* go along and enjoy yourselves. I promise that I shall be quite all right."

"No, *I* shall stay with you, my dear," Lady Carrier said

bravely. "I am your hostess, after all, and—"

A chorus of voices interrupted, all volunteering to give up their evening of pleasure to keep Meg company. "Be still, the lot of you!" Geoffrey said coldly. "It's obvious that the absence of any one of you would be more greatly noted than my own, especially since Lady Habish has never *yet* seen me at her table and probably has no expectation of seeing me there tonight. On the other hand, it's I who will be of greater assistance to our invalid here than any of you. So go along at once, make our excuses and leave us in peace."

He got up and lifted Meg into his arms again. The others, realizing that Geoffrey's words were both reasonable and adamant, said apologetic and reluctant goodbyes to Meg and went out to the waiting carriage.

Geoffrey, without another word, carried his burden to the library where he dropped her unceremoniously upon the sofa, turned his back on her and began to remove his greatcoat.

Meg watched him warily. He seemed to be showing more anger than concern over her new "accident," and his coldness frightened her a bit. "I'm sorry to have caused you to miss the festi—"

"Don't bother to continue the pretense, ma'am," he barked, tossing his greatcoat aside and turning on her abruptly. "Did you think me so simple-minded that I'd not see through your little scheme? Was it Trixie who devised this feather-headed plot to keep me at home, or was it a fabrication of your own?"

"It was my idea," she admitted, pulling herself up to a sitting position and facing him bravely. "How did you guess?"

"How could I *fail* to guess?" he sneered. "With Trixie in a state of high excitement instead of flat despair, and with you suddenly so insistent on using a grossly inadequate crutch to hobble about with, it was plain as a pikestaff that you'd concocted *some* scheme to thwart me."

"Yes, I can see now that I underestimated you. But Geoffrey, I don't understand. If you weren't fooled, why did you play along with the plot? Why didn't you expose me?"

"What? *Expose* you? Before my mother and your aunt? That would hardly be the act of a gentleman."

She smiled faintly. "I've known you to act ungentlemanly before this, and with less reason."

"Perhaps, but this time..." He hesitated and turned away from her, crossing to the fireplace and stirring up the flames.

"This time?"

"This time I did not wish to give you *another* excuse to . . . hold me in abhorence," he said quietly, his eyes fixed on the fire.

She felt her heart make a little leap. "I don't hold you in abhorence," she said, realizing with surprise that the words were suddenly quite true.

"Don't you?" He turned and gave her a mocking smile. "Yet surely a man whom you describe as an arrogant tyrant must be abhored."

She lowered her eyes. "I . . . I may have overstated the case," she said shyly. "Perhaps those words are a bit too . . . strong. Aunt Bel has often accused me of being rash in my judgments."

His smile became wry. "You are still being rash. Only a few minutes ago, you were endangering yourself by taking a foolishly headlong spill just to keep me from what you undoubtedly considered an act of tyranny over my sister. In your sudden gratitude toward me for not exposing that deception, are you now ready to take a completely *opposite* view of my character?"

She looked across at him with a brow knit in perplexity. "I don't know. I truly don't know *what* to make of you. If you're not a tyrant, then you must have had a sound reason for wishing to prevent your sister from a perfectly proper association with a young man. If you had such a reason, why did you remain behind when you knew I was really perfectly well?"

He shook his head. "I don't know either." He turned back and resumed his contemplation of the flames. "Perhaps I felt a need to justify myself to you. Kneeling down beside you on that stone floor, I at first felt terror-stricken that you'd done yourself a terrible injury. When I realized, from that artificial fluttering of your eyelids, that you were counterfeiting, I wanted most urgently to wring your neck. But I wished, too, to shake you into some understanding of what you were doing." He looked over his shoulder at her, his smile gone. "Do you realize, girl, that your interference in family matters that you know nothing of is as high-handed and arrogant as any act of mine?"

"But . . . Trixie confided in me all the pertinent details—"

"Yes, I realize that. But do *you* realize that there might be *two* sides to the story?"

"I had thought of that, of course. But it seemed to me that

a brother who disparages every one of his sister's beaux except the one he chose for her himself had very little justification on his side," she said in self-defense.

"Yes, my dear, but you've never met any of Trixie's beaux. You're not acquainted long enough with my sister to know that she loses her heart—with the most unrestrained enthusiasm—at least once a month. This fact is even more alarming when you take into account that this is a society very thin of company. When we were in London, where there are many more young idiots for her to adore, she fell madly in love at least once weekly."

"Come now, Geoffrey, you're surely exaggerating."

"I was certain you would think so. Damnation, I don't know why I feel impelled to discuss these matters with you at all! But fate has seen fit to thrust you into our midst, my family has seen fit to embroil you in our problems, and *you* have seen fit to act upon the information they've supplied. Therefore, you may as well listen to the whole tale. If you are determined to interfere, your actions will be less troublesome if they're based on sounder knowledge."

She hung her head. "You needn't say anything more, Geoffrey, if you don't wish to. It was wrong of me to have interfered, and I shan't do so again."

"But I *do* wish to. I feel this uncommonly compulsive need to make you understand me," he said ruefully. "That's why I didn't leave you out there on the floor, as I should have done, and go along with the others to the Habish domicile to keep an eye on my sister."

He sat down on a wing chair near the fire and stretched out his legs, putting his hands behind his head and leaning back in reflective relaxation. "It's not a very long story," he began. "I need go back only to last year—though it seems more like a decade since—when I was serving in the peninsula with Wellington. I'm sure you can understand how different that life is from any which you and my family are accustomed to. It is, at best, a very Spartan existence, even when one is not involved in the smoke, the filth and the noise of battle. A soldier grows accustomed to doing without the niceties. Many of us grew almost to prefer a tent and a camp-cot to the featherbeds and lace hangings of our bedrooms at home.

"We were in the midst of the drive for Salamanca when the news came of my father's sudden demise. I was given leave, of course, but when I arrived home and saw the state of affairs my father had left behind, I knew I had only one course open to me—to sell out. I don't suppose one who has not been a soldier can appreciate the pain of being forced to desert one's post in the middle of a major campaign, but I realized that my family's needs were my first responsibility. Fortunately, the news of the victory at Salamanca came in time to keep me from falling into complete despond. And the subsequent successes of the peninsular campaign made it perfectly obvious that the army had done very well without me."

He fell silent for a moment, his eyes fixed on the portrait over the mantelpiece with an unseeing stare. Meg felt her throat constrict in sympathy for the soldier who'd been snatched from the fray before the victory and who had had to hear the bells peal from a lonely lace-hung London bedroom, far from his comrades-in-arms and without being given the satisfaction of feeling that his years of sacrifice in his country's behalf had done anything to bring that victory about.

But he proceeded with his tale without the slightest hint in his voice of regret or self-pity. "My father's woeful management of what had been fairly extensive holdings had left us with a heavily mortgaged town house, a pile of gambling debts amassed by, of all people, my *mother* (who has absolutely no sense of the value of money), and the lands and buildings of Knight's Haven which, miraculously, were still unencumbered. I must confess, Meg, that Knight's Haven has always been, to me, the most beautiful place in the world, but that is not the only—or even the major—reason for my choosing this for our home. Once I'd gone over the records and accounts, it seemed plain to me that our only recourse was to sell off the London property and put what was left of our assets into making Knight's Haven a productive estate.

"In this decision I was vociferously opposed by my mother and sisters. They loved their London life as much as I detested it; they disliked Knight's Haven as much as I loved it." He turned in his chair to look at Meg with eyes that sought plainly for her understanding. "I *tried* for a while to oblige them. I paid off the debts and put the family on a strict budget, warning them that unless they followed it to the letter, we would be forced to move to the country. But I had no idea of the extent of women's propensities for frills and fripperies. They were always in dire need of new gowns, new gloves, new slippers, new draperies, new furnishings. Mama couldn't understand how it was *possible* that she'd lost three hundred guineas in one evening's game of silver-loo.

"Meanwhile, Sybil spent her afternoons being checked by every new doctor she could discover, and Trixie was busily engaged in any number of romantic encounters, each one of her swains more foolish and impecunious than the last. At one point, she managed to get herself betrothed to two of them at once, while making a third believe that it was only a matter of time before she would accept *him*. It was when she pleaded with me to extricate herself from all three of these commitments, having discovered a *fourth* who was *truly* her one-and-only love, that I realized that London was not a beneficial place for any of us. In the country our expenses would be decreased, my mother's opportunities for extravagance and gambling would be limited, Sybil would have to make do with only *one* medical man, and Trixie would find it difficult to become betrothed more often than monthly.

"I admit, Meg, that by that time, I'd completely lost patience with all of them. I admit that I found the fair sex, as a whole, to be exasperating—so exasperating that, at times, I run from the house and seek refuge in the taproom of the Horse With Three Tails. I admit that I'm churlish and unsympathetic when it comes to your female preoccupations with matters of dress and appearances. I even admit to being an arrogant tyrant in implementing my decision to move my family here and in compelling them to live in a more restrained style. But I'm convinced that what I'm doing is for the best."

For a long moment they both fell silent. Meg, while still deploring his tendency to belittle her sex, could nevertheless recognize how difficult it must have been for him to move from the masculine world of the battlefield to the female-dominated one of his London household. Now that she understood the causes of his bitterness, she could no longer maintain the feelings of resentment she'd marshalled against him. "You make me ashamed of myself, Geoffrey. I should never have tried to interfere."

He gave her a rather twisted smile. "Then you admit that there *is* another side to Trixie's complaint?"

"Yes, but, Geoffrey, I can't say you've completely won me over in that regard. Wouldn't it be better to permit Trixie to marry this fellow? Perhaps the responsibilities of wedlock will settle her down and help her to mature?"

"I would truly be delighted to see my sister wed. But her concept of an appropriate spouse is completely impossible. Go and see for yourself."

"What?" Meg looked at him in bewilderment. "What do you mean? Now?"

"Yes, right now. I'll have Hackett take you to the Habish party at once. It's still not too late for you to salvage *some* part of this evening. And you'll be able to judge with your own eyes if Mortimer Lazenby is a proper sort of suitor for my sister."

Meg was aware of a sinking feeling of disappointment. She'd been intently absorbed and very content in his company. She had no wish to leave now. "Will you . . . come with me?" she asked.

"What for? Once you see Mortimer Lazenby for yourself, you'll be as assiduous as I would have been in keeping them apart. There's no need for me to go at all." He gave her one of his quick, unexpected grins. "I'll send the footman along to carry you."

She made one last attempt to salvage the evening. "I'd rather not go anymore tonight, Geoffrey. How can I explain to Lady Habish—?"

"There's nothing to explain. You need only say that you are feeling better. They'll be overjoyed to welcome you. Come, my dear. In addition to my guilt for having kept *you* away from the festivities for more than an hour, I feel guilty for depriving my good neighbors of the sight of you. We can't permit you to have donned that magnificient gown for the benefit of my eyes alone. Go along and show yourself to the others. It would be a shame for so much loveliness to go to waste."

It was not until she'd been bundled into the carriage and was trundling over the remaining mounds of snow covering the road toward the Habish residence that she realized that there had been a sharp barb hidden in his apparent compliment on her appearance. *Had* her "loveliness" been wasted on him? Had she dressed herself in her most enticing gown, drenched herself in her most seductive perfume and spent the better part of an hour applying the most subtle colors to her eyes and cheeks for nothing? *Dash it, Geoffrey Carrier*, she asked herself angrily, *what must I do to win your admiration—put on a uniform and volunteer for battle?*

Chapter Eleven

Lady Habish's guests were still seated at the dinner table when Meg made her late and awkward entrance, hopping in on one shod foot while she leaned heavily on the arm of an overdressed footman so that she could keep the injured, stockinged foot off the ground. Blushing with embarrassment and exertion, she made excuses for her late arrival, but the warmth of her reception and the genuine excitement she seemed to stir among the assemblage soon put her at ease. Before she knew it, she'd been helped into the seat in the place of honor at Lord Habish's right and found herself surrounded by servants eager to heap up her plate.

Lady Habish might not have been one of London's *ton*, but her table was set with crystal and plate that would have done justice to any of them. Her servants numbered in the dozens, their livery impressive and their manner flawless. As for the food, it was equal to the most lavish of London dinners. Meg had missed the first course, but the second contained as many as nine different meats, four fishes, a dazzling array of side dishes and at least fifteen varieties of biscuits and pastries.

Lord Habish, a florid, white-whiskered man in his fifties, fixed his attentions on Meg with such affable persistence that, through most of the dinner, she was scarcely able to speak to anyone else. She would not have minded (for his remarks were all innocuously pleasant, and he laughed very appreciatively at all her quips) except that he never moved his eyes from a rapt contemplation of her décolletage, which made her feel as if her responses were coming from her bosom rather than her mouth.

Being so busily engaged by her host, Meg had little opportunity to observe Mortimer Lazenby at close range, but her first impression was of an overdressed popinjay. He was seated too far down the table to permit her to converse with him, but even from that distance she could see that his apparel was ridiculous. The fellow may not have shown more than two colors in his waistcoat, but everything else about him was overdone. His shirt-points were so high he could barely turn his head, the fold of his neckcloth so intricate that it seemed a jumbled confusion, his hair was curled and crimped in such profusion that Meg suspected his valet had spent half a day working over it with a hot iron, and, when he stood up to make his bow to her, she'd noted that he wore six fobs on his watch-chain where one would have done quite well.

Nevertheless, Meg did not find Mortimer's foppish appearance to be sufficient grounds to make him ineligible as a suitor for Trixie. She could readily see that Geoffrey, with his country-squire, army-bred Spartan tastes, would find the fellow's attire revolting. But if Trixie didn't mind living the rest of her life with a man who'd spend all his time fussing over his *toilette*, Meg didn't see why her brother should make the matter a major objection. Dandyism was, after all, a rather minor vanity.

Later, however, when the party assembled in the music room for card games and talk, she found the fellow even less to her liking. Trixie, her eyes shining with excitement, brought the young Lazenby to be presented. Meg offered her hand, smiling pleasantly and feeling very willing to be won over. "I've been hearing a great deal about you, Mr. Lazenby," she said.

Mortimer made his bow. *"Bound* to have heard of me, your ladyship," he said with perfect seriousness. "Mortimer Lazenby's very well known in these parts. Very well known. Especially since winning the fifteen-miler against Gap-toothed Garrelson last year. Talk of the county, wasn't it, Trix?"

"Oh, yes," breathed Trixie effusively. "Mr. Garrelson and Mortimer raced a pair of high-perch phaetons from Leyburn to Masham, and Mortimer beat him by a full three minutes. It was the most *thrilling* thing (though of course I wasn't permitted out to watch it), but *everyone* was talking of it."

"Think it was four," Mortimer corrected superciliously, fingering his neckcloth idly.

"Four?" Trixie asked, not following.

"Beat him by four, not three. Timekeeper assured me."

"Oh, yes. Think of it, Lady Meg! He won by *four whole minutes!"*

"How very exciting that must have been," Meg said, studying Mortimer intently while her feelings swung from amusement to dislike. She could easily excuse the young man's foppishness on the grounds that he was ill-advised by his parents and his valet; excesses in that regard might even be considered foolishly appealing. But an excess of self-consequence was another matter.

"Live in London?" the young man was inquiring. His shirt-points were so high that he found it difficult, standing before her, to lower his head sufficiently to look her in the eye as he spoke, and he addressed all his remarks to an area over her head. What with Lord Habish's tendency to focus on a *lower* area and Mortimer's on an *upper,* Meg began to feel that no one in the room would ever look into her *face.*

"Won't you sit down, Mr. Lazenby? And you, too, Trixie. There's plenty of room for you both on this sofa. Yes, I *do* live in London, sir. On Dover Street. Do you know London at all?"

Trixie perched on her right, beaming happily at Meg in complete confidence that the older woman who'd become her idol was showing approval of her *innamorato.* Mortimer flipped up his tails and sat down on Meg's left, twisting sideways stiffly so that he could look at the ladies without turning his head. "Oh, yes. Know London quite well. Went down for the season last year, you know. Didn't like it above half."

"No? Why not?"

"Too deucedly crowded, if you ask me. A crush everywhere

one went. Parties paltry, too. Ladies set better tables here in Yorkshire than they do in town."

"If tonight's dinner is typical, you may well be right," Meg said, trying to be agreeable. She'd noticed many times in the past a tendency among the Dandy Set to drop the subjects of their sentences (probably to convey an impression of un-book-ish masculinity), but Motimer was pushing the style—as he did in matters of dress—to its ludicrous extreme. "But there must have been *something* in London which met with your approval," she said wryly. "How about our places of interest, like Covent Garden?"

He shrugged. "Ain't devoted to plays and opera and such. Was mighty happy to come home, I can tell you. No place in the world like Yorkshire, eh, Trix? Why, even our tailors are better here." He fingered the lapel of his coat fondly. "Fully expected to be bowled over by the London tailors, y' know? Been told that Stultz and Weston and the other needle-men in town are top-of-the-trees. But, no. Didn't show *me* that they could execute the latest styles. If you ask me, my Mr. Stome— at Ripon, y' know?—is better than the lot of London tailors."

He looked at them for instant agreement. "You must be right, Mortimer," Trixie said obligingly, "for there isn't a hand-somer coat in the room than the one you're wearing, is there, Lady Meg?"

Meg, who'd found the coat (with its overly padded, puffed-up shoulders and ridiculously wide lapels) almost vulgar in its insistent exaggeration of every stylish tendency, was saved from having to answer by the approach of her host with a plainly dressed, elderly couple in tow. "The Mundeys have been asking to meet you, your ladyship," Lord Habish said, pulling them forward.

Trixie and Mortimer reluctantly surrendered their places to make room for the newcomers. And when the Mundeys showed signs of settling in for a lengthy conversation, Trixie and Mortimer wandered off, much to Meg's relief.

Mr. and Mrs. Mundey were a simple, unaffected couple whose property, they told her, marched along with the acreage of Knight's Haven, and an interesting quarter-hour passed while they related to Meg their enthusiasm for Sir Geoffrey as a neighbor. "Most sensible fellow in these parts," the apple-cheeked, grizzled old fellow told her. "He's making improvements in the property that the rest of us are all beginning to imitate." Meg found herself fascinated with their talk of tenant farmers, leases, crop management and enclosures, although at one point she was momentarily distracted from their conversation by the sound of Lady Carrier's tense voice reaching her from the opposite side of the large room.

Meg couldn't help turning to see what had disturbed Lady Carrier. Although there were a number of tables set up around the room, all occupied with engrossed card players, one table seemed to have attracted a great deal of attention. A small crowd had gathered about the table where Lady Carrier, Lady Habish and Mr. and Mrs. Garrelson were engaged in intense play. Meg could not detect exactly what was being played, but she thought she'd heard Lady Carrier say, "My diamond, then. I'll wager the diamond."

Meg turned her attention back to the Mundeys, trying to dismiss those words from her mind. Geoffrey had told her that his mother had no sense of finance, but surely even *she* would not be so foolish as to hazard her valuable brooch on a little card game at a private party. Meg must have been mistaken in what she'd heard.

The Mundeys stayed at her side, chatting pleasantly, until they were supplanted by an insistent Mrs. Lazenby, who proved to be as vulgar and self-important as her son. Meg found her loud voice and endless monologue (about how favorably her drawing room, her cook and her china compared to Lady Habish's) tedious and annoying, but she had no way to extricate herself from the lady's presence. After a while, the card game behind her came to an end, and Lady Carrier passed her by, the diamond brooch missing from her turban. Meg was appalled but not surprised. She was beginning to realize that Geoffrey's evaluation of the females who surrounded him was more accurate than hers had been.

She hoped that, by midnight, the party would end. Surely a country assemblage would not keep late hours. But at midnight Lady Habish announced that a buffet supper had been set up in the upstairs sitting room and was now being served. All of the company began to move toward the stairs, no one in the room showing the slightest interest in making an end to the festivities. The host and hostess approached Meg to tell her that the footman would carry her up the stairs to the table, but she firmly declined. "I've had more than enough to eat already," she insisted. Her host, however, was driven to urge her again and again to change her mind.

Mr. Mundey, overhearing his harangue, came to Meg's

rescue. "Let the lady *be*, Habish," he said. "I'll be happy to keep her company while the rest of you make gluttons of yourselves over Lady Habish's apricot souffles and banana creams."

The plan suited Meg very well, and the others trooped up the stairs while Mr. Mundey took a place beside Meg and began to recount the circumstances of his friendship with Sir Geoffrey. It took very little urging from Meg to encourage him to expand on the details of his dealings with his admired neighbor. The conversation proved to be very informative. Meg learned a great deal about the problems of estate management and how the war had affected the economies of farming. Mr. Mundey was just launching into a complicated explanation of the meaning of enclosure when they were distracted by the arrival of Mortimer Lazenby from upstairs. The fellow strolled into the room carrying a fully laden platter of tidbits and sweets. "Brought you a bite of supper, your ladyship," he announced, interrupting the old man in mid-sentence. "I say, Mundey, why don't you go upstairs and get some supper? I'll keep Lady Margaret company in your place."

"But Mr. Lazenby," Meg objected, "you've cut in on a very interesting—"

Mr. Mundey, blinking curiously at Meg, smiled deprecatingly and shook his head. "Not so very interesting as the kind of talk that you *young* folk will engage in," he chuckled. "You've been kind to an old fellow for long enough, my lady. It's time I took myself off."

Meg's objections were of no avail, and Mortimer, handing Meg the platter, took Mr. Mundey's place with a self-satisfied smirk. "Didn't think I'd let the evening pass without finding a way to see you alone, did you?" he asked familiarly as soon as old Mundey was out of hearing.

Meg's eyebrows rose. "I beg your pardon?"

"I mean, you *did* realize a fellow like me would manage it, didn't you? Even if you *are* the guest of honor and were bound to be surrounded?"

"I can't say I gave the matter any thought at all," Meg said coldly. "Did you have a special reason for wanting to see me alone? Is there something you wish to confide in me regarding Trixie?"

"Trixie? Don't see why you think I'd want to speak of Trixie."

"Well, I thought..." She put the platter down on the table behind the sofa, folded her hands in her lap and looked over the young man with an expression calculated to depress his pretensions. "Then what business *do* you have with me, sir?"

His pretensions were not in the least depressed. He leered at her and put his arm on the back of the sofa with a swaggering self-confidence. "Wouldn't exactly call it *business*. Business isn't what I have in mind."

"Then what *do* you have in mind?"

"You can guess, your ladyship. I mean, Margaret. Better call you Margaret, eh? Can't keep saying 'your ladyship' when I'm arranging to call on you."

"You may *not* call me Margaret!" she said in disgust. "And why on *earth* would you want to *call* on me?"

Unaffected by her tone, he grinned again. "Silly question. Why does *any* fellow call on a girl?"

"Girl!" She could hardly believe her ears. "Perhaps I don't fully understand you, Mr. Lazenby. Are you not promised to... that is, haven't you and Trixie an understanding?"

"Oh, is *that* what's worrying you?" With fatuous presumption, he patted her shoulder soothingly. "Ain't a thing between Trixie and me that can't be ended like *that!*" And he snapped his fingers together with so loud a sound that Meg jumped.

She thrust his hand from her shoulder with revulsion. "Mr. Lazenby," she said icily, "I cannot *imagine* what I've said or done to give you the impression that I would welcome a visit from you. Even if you should come to call merely to confide in me your love for Trixie Carrier, I would refuse to see you. Let there be no possible misunderstanding between us, Mr. Lazenby. I tell you quite bluntly that I will not admit you over my threshold under *any* circumstances."

His eyebrows rose in mild surprise. "Is this the way London ladies keep a fellow dangling? No need to play that game with *me*, my dear, I assure you. Already have me hooked, y'see. Smitten the minute I saw you, word of honor!"

If she weren't so exasperatedly furious with him, she would have laughed. Never had she met anyone so incapable of self-doubt. "I give you *my* word of honor that I'm not playing a game. The truth is that I find you completely unacceptable as a suitor. And if you persist in this foolishness, I shall be forced to tell Trixie what has transpired here tonight—and in complete detail. Do you understand me, sir? One more idiotic word from you on this matter and I shall tell her everything you've—"

"Meg?" came a faint voice from the doorway. "Meg, my dear..."

Meg turned quickly toward the new sound. Isabel, strangely flushed, stood leaning on the door jamb. "Aunt Bel!" she exclaimed, rising to her feet in alarm, "Good God, what's—"

"I'm afraid I'm...not feeling at all...well. Do you think...someone...might take me...home?"

Ignoring her own pain, Meg limped as rapidly as she could across the floor. "My poor darling!" she cried, taking her aunt in a tight embrace. "What is it?"

But she could feel the waves of heat emanating from her aunt's flushed cheeks. The woman was burning with fever!

"I don't know what's wrong with me," Isabel muttered through dry lips. "I feel so...dizzy." She sagged against Meg heavily and began, shockingly, to shiver. "Do you think, my dearest...that that irritating doctor...can have been...right?" And, her body going completely limp, she slid slowly from Meg's hold and slipped to the floor in a swoon.

Chapter Twelve

Dr. Fraser was summoned to Knight's Haven in the wee hours of the morning. Despite the hour, he came promptly through a chilling rain to examine the woman who had so adamantly refused to accept his advice two days before. Isabel was not even aware that he'd come—her high fever had driven her mind into a foggy, half-conscious state somewhere between sleep and delirium.

From their places at the foot of her bed, Meg, Geoffrey and Lady Carrier watched anxiously as Dr. Fraser felt Isabel's pulse and listened to her labored breathing. It was clear even to the untutored observers that the poor woman was in pain. Her breath seemed to come in shallow little pants, but periodically the shallow breaths were inadequate, and she gulped deeply for air. At those times, her hand fluttered to her chest as if to keep the pain in check.

"It's the pleurisy," the doctor said, turning from the bed and leading the onlookers from the room. "The vauntie female, like as no, has had pains in her side fer days."

He explained that the only treatment he could provide was to strap her chest to keep her from breathing too deeply, thus limiting the pain. Other than that, there was nothing much to be done but to try to draw the fever down and to keep the patient calm and quiet. "She has a strong constitution," he told Meg reassuringly. "Gi'e the lass time and care . . . she'll come round." He then requested Geoffrey's assistance for the strapping and ordered the women to their beds. Lady Carrier obeyed, but Meg insisted that she would sit up with her aunt till morning and that *she* was capable of assisting the doctor in Geoffrey's place. Unable to dissuade her, the two men accepted the inevitable and assisted her back into the sickroom.

Meg held the limp Isabel up against her shoulder as the doctor and Geoffrey tore a sheet into strips and wound them tightly about the patient's chest. The discomfort of the handling and the constricting effect of the strapping woke Isabel from her stupor for a moment. After a paroxysm of coughing, her eyes fell on the doctor. "You!" she muttered faintly. "Go 'way! Don't want . . . your . . . assis . . . assis . . . help."

"Wheesht, woman, stop yatterin'!" he ordered curtly as he continued his labors, the seriousness of her condition having not the slightest softening effect on the brusqueness of his manner. "Some folk dinna ken when 'tis time t' save their breath."

In a few moments, the task was completed, a strong sleeping draught had been forced down the patient's throat, and she'd been settled back upon a pile of pillows with a comforter pulled up to her neck and a cool, wet cloth placed on her forehead. While Geoffrey accompanied the doctor to his waiting curricle, Meg settled herself on a chair near enough to the bed to enable her to change her aunt's compresses without getting up. When Geoffrey returned, a whispered debate ensued about which one of them was more capable of remaining awake through the rest of the night to care for the patient. The argument resulted in a stalemate. Geoffrey took a chair on the other side of the bed, and the two exchanged not another word for the rest of the night.

Some time after dawn, Meg must have drowsed off, for the next thing she knew it was daylight, and Geoffrey was lifting her in his arms. "Hush, my dear. Don't say anything," he whispered as he carried her out of the sickroom. "I'm taking you to your room so that you can get a few hours of sleep. Mrs. Rhys is with your aunt now. Poor Isabel is so soundly drugged that she won't wake for hours. I assure you that you'll not be needed."

Meg was too weary to object. She was exhausted from lack of sleep, her ankle ached from the abuse she'd given it earlier, and her spirits were utterly depressed. Her thoughts were a confused jumble of nightmarish fears and guilts. They seemed to circle in her mind like a chorus of accusing voices. Her aunt might *die* because of her own weakness and neglect. If only she'd forced Aunt Bel to obey the doctor . . . if only she'd seen the illness growing in her aunt's chest . . . if only she'd stayed the night at the Horse With Three Tails Inn like a person of sense . . . if only she'd remained at Isham Manor and faced the consequences of breaking her engagement like a woman of character . . .

Geoffrey carried her into her room and laid her gently on the bed. "Don't look so terrified, Meg. Dr. Fraser assures me that there is every chance—"

She had not yet taken her arms from round his neck, and his face was very close. Never before had she seen in his eyes such a look of tender concern. Something inside her—some last vestige of strength or self-control—gave way, and as her arms slipped down from his shoulders, she suddenly found herself clutching in panic at the lapels of his coat. "G-Geof—" she stammered fearfully and, without the slightest warning signal either to him or to herself, dissolved into a flood of despairing sobs.

He sat down on the edge of the bed and let her head fall on his shoulder. "Don't, Meg," he said softly into her hair. "It will all come right, I promise you."

Shaken as she was, she could feel the tightening of his arm around her waist. With a surprising sense of comfort, she let herself sag against him, weeping unrestrainedly into his shoulder. It was a strange sort of unburdening; a tension which had held her emotions in a frozen grip for many hours suddenly seemed to melt. She had never before leaned—either emotionally or physically—on anyone else in time of trouble. There was something soothing and secure in this unfamiliar act of sharing her distress with someone else. She *liked* the support of his shoulder, the strength of his arm, the pressure of his face against her hair. She felt a large part of her inner turmoil pour out in what seemed an endless flow of tears.

But this behavior was completely unlike her, and when at last she was able to bring herself back into some sort of control, she lifted her head and turned her face away from him in deep embarrassment. "I'm t-terribly sorry," she said, wiping her eyes awkwardly with the back of her hand. "I don't know what came over me . . ."

He took her chin in his hand and turned her face to him. "What came over you, my dear, is only weariness and worry," he said brusquely, brushing her tousled hair back from her forehead. He stared at her for a moment and then abruptly let her go. Getting to his feet, he added, half to himself, "We should neither of us refine on it."

"I suppose you're right." She looked up at him with a shaky, rueful smile. "But isn't it ironic that, immediately after you'd confided in me your difficulties with the women in your family, I should *add* to your conviction of female incompetence by collapsing in your arms and bursting into tears in that missish way?"

He shrugged and turned to the door. "If you think that I find a perfectly understandable display of emotions to be a sign of female incompetence, you have a great deal to learn of me, ma'am." He paused a moment at the door and glanced back at her. "Shall I send a housemaid to help you undress?"

She peered at him for a moment before answering. There was something in the coolness of his tone that gave her a twinge of pain. Before her display of waterworks, she had been sure she recognized the signs of real tenderness in his face; now, however, he seemed suddenly curt and distant. Was it possible that, despite his reassurances to the contrary, he'd been repelled by her show of weakness? Was he truly as much of a misogynist as all that?

But with a brush of her hand across her forehead she dismissed the questions from her mind. Geoffrey Carrier was not her concern. Her beloved aunt lay on a sickbed down the hall, struggling for her very breath—*that* must be her first and only concern. Anything else was a superfluous and inexcusable distraction. "No, thank you, sir," she said, weary but firm. "I shall manage very well on my own."

Isabel's fever remained alarmingly high for two days, and the poor creature appeared to be burning up. Her lips were dry and parched, and she muttered incoherently as she moaned and tossed about through the dark hours of the night. Unless drugged with laudanum, she was unable really to sleep, and she tugged and pulled weakly at the bands which constricted her chest. Watching her, Meg felt herself torn apart with fearfulness and helpless sympathy.

She left the bedside only when forced to do so by Geoffrey or Mrs. Rhys. Actually, Mrs. Rhys was of greater use in the sickroom than she. The housekeeper had an inborn talent for nursing. She kept the room aired without permitting the slightest chill to reach the area of the bed; she managed to prevail upon the patient to drink her medicinal draughts and liquid nutriments when no one else could do so, merely by propping Isabel up on her arm and keeping up a stream of meaningless but cheerful chatter as she poured the liquid down Isabel's throat; and she changed the damp bed linen so frequently and with so little disturbance to the patient that Meg could only gape with admiration.

Geoffrey, too, was overwhelmingly helpful. Somehow he always seemed to take over the sickroom in the late-night hours, demanding that Meg and Mrs. Rhys snatch a few hours of sleep. Meg, who always found him dressed and available whenever she needed him, wondered when he himself managed to get to sleep.

Dr. Fraser was the only other person whose presence Meg found comforting. He came to the sickroom twice a day to see his patient. The only thing he did was feel her forehead, take her pulse, peer at her and grunt. He would say nothing in response to Meg's persistent questions and alarms, but she nevertheless felt reassured by his presence and by the matter-of-fact imperturbability of his manner.

Lady Carrier, on the other hand, never failed to annoy Meg when she visited the sickroom. She was always full of concern, whispering the most sincere good wishes and asking interested and anxious questions regarding the patient's progress, but she was obviously unwilling to step over the threshold. And as for her daughters, she explained that it was she who kept them away. "I told them with the strictest firmness to stay away," she admitted. "After all, neither one of them would be of the slightest use to you. Sybil's constitution is too delicate, you know, and Trixie, with her mind so preoccupied with the impediments her brother keeps throwing in the path of her romance, is completely absent-minded. Besides, there's little point in endangering their health at a time like this. The very last thing we need in this house is another invalid."

While Meg couldn't blame Lady Carrier for protecting her daughters' health, the woman's lack of graciousness did not endear her to Meg's heart. Even though she was relieved not to have the girls underfoot in the sickroom, she wished that Lady Carrier could have shown a greater generosity of spirit. She never failed to make Meg feel like a troublesome intruder, while Geoffrey went out of his way to *keep* her from feeling that way. Matters seemed to have taken a complete reversal in that regard. Suddenly it was Geoffrey who was trying to make her feel at home and the others who were behaving churlishly.

But aside from his exceptional devotion to her aunt's needs and his scrupulous kindness as a host, Meg found Geoffrey's behavior puzzling. The intimacy which had developed between them on the evening of the Habish's dinner party had somehow dissipated. He was invariably thoughtful of her needs, but he seemed to keep a distance between them. It was as if he regretted ever having let her see the side of him that was open and warm. Was it fear of entangling himself with yet another troublesome female that had caused him to withdraw? Was he afraid of her . . . or of himself?

No matter how many times the question popped into her mind, she pushed it aside. She couldn't let herself think of anything but her aunt's recovery. It was a very foolish, superstitious sort of feeling, she knew, but if she ever let her mind wander from the problem of her aunt's illness, she was beset with guilt. It was as if she'd set herself the task of *willing* her aunt back to health, and the task required her complete concentration.

By the third night of Isabel's illness, her fever seemed worse than ever. Isabel alternately shivered and perspired, crying out hoarsely after long silences words that made no sense. Meg hobbled anxiously about the room (for her ankle had been feeling stronger during the last two days, and Geoffrey had provided her with his walking stick), jumping with a nervous start every time Isabel made a sound. At last, Geoffrey, who'd been watching her from a chair near the fireplace with knit brows, ordered her to bed in a voice that brooked no argument. She threw herself upon her pillows, too exhausted to remove her dress and, after a bout of weeping, fell into a stertorous sleep.

She awakened in broad daylight, with no idea of how long she'd slept. Throwing open the draperies, she looked out upon the dreariest prospect she'd ever viewed. A steady rain was falling from leaden skies, washing away the last vestiges of the snow which had brought her to this pass and driving down all but a few of the remaining autumn leaves. Those that still managed to cling to their branches had lost their color. The little specks of gold and red that had pleased her eyes only a few days ago had now regressed to a faded brown, adding a final note of gloom to the ravaged landscape. *Good Lord!* she thought in horror, *is this some sort of warning . . . a foreboding of the day ahead?*

Without changing her gown or combing her hair, she hobbled down the corridor as quickly as her injury allowed and threw open the door of the sickroom. There on the bed, sitting erect, was a wide-awake aunt, sipping contentedly from a glass that Geoffrey was holding at her lips. "Aunt Bel!" Meg cried in delight. "You're awake!"

Over Isabel's head, Geoffrey (looking completely disreputable with a two-day growth of beard) gave her one of his rare, disconcerting grins. "The fever's broken, Meg. I think your aunt is going to be all right."

This opinion was seconded by Dr. Fraser when he arrived shortly afterwards. At his first glimpse of Isabel's alert eyes, he gave her a twisted little smile. "So, lass, ye've broken yer fever at last. It's aboot time, too. Ye've been keepin' us all in a curfuffle owre ye, ye ken."

"Meg," Isabel asked weakly, drawing back fearfully against her pillows and pulling her comforter up to her neck, "you haven't permitted this dreadful man to . . ." But a fit of dry, hacking coughs kept her from finishing.

"Aye, after the fever comes the coughin'," Fraser said to Geoffrey with a knowing nod, ignoring Isabel's insult.

"Dr. Fraser's been a wonderful help to you, my dear," Meg said to the horrified patient softly. "Don't think so harshly of him. It's not like you to hold a grudge."

"A grudge?" Isabel echoed, too weak and bemused to argue the issue with her usual spirit. "It isn't a grudge . . . but . . . is there no other medical man in the vicinity whom we could call . . . ?"

"Hold yer clack, woman," the doctor ordered in considerable asperity. "There's no better medical man in the whole of Britain, and dinna ye forget it. Geoffrey, lad, take yersel' oot, if ye please, and *you,* ma'am, will lower yer nightie frae yer shoulder so I can look at yer chest."

"Never!" Isabel sputtered, coughing and burrowing fearfully into the mound of pillows like a frightened rabbit.

"Lady Meg, yer aunt is a gowky wanwyt! Hark ye here, ma'am. Y're too auld and I'm too thrang to spend time wi' sich foolishness. Do ye think the sight o' yer bare bosom will egg me on t' *ravish* ye? I've seen ye afore, ye ken. Who do ye think it was put the strappin' on ye, eh? Gi'e owre, and let me harken to yer chest!"

Isabel, her eyes wide as saucers, stared at him numbly while Meg, biting her underlip to keep from laughing, pulled down the shoulder of her aunt's gown. The doctor briskly examined his patient, muttered a few directions to Meg about the ingredients he required for a hot tisane to be administered to his patient four times daily, snapped his bag shut and stamped from the room.

Isabel, her chest heaving with rapid breaths, sank back and stared wide-eyed at the door. Meg prepared herself to deal with her aunt's outrage. Isabel might chafe and stew from the sting of the doctor's blunt manner, but as far as Meg was concerned, the Scotsman had brought Aunt Bel through a dangerous illness and would therefore always have her loyal support. "He called *me* a gowky wanwyt once when I dropped a glass," Meg offered comfortingly. "I don't think he means to be insulting."

Isabel turned slowly and looked at her niece with a thoughtful intensity. "You know, Meg," she said in a voice that was weak but surprisingly calm, "I've been wondering if, when I'm better, it might not be a good idea, after all, for me to dye my hair."

Chapter Thirteen

A week later, Meg awakened to a very different sort of morning. Though the prospect from her window was as November-bare as before, the sun seemed to put a sparkle on everything, even the bare trees. A brisk wind made the branches dance and sent little white clouds scurrying to the horizon across the vast expanse of bright blue sky. As she stood in the window embrasure, lifting her tumbled, thick red hair away from her neck and letting it sift through her fingers, her eyes roamed over the south fields that, except for the section of home woods to her left, spread out before her in unbroken, undulating swells that seemed to reach to the ends of the world. She had a most uncommon urge to dash out just as she was, in nothing but a thin nightdress, and run madly across the fields to the far horizon, the wind in her face and her hair streaming out behind her. The impulse made her laugh at herself. She had better restrain such wildly romantic fancies—that was just the sort of nonsensical urge that had ruined Caro Lamb.

Just then her eye fell on a little brown rabbit which had come out of the woods and was hopping across the fields following the very route on which she'd chosen to make her imaginary run. While she watched, the tiny animal stopped, turned its head, lifting its twitching nose in the air and sniffed. She could almost believe the little creature was looking right at her. "Why don't you come?" it seemed to be saying. "Come out and have an adventure."

Why not? she thought. She needn't run about in a night dress, but she *could* venture out into the air. She'd been cooped up long enough. Today, with a bit of luck—and *that* depended on finding Geoffrey Carrier in the right mood—she would do just what the rabbit advised: go out and have an adventure.

She dressed herself quickly in the green jaconet (for it was the one dress Geoffrey had ever said he admired), brushed her hair, pinned it up into a careless knot at the top of her head and went down the hall to see her aunt. Just as she was about to enter the room, Dr. Fraser came out. The dear man had been wonderfully faithful about continuing to call on his patient in spite of the fact that Isabel, mending rapidly, never failed to say something abusive about him in his presence. "Good morning, Doctor," Meg said cheerfully. "Have you seen Aunt Bel already?"

"Already? 'Tis past ten, lass. I've been makin' calls these past three hours."

"Past ten? Oh, dear, I *am* a slugabed. How does my aunt today?"

"Thrivin', fair thrivin'. We'll ha'e her aunt up and aboot in no time," he said, clapping his battered old hat upon his head and striding off down the hall with a step that she would have described as almost capering. She watched him as he disappeared down the hall, wondering what had caused the usually dour Scot to be so cheerful, when a completely surprising sound assailed her ears—the good doctor was *whistling!*

"What on earth did you say to Dr. Fraser to set him in such high spirits, Aunt Bel?" Meg asked as soon as she entered. "I've never seen him quite so cheerful."

Isabel was sitting up against her pillows, a breakfast tray on her lap. Her hair had been brushed neatly back from her face, and she'd been dressed in a fresh, lace-trimmed nightgown that made her look almost girlish. In fact, Meg found her appearance very encouraging. Isabel's eyes were clear and the sick pallor of her complexion had almost disappeared. Except for a persistent, dry cough and a tendency to tire in the late afternoon, Isabel showed small trace of the illness that had laid her low.

Isabel didn't immediately respond to Meg's question. Instead, she raised her teacup to her lips and took a sip of the still-steaming brew. *"Was* he cheerful?" she asked after a moment.

"Out o doot, as he'd say himself. Why, the fellow actually *pranced* down the hall, and, Bel, you'll never credit it when I tell you what he was doing."

"What *was* he doing?" Isabel asked, lifting her eyes from her cup to throw a quick, darting glance at her niece.

"He was whistling! Actually whistling. What did you say to him, my love?"

"Nothing at all," Isabel said sourly, a spot of color appearing in her cheeks. "Why should Dr. Fraser's good spirits have anything to do with me?"

"I don't know. I only hoped that perhaps you'd been kind to him for once. He really is the dearest man. I don't know why you persist in holding him in dislike."

"The man is a presumptuous lout, and I don't see why we spend so much time talking about him. May we not speak of something else for a change?"

"Of course, dearest, if that's what you wish. Just let me tell you that the doctor gave me good news of you. He says you'll be up and 'aboot' in no time."

"I'm glad to hear that," Isabel said, her eyes fixed on her cup. "That means we shall soon be able to leave here and return home."

Meg, about to pick up Isabel's breakfast tray, stopped in her tracks. *Return home.* Of course! If the doctor's prognosis was correct, it was likely that Isabel would be ready for travel by the time the week was out. Meg sank into a chair, her mind in a whirl. She hadn't been thinking of home for *days*. How strange, when reaching home had been her primary goal from the moment she'd decided not to wed Charles Isham. Stranger still, why should the prospect of an imminent departure depress her spirits?

She'd been away from home for more than a fortnight and

hadn't troubled to send word to any of her friends about her situation. They must all be wondering what had become of her. And if Isham had already returned to London and let slip the news that their betrothal was at an end, all her friends would be in a turmoil. They were completely ignorant of her whereabouts and would surely be in a flurry of concern. She must begin to plan her return home as soon as possible. But, she realized with a shock, she was not yet ready to take her leave of Yorkshire and this house.

"Is something the matter, love?" Isabel asked.

Something was very much the matter, but Meg didn't want to think about what it was. "No, Aunt Bel, just thinking," she said, shaking herself into action. "I'm afraid my head is full of cobwebs today. Do you know what I'm going to do this afternoon? I'm going to go *riding!* There's nothing wrong with me that a few hours in the open air won't cure."

A brief conference with Roodle revealed that, since the bruised foreleg of the wounded chestnut had nicely healed, either one of the pair of horses she'd "stolen" would make an adequate mount for Meg to ride. All she needed was permission from Geoffrey to use one of the saddles. If she found him in the right mood, she would get that permission . . . and his company as well.

She found him in the library, seated behind a long table and busily absorbed in studying a number of documents and maps spread out before him. Remembering her conversation with the elderly Mr. Mundey, Meg realized that he was planning the "enclosures" which Mundey had spoken of. "Am I disturbing you, Geoffrey?" she asked hesitantly. "You appear to be thoroughly engrossed."

He got to his feet at once. "Please come in," he said politely, although she could see that he tore his eyes from his work most reluctantly. "Is there something I can do for you?"

"I think it's time I took some air. It's such a lovely day that I'd like to ride. May I make use of one of your saddles?"

"Yes, of course you may. And one of my horses, too. Surely you're not thinking of riding one of your chestnuts? I hardly think them suitable for a lady."

She raised an eyebrow in cold rebuke. "Since you know nothing of my ability to sit a horse, is it not presumptuous of you to assume—"

He cut her off with an impatient gesture of his hand. "I

don't wish to argue with you, Meg. You may, of course, do just as you like. However, I've not forgotten that you acquired the animals with the carriage on the night we first encountered each other. You therefore haven't had the opportunity to become familiar with their habits. It seems to me that caution would dictate your choosing a horse of *my* recommendation rather than taking a chance on an animal which neither one of us has tried."

Meg clenched her teeth angrily. "I've never encountered a horse I couldn't—" She stopped herself in mid-sentence. A dispute with Geoffrey was not at all what she'd intended. "I'm sorry," she said, suddenly meek. "I'm afraid that caution is not a quality which comes easily to me."

If her change in tone surprised him, he didn't show it. "Ask my groom to saddle Guinevere for you. And you needn't look at me with such suspicion—the mare is no slug, I promise you. She's quite spirited enough to give you a perfectly enjoyable ride."

"Are you certain, then, that I won't be thrown?" she asked sarcastically. "After all, you have only my word that I can ride. Doesn't your caution warn you that, with a horse of spirit, I may be in danger?"

"Guinevere is spirited but not wild. Besides, you'll take the groom along with you, of course."

"Take the groom with me? I shall do no such thing!"

"See here, ma'am—" he said in irritation.

"I shall *not* 'see here.' Having a groom plodding alongside is the greatest bore. If you're so concerned for my safety, come along with me yourself."

He sighed in barely controlled impatience. "You can see, ma'am, that I'm quite busy at the moment. Why don't you coax Trixie into going along. She sits a horse fairly well. If she spent more time at it, she would make an admirable horse-woman." He lowered his eyes to his papers, trying to indicate that the interview was at an end.

But Meg was not so easily dismissed. "I would gladly seek her company, but she's gone out."

Geoffrey's head came up abruptly. "Out? Where?"

"I don't know. Lady Carrier didn't mention—"

"Damnation!" He slammed his fist on the table in fury and then turned and strode to the window where he stood staring out on the sunny fields.

"Oh, dear," Meg murmured, "is it Lazenby again?"

"I'm afraid so." He turned around to face her, his temper under control again. "We've not had the opportunity to discuss your opinion of my sister's latest flirt. Now that you've met him, do you still believe I'm tyrannical in trying to halt the affair?"

"To be frank, Geoffrey, I don't. He's a vain, silly, impossibly smug young man, and I think you're quite right in wishing to keep your sister away from him."

"You don't say!" His expression softened almost to a smile. "Is it possible that you and I have found something upon which we can agree at last?

"Come now, sir, we've not been as contentious as all that. But I must tell you that I *don't* agree with your method of handling your sister. Don't you know that when a young woman is ordered to keep away from a young man, that is the one she will wish to see above all?"

"Yes, I see your point. Women are the most contrary creatures. In that case, Meg, what am I to do? Stand aside and pretend to approve of the match?"

"I don't know. It may be too late for you to employ that strategy now, although if you'd done so earlier, a girl of Trixie's intelligence might have discovered for herself, as her sister Sybil has, that the fellow is a twiddle-poop."

"Is that what Sybil calls him?" He gave an appreciative laugh. "I didn't think Sybil had so much sense. Very well, ma'am, I admit I was high-handed with Trixie in this matter. What do you suggest I do about it now?"

"I have no suggestion . . . but there must surely be a strategy you can devise . . ."

"Strategy? I'm afraid that when it comes to dealing with women I haven't the least notion of how to devise strategies. Now, if it were a military campaign—"

"No, women do *not* behave 'like armies in the field. But Geoffrey, I don't desire to stand here on my weak ankle and discuss strategy. If you really wish to continue this conversation, why can't we do it on horseback?"

He raised a quizzical brow. "This is what you've wanted to accomplish from the first, isn't it, ma'am? I very much fear that I've been the victim of strategy myself. Very well, I'll ride with you. But if you plan to show me up by outracing me across the fields, I warn you that I was a member of a *cavalry* regiment, and even among those experts I was a hard man to beat."

She laughed and went quickly to the door. "Good. There's nothing I like more than a challenge. But first, let's see who'll be quicker at dressing. If you're not at the stables in half-an-hour, I shall start without you."

They raced across the fields with the high-spirited abandon of bred-to-the-bone riders who'd been kept too long from the saddle. They found themselves laughing aloud in pure joy as the wind whipped their faces and the ground seemed to fly away under their horses' hooves. Meg couldn't remember when she'd enjoyed a ride more. Never before had she ridden with anyone so attuned to her rhythms—she was neither forced to hold back nor urged to speed up her mount's gait to match his. They flew over the wide terrain in complete harmony.

Only once during the afternoon's ride did she drop away from his side. She'd become winded and had pulled up, motioning him to take a turn alone. As he'd galloped away down the slope, she'd watched him with wide, admiring eyes. His horse was a beautiful roan he'd brought back from Spain, and the width of Geoffrey's shoulders and his impressive height were in perfect balance with the size of the animal. He seemed, from this distance, to become one with the horse as man and beast moved in remarkable congruity over the landscape. It must have been just such a scene, she imagined, that inspired whatever ancient Greek it was who conceived the idea of the Centaur.

When he came thundering back and pulled up alongside, she felt herself blush. To have been watching—and with such unabashed appreciation—a man's physical form was completely brazen behavior for a lady. She hoped he had not been aware of her rather depraved enjoyment.

"Are you tired, or do you have the stomach to ride up there?" he asked, pointing to a promontory that rose behind them, his eyes shining with the pleasure of his exertions. "It's Hauberk Hill. It's an easy climb to the top, and I promise you that the view is worth the effort."

He didn't have to ask; if Meg could have her way, the afternoon would never end. The horses easily made the climb, and the view at the top was indeed breathtaking. They could see for miles to the north—Geoffrey pointed out that the group of habitations to her left was Masham. He helped her to dismount, and while the horses grazed she seated herself on a boulder and looked about her, the chill of the wind not in the least troubling her. Geoffrey sat down on the ground beside her, leaning back against the boulder and taking deep breaths of the crisp air. "We haven't yet taken time to talk about Trixie," Meg said after a few moments of companionable silence. "Perhaps we should try to concoct some sort of—"

"I don't want to talk about Trixie," he said, "and neither do you. That's not why you coaxed me to take you riding. What have you on your mind, my girl?"

"You can be quite disconcertingly blunt, sir."

"Blunt, but not wrong."

"No, you're not wrong. I *do* have something on my mind that I've been wishing to discuss with you."

"Then out with it. There will never be a better time. I'm completely at peace with the world at the moment and would probably agree to get you the moon if you asked it of me nicely."

"I don't want the moon. I only want to know why you've been avoiding me since the night of Lady Habish's party."

He threw a quick glance at her over his shoulder and then turned back to fix his eyes on the toes of his boots. She could almost feel his indecision. He could answer her question and find himself embroiled in a relationship with her, or he could avoid the question by claiming that she was imagining things and take her home—thus closing any doors to future intimacy. Her heart beat rapidly as she waited for an answer.

He was silent for a long, long moment. "I should have thought that a woman of your intelligence—your experience in the ways of the world would have guessed the reason."

"But I haven't. You haven't provided me with any clues."

"Come now, Meg," he said, turning so that he could see her face, "it doesn't become you to play the coy innocent. You *must* have guessed by this time that I've grown terrified of you."

"Terrified? But, Geoffrey, why?"

"You know perfectly well why. You've played with my emotions since the first moment I laid eyes on you. It's your skill at the game that frightens me. I've had very little to do with ladies of fashion, you know. I'm not familiar with the sort of skirmishing which goes on between the sexes in your London society. I don't know the rules of play. I might too easily find myself the loser."

She giggled. "Poor, helpless Geoffrey. I might almost pity

you, except that you're not a boy of nineteen but a quite clever, very sharp-tongued, completely self-possessed and not-a-bit unworldly man of . . . of . . ."

"Thirty-six," he supplied.

"Of thirty-six. Are you trying to pretend that a man who has faced Napoleon's armies without a qualm is fearful of dealing with a mere female?"

"I'm not pretending, my dear. The prospect of 'dealing' with you has me quaking in my boots."

"I think, Geoffrey, that you're putting it on much too rare and thick. What sort of harm can come to you, do you imagine, if a friendship should develop between us?"

"Friendship?" he inquired sardonically. "What has friendship to do with it?"

"Why, everything," she said, surprised. "What do you think we've been speaking of?"

He gave her a smile of complete disdain and got to his feet. Reaching down, he grasped her hands and pulled her to her feet. Before she realized his full intent, she was locked in his arms. "I'll show you what we've been speaking of, my dear," he muttered and lowered his face to hers.

Meg had, of course, been kissed before. Many times. And she knew just what to do when a man's passion carried him to extremes of misbehavior. It was quite easy when one saw it coming and could turn the ardor aside by a laugh or a quip. Even when matters became more difficult, as in the present situation, Meg had always been able to control matters. She was quite adept at stiffening, at thrusting the man away and administering a firm and stinging slap to the cheek. But this time she found herself completely unable to act. Instead of stiffening, she seemed to melt. Instead of pushing him away, she discovered that one of her arms had slipped about his neck and the other was clutching at his back with quite the opposite purpose. His lips were pressing down on hers with an almost angry urgency, so passionately insistent on an equal response from her that she wondered why she didn't find the act infuriating. But she was not infuriated. She was exhilarated, quickened, aroused. She'd had no idea that a kiss could affect her in this way. She wanted it never to stop.

But quite soon he let her go. Breathless, they stared at each other, each equally shaken by the effect of the embrace. "So you see, my dear," he said when he'd caught his breath, his smile gone, "it's not friendship that frightens me."

"If this is a game, Geoffrey," she answered softly, "then I don't know the rules either."

He came up to her again, put his palms against the sides of her face and tilted it up. "I wish you weren't quite so beautiful," he murmured. "Perhaps then it would be easier for me to think clearly. Confound it, woman, I've no place in my life for these affairs of the heart."

She didn't know how to answer him. If he truly didn't wish to become entangled with a woman, there was nothing she could do. Besides, her own feelings were in too great a turmoil to make sense of what was happening. She only knew that she wanted him to lower his head and kiss her again. Her eyes closed in dizzy anticipation.

"No, not again," he said firmly, letting her go. Picking up the reins, he led the horses to the path and lifted her on her mount, remaining abstractedly silent all the way down.

When they reached the stable-yard, he jumped down from his roan and walked around to help her down. As his hands reached up to grasp her waist, he grinned up at her. "Don't look so worried, my dear," he said comfortingly. "After this afternoon's encounter, I'm much less-terrified than I was."

She slipped down into his arms, her heart beating fearfully as he set her on her feet. Looking up into his face, she said ruefully, "Yes, but now, you see, *I* am much *more* so."

Chapter Fourteen

Keating was waiting for them when they came into the hall. "There are two gentlemen come to see you, Sir Geoffrey," he said. "I've put them in the sitting room."

Meg turned to Geoffrey with a shy smile, feeling since their return very young and vulnerable in his presence. "I'll go upstairs, then, if you'll excuse me, and see how Isabel does. Thank you for the ride." And without waiting for a response, she ran up the stairs.

He watched until she'd disappeared from sight. Then, forcing his mind to attend to business, he turned to the butler. "Who *are* the callers, Keating, did they say?"

"Yes, sir. One is Lord Isham of Isham Manor near Masham. The other is a Mr. Arthur Steele of London."

Geoffrey rubbed his chin thoughtfully. "Isham's a familiar name, but I can't think where I've heard it. And as for Steele,

I haven't the slightest recollection of ever having heard of him. Very well, Keating, I'll go in and see what this is all about."

The two men awaiting him showed two very different aspects. One—a tall, lean, distinguished-looking gentleman—stood brooding at the fireplace. The other—shorter, quite stocky and with a cheerfully open face—sat in relaxed ease in a deep wing chair playing idly with the silver head of his walking stick. "Lord Isham?" Geoffrey asked the seated one.

"No, I'm Steele," he said with a smile, getting up and offering his hand. "You, I take it, are Sir Geoffrey Carrier?"

They shook hands. Geoffrey turned to the tall gentleman. "Then you are Lord Isham. I think I've heard the name. You reside in this district, my butler tells me."

"Yes, a bit north of here," Isham said in a cold, lordly tone.

"Please sit down," Geoffrey said politely, "and tell me what it is I can do for you."

"I prefer to stand," Isham said, frowning at his host darkly. "And what you can do for us is to tell us how you managed to get hold of a certain carriage which I discovered at the wheelwright's in Masham, being mended by your order."

"The carriage? At the wheelwright's? Oh, I *see*." He studied the visitors with an intensified interest. "Before I answer, may *I* ask a question?"

Isham bowed his head in dignified assent.

"How does the carriage concern you?"

"It *concerns* me, sir," Isham answered furiously, "because the carriage just happens to be mine!"

"Oh. Yours. I see! Then I suppose, of course, that you have every right to know how I came by it."

Arthur Steele couldn't help smiling. "I would say he *does*, yes."

Geoffrey's mind raced around to find a way to explain matters without involving Meg. "The truth is, my lord," he said smoothly, "that my coachman came upon it during the first night of the recent snowstorm. He, I regret to say, locked wheels with it and forced it into a ditch. When I examined the wreckage the next day, I thought it better to have the equipage taken in for repairs than to leave it lying about in the road. I was certain, of course, that *someone* would come to claim it sooner or later. And here you are!"

"And is that all?" Steele pressed.

"All? I don't know what you mean."

"You heard him," Isham said irritably. "Is that all you have to tell us?"

Geoffrey shrugged. "Well, I can only add that, since you claim to be the owner—and I don't for a moment doubt your word—I haven't the least objection to your picking up the carriage from the wheelwright whenever it suits you to do so. Naturally I will take care of the bill myself, since it was my coachman who caused the accident." He got to his feet and smiled with meticulous propriety. "I trust that concludes our business, gentlemen?"

"Not by a long shot, old man," Steele said calmly.

"Not by a long shot," Isham echoed threateningly.

"Is there something else?"

Arthur Steele leaned forward, watching Geoffrey's face intently. "What about the passengers?" he demanded.

"Passengers? *Were* there passengers?" Geoffrey asked innocently.

"Well, the carriage could scarcely have been traveling along the Harrogate Road all by itself," Steele pointed out.

"It certainly couldn't," Isham agreed sourly.

"No, of course it couldn't," Geoffrey said soothingly. "But the passengers *could* have gone off somewhere and *left* the carriage. The snow had made the going very difficult that night, you know."

"Yes, we had considered that possibility," Steele admitted, planting his walking stick firmly on the ground and leaning his chin on its silver head. "As a matter of fact, we've been making inquiries all over the neighborhood for more than a week. They—the passengers, that is—couldn't all have vanished into thin air."

"All?"

"Two ladies and a groom."

"Ah, two ladies and a groom," Geoffrey echoed blandly. "Relatives of yours, Lord Isham?"

Lord Isham threw Arthur Steele a forbidding frown. "Not exactly."

"They're not related to his lordship *at all,*" Steele said firmly, looking mockingly at his lanky companion. "Not at all."

"Oh, I see. *Your* relations, then, Mr. Steele?"

"They're not related to *him* any more than to me," Isham informed Geoffrey with lordly superiority, "though I fail to see how the matter concerns you, sir."

"It doesn't concern me, I admit. I only wish to point out that, if one had some knowledge of the whereabouts of the missing passengers—and I am not saying that I have such information myself, mind you—but if one did, one would not wish to reveal such information to every tomdoodle who happened by. Ladies, I'm sure you'll agree, ought to be protected."

"The man's right, you know, Isham," Arthur Steele said. "We could be abductors, for all this fellow knows."

"Nonsense," Isham said in injured pride. "He must know perfectly well that I'm not an abductor. Isham Manor is known all over the neighborhood. You said before that you've heard of it, didn't you, Sir Geoffrey?"

"Possibly. Nevertheless, I find your persistent questioning quite suspicious."

"Suspicious?" Steele asked. "Why? I was only funning when I suggested we might be abductors. Surely you can't think—"

"Perhaps not abductors, but your strange behavior could have other explanations—"

"I fail to see," put in the aggrieved Isham, "what is so strange about our seeking the persons who made off with my property!"

"Made off? Are you saying that these 'persons' *stole* your property?"

"Well, one needn't use as strong a word as that," Steele said placatingly.

"What word would *you* use?" Isham demanded. "Stealing is stealing, whatever word you choose."

"But you have your carriage back now," Geoffrey reminded him, "so there's no need to seek the . . . er . . . culprits any further, is there? There's not much point in it."

"What can *you* know of my reasons, sir? Besides, there's the matter of a pair of horses, too!"

"Oh, yes, horses." Geoffrey rubbed his chin. "I'd completely forgotten about them."

"Well, I haven't. Those chestnuts are worth a fortune."

"Isham, for heaven's sake," Steele said impatiently, "aren't we getting a bit off the track here? We're looking for the ladies, not the horses!"

"Well, I'd like to find the confounded horses, too," his

lordship said petulantly, throwing himself into a chair.

"If I were to tell you, Lord Isham, that I have your chestnuts safe in my stables, would that satisfy you?"

"What's that?" Both men sat forward and gaped at him.

"*Have* you my horses?" Isham demanded.

"Safe in my stables. Both of them."

Arthur Steele peered closely into Geoffrey's face. "Now *I'm* suspicious. Do you expect us to believe that you have the horses *and* the carriage in your possession but know nothing of the passengers?"

Geoffrey leaned back and smiled into Steele's eyes with cool aplomb. "I haven't the faintest interest in *what* you believe."

Steele's eyes flickered uncertainly. The fellow was a cool one, but Steele was suddenly certain that he knew more than he was saying. With another piercing look at Geoffrey's face, he said to Isham, "He's seen 'em all right."

"I shouldn't be at all surprised. Come now, sir, I demand to be told exactly what you know. You have no right to withhold information from us."

"You have yet to convince me, your lordship, that you have a right to ask."

Isham was nonplussed. With a sidelong glance at Geoffrey's impassive face, he said to Steele in an undervoice, "I suppose there's no harm in telling him who they are."

Steele looked dubious. "No, but it seems to me that Sir Geoffrey here is learning more from *us* than we are from *him*. Why, Sir Geoffrey, are you so reluctant to talk to us? These people can't mean anything to you."

"Even if I had any information, gentlemen, I should certainly not reveal it to you merely for the purpose of helping you to prosecute a pair of ladies who, for all I know, meant no harm. You have your carriage back, and your horses, too. What purpose would be served in bringing in the magistrates?"

"Magistrates?" Isham repeated bewilderedly.

"Who said anything about magistrates?" Steele asked.

Geoffrey, puzzled, looked from one to the other. "But didn't you say . . . ? You told me yourself that they'd *stolen* the equipage from you—"

Steele threw Isham a look of disgust. "I *told* you not to use the word steal! Now you've got the fellow thinking we want to have them hanged!"

"I assure you, Sir Geoffrey," Isham said in sincere dismay, "we have not the slightest intention of involving magistrates in this matter. Prosecution is the farthest thing from our minds."

"I don't understand." Geoffrey was beginning to realize that there was more to this matter than he'd supposed. He had deduced that Meg had mischievously absconded with a stranger's vehicle. He'd been trying to protect her. But there seemed, from these gentlemen's attitudes, to be some sort of personal involvement here. Was Meg in deeper trouble than he'd suspected? He leaned forward in his seat. "If you don't intend to prosecute . . . and you've regained your property . . . what on earth do you want the information *for?*"

"Why, to find them, of course! What else would we wish to do?"

"But . . . if you're not related—"

"Don't be an idiot," Steele broke in. "If there wasn't a connection, would we be dashing about the countryside in this way looking for them?"

"You mean there is a connection between you and the ladies? They are *known* to you?"

"Of course they're known to us!" Isham said curtly. "I, for one, am almost beside myself with worry. For all we know . . . they . . . are lying dead somewhere—"

"Balderdash," Steele insisted. "There's no need to become frantic. If they were dead, the bodies would have been discovered by this time." He looked across at Geoffrey with unruffled nonchalance. "Probably the girl's hiding away somewhere so that this jobbernowl won't find her."

"That, Steele, is only *your* interpretation," Isham retorted. "I hope, Sir Geoffrey, that you'll not give any credence to anything this fellow says."

Geoffrey lifted an eyebrow. "I thought you two were together in this. Are you making a *separate* search?"

Steele grinned at Geoffrey's bewilderment. "Oh, we're in the search together, all right. It's just that Isham doesn't like my presence. I forced myself upon him, you see."

Geoffrey sighed. "I wish I did see."

"All this is neither here nor there," Isham muttered. "The fact is that a woman can't just disappear. If you do know something, Sir Geoffrey, something to help us get to the bottom of this—"

"Perhaps I do. But I still haven't learned just what your

connection is with the ladies in question."

Isham cast a defiant look at Steele before he answered. "The younger of the pair is Lady Margaret Underwood, and she was traveling with her aunt . . ."

"Yes? And the connection?"

"She happens to be—" He threw another look in Steele's direction before he continued. "She happens to be my betrothed."

"On the contrary, Sir Geoffrey," Steele said, standing up and throwing a scornful look at Isham, "she is mine!"

The two visitors, glaring at each other with dislike, failed to notice that Geoffrey had whitened about the mouth. "Betrothed?"

"Yes," Isham said, rising and facing Steele, glowering down at him from his superior height. *"My* betrothed. May I remind you, Steele, that she was a guest at my home, and that we were about to make the announcement of the forthcoming nuptials when the girl disappeared?"

"There's no need to remind me. I must point out to you, however, and for the hundredth time, that she left you a note breaking it off."

"I don't take that note to have any more significance than an exhibition of momentary pique. When we find her, I'm certain she will explain to you that she ran off in a fit of temper and had every intention of returning in time for the betrothal dinner."

"And what about *my* note, eh?" Steele demanded, his usual calm fraying at the edges. "Does *that* give any indication that she intended to return to you?"

"That note proves nothing. It doesn't even make sense to me." With that, Isham made a dismissive gesture of his hand and impassively resumed his seat.

Steele, in disgust, turned to Geoffrey. "I can't reason with the man. Here, Sir Geoffrey, look at this note. Wouldn't you say it supports my claim?"

Geoffrey, his head spinning with confused emotions, took the note which Steele held out to him and stared at it dazedly. *Dear Arthur,* he read, *You win. Be at the White Hart, Harrogate, tomorrow evening. I shall be waiting. Meg.* His heart sank. What sort of woman was Meg Underwood anyway? How could she play games with so many men at once?

"Well?" Arthur urged. "Does that sound like a note written

by a lady betrothed to someone else?"

"I don't . . . know . . ." Geoffrey muttered, his eyes fixed on the paper he held in a hand he was hard-pressed to keep from shaking.

"Aren't we straying from the point again?" Isham inquired coldly. "I thought our purpose here was to discover the lady's whereabouts, not to debate the nature of her precise relationship to us."

"You're right," Steele agreed, taking back his note and pocketing it. "This discussion is taking us from our object. If you know where she is, Sir Geoffrey, speak up. You must have heard enough by this time to believe that we have every right to know."

Geoffrey didn't seem to hear. He was staring off into the middle distance, his brow furrowed in deep thought.

"Did you hear what Steele said to you?" Isham demanded, rising to his feet again and joining Arthur Steele in confronting their abstracted host. "What do you know about the girl's—"

He was interrupted by the opening of the door. "Geoffrey, I just had the most *ingenious* idea about Trixie's—" Meg said from the doorway.

"Meg!" Arthur Steele and Charles Isham gasped in concert.

"Ch-Charles! Arthur!" Meg's eyes widened in complete astonishment. "Good God!"

Chapter Fifteen

It seemed to Geoffrey that the room was full of noise and confusion, and all he wanted to do was to get away from it. Lord Isham, red-faced and angry, was demanding from Meg a proper explanation of her actions. Arthur, with the air of an overprotective solicitor, was brandishing his silver-headed cane at Isham and telling Meg that she needn't explain anything at all. Meg was attempting to quiet them both, but they didn't stop their shouting long enough to permit her to utter a full sentence. Geoffrey, convinced that he'd heard more than enough, rose and headed for the door.

"Geoffrey, wait!" Meg called, darting after him. "Don't you want to hear what I—"

"No, ma'am, I don't. I think you know me well enough to understand that I do not like to become embroiled in ... er ..."

"Women's wranglings?" she teased, making a face at him.

"Exactly," he agreed, not amused. "I'm sure the gentlemen will excuse me. They cannot wish to be observed by a stranger while you all try to settle what is obviously a private matter among the three of you."

Meg, who until this moment had not taken this incident to be in any way catastrophic, was chilled by the coldness of his tone. "But . . . you don't understand. There's nothing much to settle, really."

"Nothing much to *settle?*" Isham asked in outrage. "I most vehemently beg to differ."

"Oh, Charles, be still!" She put a restraining hand gently on Geoffrey's arm. "I want you to stay, Geoffrey, *please.* You'll see that the fuss is just a great deal of noise about a small misunderstanding."

He shook his head. "From what little I've heard already, I think it's much more than that."

"But you don't know what—"

"Please don't explain. Not to me," he said, adamant. "Do you remember that we discussed this carriage business before? At that time you told me that you'd managed your affairs very well for years without my help and that you had every intention to continue to do so. Well, then, ma'am, *manage* them! I wish you luck."

He lifted her hand from his arm in deliberate, icy rebuff and walked from the room. Meg stared after him, aghast. How could this silly *contretemps* have so greatly altered his mood since this afternoon?

"Can't say I like the way that fellow spoke to you, Meg," Arthur said, looking at the door with a puzzled frown. "What *is* he to you?"

"That's just what I'd like to know," Isham agreed. "And what are you doing in this place? I find it quite shocking, now that we're on the subject, to find you apparently taking up residence with a complete stranger."

Arthur jumped immediately to her defense. "Come now, Isham, climb down from your high ropes. 'Taking up residence' is putting it much too strong. Besides, it isn't your place any longer to comment on Meg's behavior."

"Isn't it?" Isham's nostrils flared. "It's *your* place, then, I suppose."

"Oh, be quiet, both of you!" Meg, who'd been staring at the door, whirled about and faced them furiously. "Why couldn't you have gone about your own business instead of coming here to seek me out? You've probably spoiled everything!"

Arthur's brows knit in sudden suspicion. "Spoiled what, my dear?"

Meg bit her lip. "Nothing. Nothing at all. Your sudden arrival has . . . startled me . . . that's all."

"That's *not* all," Arthur said, his eyes narrowed. "Seems to me that you and this Carrier fellow are thick as thieves. Haven't I a right to know——"

"No, you haven't," Meg said bluntly.

"Aha!" Isham's exclamation resounded loudly round the room, ringing with mirthless satisfaction. "So it isn't your place *either* to make inquiries. Who has to come down from his high ropes *now?*"

"See here, Isham, I'm a patient man, but these last few days of being forced into your company have shortened my temper! I've had more than enough of your lordly disparagement, and if I hear much more, I shall be strongly tempted to plant a facer on your lordly nose!"

"Why were you forced into his company?" Meg asked curiously.

Arthur looked at her with some surprise. "So that we could join forces to look for you. What did you think we were doing?"

"I don't know why you had to look for me at all."

"Really, my dear," Isham said, "didn't you expect me to wonder what had become of you?"

"No, I did not! I expected you to believe that I'd gone home—which is what I fully intended to do."

"But what about me?" Arthur inquired. "Didn't you think, when you failed to appear at the White Hart, that *I* would be concerned for your safety?"

She cast him a guilty glance. "I . . . I'm sorry, Arthur. I just . . . forgot about you."

"Ha!" Isham chortled sourly. *"Your* betrothed, eh?"

"Confound you, Isham, hold your tongue!" Steele barked, his usual good nature pushed beyond its limits. "As for you, Meg Underwood, that is the most unkind thing I've ever heard you say." And he cast himself into a chair in morose disenchantment.

"I'm truly sorry, Arthur," Meg said, taking a chair beside him. "I never dreamed matters would take this turn. You see,

I *was* on my way to the White Hart when the snow came. We were unable to proceed, there was an accident, and we were taken here. First we thought my ankle had been broken, and by the time that problem had solved itself, Isabel fell ill. During all those difficulties, I had little opportunity to think about anything else. I simply assumed that you would have returned to London, and I put the matter out of my mind. It didn't occur to me to suppose that you'd take the trouble to go to Isham Manor to seek me out."

The explanation brightened Arthur's mood considerably. "So you were injured, eh? Then that explains everything. It wasn't *your* fault if you couldn't walk."

"Not quite everything," Isham reminded him, taking a stance at the fireplace and looking down at them both in haughty disapproval. "There is still the matter of Meg's absconding from Isham Manor on the eve of our betrothal dinner without so much as a by-your-leave—"

"Yes, I owe you an explanation for that," Meg agreed, her eyes lowered to her folded hands. "More, I owe you a most sincere apology. It was a dreadful thing to have done. To break a vow . . . a betrothal . . . so thoughtlessly and abruptly, too . . . it was quite unforgivable. I was cowardly to have done it, and for whatever pain my behavior has caused you, I am truly sorry."

Arthur studied her with raised eyebrows. "I must say, Meg, that was sweetly said. Very contrite. Very penitent. Very humble. And not a *bit* like you! I don't know what's happened to you in this place, but I'd better get you back to London before you become completely unrecognizable."

"Just a moment, Steele, just a moment. Let's not jump to any unwarranted conclusions," Isham cautioned. He crossed the room in his dignified, measured pace and took a chair facing Meg. "I wish to say, my dear, that I am quite willing to forgive and forget. You ran away. It was probably just momentary panic . . . an attack of maidenly shyness . . . it doesn't matter. But you've learned your lesson. As even Steele recognizes, you've truly repented. I'm willing to overlook the transgression. Come back with me to Isham Manor. I'm sure that even Mama will find it in her heart to forgive you when you explain it all to her."

Arthur hooted. "Isham, you must be touched in your upper

works. Can't you understand that she's done with you?"

"Please, Arthur, let me speak for myself," Meg said. "Charles, I know I was wrong in the *way* I acted, but I wasn't wrong to act. In substance, if not in manner, I was right. Don't you see? It surely *must* be clear to you by this time that we should *never* suit. Our temperaments are completely opposite. I'm sorry that I didn't realize sooner how unsuited we are, but you must agree that a little pain at *this* time is better than having to endure a lifetime of it." She leaned forward and patted his arm. "You'll see it for yourself when the shock wears off."

Isham stared at her for a moment, his lips compressed into a tight line. Then he got up stiffly. "Is that your final word on the subject, my dear?" he asked.

"I'm afraid it is," Meg assured him, lowering her eyes to her hands again.

"Very well, then. Steele, it seems you've been right all along. No doubt you'll wish to make plans with the lady without my presence. Since we came here in my curricle, you'll need to go back with me to Isham Manor to get your carriage. I shall, therefore, wait for you outside."

"Just a moment, Charles," Meg said firmly. "I don't know of anything that Arthur has to say to me that can't be said in your presence."

Arthur, who'd been grinning in self-satisfaction, found his smile fading quickly. "What do you mean? Doesn't your jilting Isham mean that you're going to wed *me?*"

"Of course not! Really, Arthur, how can you ask such a thing? Didn't I distinctly tell you in London that you and I can only be good friends?"

"Yes, but *I* said that good friends make good husbands."

"Perhaps you did, but I didn't agree with you."

"But... your note!" He pulled it from his pocket. "Right here! You said, 'you win.' Doesn't that mean—?"

"How can you be so foolish?" Meg asked impatiently. "It means you win the *wager*. Don't you remember? A hundred guineas to my one that I wouldn't go through with my betrothal to Charles?" She looked up at Isham guiltily. "Sorry, Charles— it was only in fun."

"You mean you sent for me only to *escort* you?" Arthur asked, deflated.

"Well, yes. You did *offer* the escort, you know."

He got up and looked down at her with a rueful twist to his lips. "And that's your final word on *this* subject, too, I suppose."

She nodded.

He shrugged in resignation. "Well, then, Isham, it seems we both were wrong. Come along, man, there's nothing more for either of us here. We've kept your horses standing long enough."

"Goodbye, ma'am," Charles said with a formal bow. "I'm sure Steele will agree with me when I say that we wish you all the good fortune and happiness that life can bestow and that the future may bring you all manner of—"

"Oh, come along, you clunch!" Arthur said, pushing him to the door. "She doesn't need your prosy speeches." He turned back and gave her a good-natured wink. "Goodbye, my dear. I'm still available to escort you to London if you should need me."

By the time the two gentlemen had taken their leave, Keating was ready to announce dinner. When the Carrier ladies and Meg had taken their places at the table, Lady Carrier explained that Geoffrey had asked to be excused. "It seems that his attentions had been diverted from his work this afternoon," she said, "and so he's making up for lost time by poring over his papers now. He says he'll be content with some cold meat and bread, sandwich-style, at his worktable in the library."

None of the ladies noticed that Meg was unusually silent during the meal, for each of them had a great deal to chatter about. Sybil had discovered a new symptom; Lady Carrier had spent the afternoon playing cards with Isabel and was full of glad tidings of that lady's improved condition; and Trixie had called on Harriet Habish, where she'd been "delightfully surprised" to discover that Mortimer Lazenby had called at the very same time. Meg, out of patience with all of them and playing dispiritedly with the food on her plate, found herself wishing that she too could take her dinner sandwich-style in the library.

After dinner, she sat with the ladies for as long as she could bear and then, excusing herself by explaining that she'd not seen her aunt since early in the day, made her escape. On the way to the stairs she noticed a light glowing beneath the library door. It meant that Geoffrey still sat over his papers. With an impulsive recklessness, she tapped on the door and burst in. "I know you're busy, Geoffrey," she said defensively, "but I must talk to you. I shall only keep you a moment or two."

He passed a hand over his brow and stood up. "Come in, Meg. I . . . I'm glad you've come. I've been wanting to speak to you, too."

He led her to a chair close to the fire and busied himself with poking up the flames.

"I suppose you want to hear about the scheme I've devised in regard to Trixie, but—" Meg began.

"No, it's not that at all. Trixie hasn't been on my mind this evening."

"Good, because she's not been on *my* mind either. I want to explain to you about that misunderstanding with Charles and Arthur."

He straightened up, replaced the poker and sat down on the hearth, one booted foot stretched out before him. "There's no need to explain anything, Meg. It's not my affair. That's what I must explain to you. The very fact that you feel you *ought* to explain to me proves that I've permitted our . . . our *friendship* to get out of hand."

Meg felt the blood drain from her face. He was about to say things she would not like to hear, and her mind raced about to find ways to forestall him. Her first instinct was to react in the usual way of a London flirt . . . to say something meaningless and coy, like "I don't know what you *mean,* sir," or, in her own, more customary style, "La, sir, I *never* permit my friendships to get out of hand." But somehow, in her relationship with Geoffrey, that sort of conversation had never been appropriate. "You're referring to . . . to what happened between us this afternoon," she said helplessly.

"Yes. I feel I must apologize for my behavior. Our ride stirred up my blood . . . there was the view . . . the wind . . . Damnation, there really isn't any excuse, but you are so deucedly beautiful, you know . . ."

Meg felt suddenly encouraged. *This* sort of conversation was very familiar to her—she knew from long experience just how to deal with it. She leaned back in her chair and smiled. "Your behavior needs no apology, Geoffrey. I was not in the least offended."

He looked back at her with knit brows. "I know that. But that's not the point. I think the afternoon . . . the feeling between us ... misled you. I know it misled me. For a while it began to seem possible that we could ..." He paused and turned to stare into the fire. "But you see, my dear, how one's true character reasserts itself. You assessed me well from the first. You remarked on how I seem to disparage the female sex. I suppose I did show signs of being a woman hater—a true mysogynist. You made me aware for the first time of this shortcoming in me. I've thought about your words many times since, and I believe you were right—"

"No, I wasn't. There's no hate in you for anyone. I see that now."

"Yes, that's what made me believe you to be wrong, at first. But perhaps a mysogynist is not really a hater but one who's merely uncomfortable with women. That is what I've discovered about myself. I don't understand the way that females behave. I find myself disapproving of their words and their acts. I can't follow the convolutions of their thoughts or the twists in their ethical reasoning."

"Are you thinking of your mother and sisters ... or of me?" Meg asked frankly.

"Of all of you. You all never fail to leave me bewildered and confused."

"But Geoffrey, in what way have *I*—?"

He stared at her. "Dash it, woman, you're the worst of the lot! Here you are, a lady of breeding, education, taste and refinement. You've been the head of a household, managed a fortune, and lived for all your years a life which Isabel tells me is a model of responsible, mature propriety. Yet I've seen you make all sorts of foolish decisions, take a number of reckless chances, embroil the people you meet in troublesome situations, get yourself betrothed to two men at once—"

"Stop, please!" Meg didn't know whether she should laugh or cry. "You make me sound like a veritable zany. There are perfectly logical explanations for every one of those mischances to which you refer."

"Yes, I'm certain that there are, but—"

"And I was *not* betrothed to two men at once! That, of all my misconduct is what most bothers you, isn't it? I'm beginning to believe, Geoffrey Carrier, that you are merely saying all this to me in a fit of jealousy!"

He gave her a sardonic laugh. "Oh, not a fit, girl. A rage. I've been suffering from a murderous jealousy ever since I first realized the place that pair of park-saunterers had in your life. But you see, it's the way of the male of the species to try to overcome such irrational indulgences, not to wallow in them. And we men certainly don't permit those feelings to get the better of our judgment or to affect the decisions we must make. So you mustn't think that my jealousy is in any way responsible for what I must tell you."

"It's the way of women, too, to try to overcome irrationality. We don't *all* wallow in our emotions, you know. So don't take that superior tone with me, Geoffrey Carrier, for I won't have it! As for what you 'must' tell me, I'm not at all sure I want to hear it."

"I'm afraid you'll have to, Meg," he said with a return to his earlier, ominous tone. "I can't let you go on in the belief that . . . that what passed between us this afternoon can continue. For you, it may have been just another of your many flirts—I'm too unaccustomed to the ways of London society to be sure—but for me it was frighteningly close to . . . to being a commitment I cannot make."

"I see." Now it was out. Now he'd said it in so many words. She stared at him for a moment, feeling strangely numb. It was like a cut on the thumb that one knows is there but can't for a moment feel. Only after the blood starts to flow does one begin to feel the throb of pain. "Would it make any difference to you if . . . if I said that this afternoon was *not* just another of my . . . flirts?"

He threw her a quick, piercing look and lowered his head. "It would be something I should be very gratified to hear, I admit . . . but it couldn't change anything. I'm meant for the bachelor life, I'm afraid. Married life is something I seem to have no stomach for. The fact is that I'm too cowardly."

Meg sat silent, unmoving. There was not a thing she could think of to say . . . he'd left nothing *for* her to say. Even the explanation of Charles' and Arthur's visit—an explanation she'd been bursting to make!—would be pointless now. There was nothing to do but to exit gracefully. That, at least, was something she could carry off without failing. She'd failed at everything else she'd tried in this house. Was it only a few days ago that she'd expected to be able to return to London carrying his heart in her pocket like a trophy? True, it was a goal she'd promptly lost interest in . . . but she'd never expected to end by leaving *her* heart as a trophy for *him*.

She got up from her chair, hoping that the trembling of her knees would not be apparent in her step. *Could it be,* she wondered, *that Charles and Arthur had felt this way when I rejected them this afternoon?* Were the Fates taking a malicious retribution? Charles and Arthur had taken their dismissal quite courageously—Charles had made a well-wishing speech and Arthur a quip. She could certainly do as well. When she reached the door, she turned back to him. He was still seated on the hearth, staring at her with a frozen, unreadable expression. "You needn't look so grim about it, Geoffrey," she said lightly. "It was only a game after all."

But when she'd closed the library door behind her, her step became unsteady and her throat burned. There had been so many times in the past when she'd rejected suitors, yet she'd never dreamed that they might have suffered like this. Now the shoe was on the other foot, and it pinched dreadfully. Why had she never before been capable of understanding that the pinch of a little rejection could cause such agonizing pain?

Chapter Sixteen

A long night provided neither rest nor comfort, and the events of the following day only underlined the dilemma of Meg's situation. Geoffrey, evidently adamant in his determination to keep himself unentangled, removed himself completely from the society of the household. Even when Isabel made her first venture out of bed—and the whole family, Dr. Fraser and most of the household staff were on hand to cheer her as she came down the stairs for afternoon tea—Geoffrey was conspicuous by his absence. Meg came face-to-face with him only once during that endless day—when she'd returned from a lonely ride and encountered him on the stairs—and he, although unimpeachably polite, made it clear from the cool dispatch with which he excused himself and passed her by that the chasm between intimacy and estrangement was wide indeed and would not be easily bridged again.

It was a completely unbearable situation in which to find herself, and the only way to ease it was to leave this house as soon as possible—the very next day, if she could manage it. The only deterrent to the plan was her aunt's condition. Although still weak, Isabel was no longer feverish and had spent part of the day downstairs. If the doctor felt that the trip would not unduly affect her health, and if the fine weather held, there was every reason to hope that they could take their leave of Knight's Haven at last.

That evening, when Dr. Fraser made his evening call on his patient, Meg came into Isabel's bedroom to ask him what he thought of her plan. "We've been here for almost a fortnight," she explained, "and that's been far too great a burden on the Carriers' hospitality. Besides, Aunt Bel and I yearn for our own surroundings, our own bedrooms, our own lives. I'm sure that Aunt Bel will agree that her recovery will be quickened by finding herself in her own home."

Isabel and the doctor exchanged surprised looks. "But... tomorrow?" Isabel asked, her voice breathless. "Isn't that a bit too sudden?"

"Perhaps, my love, but if you're well enough, don't you think the sooner we go the better?"

"Well, I... suppose so," Isabel answered, her fingers clenching nervously at the coverlet, "if... er... Dr. Fraser thinks it's all right for me to go."

Dr. Fraser was glowering at Isabel with unusual ferocity. "Ye wish me t' tell the lass ye need anither week o' recovery, is that it? Pawky female, what good would *that* do? Ha'e ye no the courage t' tell her the truth?"

Meg looked from one to the other in stupefaction. "What truth?"

Her aunt was glowering back at the Scotsman. "Donald MacPherson Fraser, you are a yatterin' gowk! I *told* you I couldn't—"

"Are you still sick, Aunt Bel? Is that it?"

Dr. Fraser ignored Meg's interruption and continued to frown down at Isabel in impatient disapproval. "Y're sufferin' from simple cowardice!" he accused. "Ye wish me t' tell her y're too ill t' travel, is that it? And then, next week t' tell her *more* o' the same? Is it a liar ye wish t' make o' me? Woman, I winna lie fer you or anyone!"

Meg could make no sense of the doctor's words. She wondered if rejection in love could make a person lose her reason. "What are you talking about, Dr. Fraser?"

"Don't pay any attention to the man, Meg," Isabel said, hitching about on the pillows to show the doctor her back. "He's just being nonsensical."

"Oho! Michty *me!* Nonsensical, am I? So ye'll be runnin' off fer *home* tomorra, then, will ye? Is that what yer sayin'?"

Isabel cast a troubled look at him over her shoulder. "Well, if you say I'm well enough..."

"Aye! Out o' doot!" he shouted, his hands waving about wildly. "Yer braw! Yald! Healthy as a horse! Go, then!"

Meg could only stare at him in stunned bafflement. Isabel looked from one to the other in an agony of indecision and then, without warning, cast herself into the pillows, buried her face and burst into sobs.

"Aunt Bel! Dr. Fraser, what *is* this?" Meg cried, dumbfounded and alarmed.

Dr. Fraser, his expression softening, gazed down at the sobbing woman for a moment in hesitation. Then, pulling off his *pince-nez* and pocketing it carefully, he sat down on the bed and took the weeping Isabel into his arms. "Wheesht, me bonnie, wheesht! It winna be so dreadful t' tell the lass."

"Oh, Donald," Isabel sobbed into his shoulder, "I'm too old for this sort of scene."

Meg could think of nothing but that her aunt was dying. "What sort of scene is she talking about?" she asked, shaken. "Tell me!"

The doctor looked up at Meg over Isabel's shoulder. "It ain't fer *me* t' tell ye, lass. 'Tis yer aunt who should be makin' the explanations."

"Th-there's n-nothing to explain," Isabel sniffed, lifting her head, pulling a handkerchief from the doctor's pocket unceremoniously and blowing her nose into it. "There, that's b-better. I'm s-sorry I lost my c-composure."

"But you *must* explain, Aunt Bel," Meg insisted. "You can't expect me to ignore—"

"You must ignore it. The doctor says I'm well—healthy as a horse, in fact—so there's nothing further to be said. We shall leave t-tomorrow, just as you wish."

"Nothin' further to be said?" the doctor asked, jumping to his feet. "*That's* yer decision, is it?"

Isabel seemed to sag. "I've already warned you this might

happen," she said to him. "I can't leave her now, completely alone as she is. When she marries, well, then we can—"

"But ye said that she and the lad might—"

"Hush, for heaven's sake! We can't discuss this now," Isabel hissed impatiently.

"I dinna ken *when* we're to discuss it, if y're to run off tomorra. Dinna ye see, woman, that things are changed? If the lass plans t' return home, it's clear yer matchmakin' scheme didna succeed. Who's t'say *when* she'll wed? If y're too old for scenes, m' dear, *I'm* too old t'be kept waitin' indefinitely."

"Donald," Isabel said in a trembling voice, "if you don't stop badgering me, I shall start to w-weep again!"

"And if you two don't tell me what you're talking about," Meg said threateningly, "I shall start to scream! If I didn't know better, from the way you two are behaving I'd think you were lovers."

Dr. Fraser broke into a grin. He looked down at Isabel triumphantly. "There, woman, y' see? She guessed!"

Isabel glared at him. "How could she *fail* to guess, with you carrying on like a madman?"

"Good God!" Meg gasped, sinking into a chair. "Do you mean to say it's true? The two of you have fallen in *love?*"

"Aye, lass, that's the gist o' the matter."

"But . . . you've been at each other like cat and dog! I can't believe my ears! When did this abrupt about-face take place?"

"There wasna an aboot-face at all!" the doctor exclaimed in surprise. "'Twas love at first sight, is that nae right, m'love?"

"Yes, quite right," Isabel agreed, nodding at Meg in perfect sincerity.

"At first sight? But you were at each other's throats!"

"Oh, no, dear," Isabel said firmly, "Donald is speaking the complete truth. I loved him from the first moment I saw him."

Meg could only gape, awestruck. "B-But you said . . . you s-said he was detest . . . detest . . ." A little laugh gurgled up from her throat. "At . . . at first s-sight—?" The little laugh was followed by a bigger one and then by a third, and before she could stop herself she'd doubled over, convulsed with laughter. Isabel watched her for a moment, nonplussed, and then began, herself, to giggle. Dr. Fraser let loose with a booming guffaw, and soon the three were howling uncontrollably, Isabel pressing her hands against her chest to keep back the pleural pain.

"I don't know what was so f-funny," Isabel said when they'd

all recovered their breaths. "I suppose a romance at our age
has its ludicrous side, but—"

"Oh, Aunt Bel, it's not in the least ludicrous," Meg assured
her. "That's not why we laughed. It's only because you seemed to dislike each other so! If you want to know the truth," she
added, jumping up and embracing her aunt warmly, "I think
it's wonderful! I couldn't be more pleased. I've felt from the
first, you know, that Dr. Fraser is a man of singular charm,
in spite of the fact that he pretends to be so gruff."

"Thank ye, lass. I *told* yer aunt ye'd not be takin' our news
amiss."

"That's all very well," Isabel sighed, "and I'm glad she
knows, but that doesn't change the fact that we're to leave
tomorrow."

"Leave? Are ye startin' that foolishness again?" the doctor
exclaimed loudly. "Woman, y're makin' me daft!"

"Donald, you're giving me the headache with your shouting.
I've told you from the first that if Meg goes, I go too."

"You will *not* go, you goose!" Meg said firmly. "I've never
heard such nonsense."

"That's a good lass!" the doctor said, cavorting about the
room with a merry little Scottish dance step.

Isabel's face brightened. "Do you mean, Meggie, my dear,
that you'll stay, then?"

"I?" Meg blinked as the full import of what was happening
struck her with a forcible blow. She couldn't stay . . . neither
in this house nor in this neighborhood. Yet she couldn't expect
her aunt to leave with her— not now. Dr. Fraser couldn't be
expected to give up his medical practice and come to London;
therefore, Isabel, if she was to live happily ever after, would
have to be convinced to remain here in the north with her
Donald. But for Meg to remain with her was out of the question.
Her happiness—whatever was left of it—depended on getting
away. "I can't stay here any longer, my dear," she said with
a sigh. "It wouldn't be right."

"Why not, Meg? Donald and I can be wed within a fortnight.
He tells me he has a huge, commodious house in which we
can *all* live comfortably. The Carriers would be delighted, I'm
certain, to have us stay with them until then."

Meg sat down on the bed and took her aunt's hand in hers.
"We must try to be sensible, Aunt Bel. You must certainly stay
here with the Carriers until you wed, and then you'll take up

residence with your husband as a proper wife should. But under no circumstances will I move in with you. My home is in London, and that's where I belong."

Isabel argued long and hard. She used tears and threats. She even swore she would give up her wedding plans rather than permit her niece to live alone. But after a while, Meg's reasoning prevailed. "Very well, Meggie, my love, go home if you must," Isabel said at last, tears running down her face. "But you must promise two things—one that you'll hire a companion—a respectable woman to live in the house with you—and two, that you'll come to visit us very, very often."

"I promise," Meg agreed. "But now, my dear, you must let me go and begin my packing. Dr. Fraser . . . Donald . . . I hope you can coax her out of the doldrums as soon as I leave you two alone. Look at her—she's become a veritable wateringpot."

"I kn-know," Isabel said, wiping her overflowing eyes with the already-soaking handkerchief. "I can't seem to s-stop. I had so hoped that you and Geoffrey would make a m-match of it. It would have been so lovely to have you living j-just down the road!"

Meg recalled those words several times while she packed. Yes, it would have been lovely indeed. As it was, her prospects were gloomier than they'd ever been before. She was returning home entirely alone, leaving behind her beloved aunt and her last expectation of happiness. She would return to London without family, without the prospect of a promising suitor and without even the hope of being able to retain her fortune after her twenty-sixth birthday rolled round.

She stared at her belongings, stacked neatly at the door of her bedroom. A bandbox and a portmanteau . . . that was all she would take with her when she left this house forever. She had her memories, of course, but even they, if they'd needed to be packed, would not have taken up much room: one windblown afternoon and one kiss on a hill. Not very much to remember of a fortnight that had altered her life.

But of course there was still Roodle. He, at least, would be glad to make the journey with her. His impatience to see London had been made manifest at every one of their interviews which he'd periodically requested to inform her of the condition of the chestnuts and to ask her plans. He realized that she had

better send for him at once and tell him to ready himself for
travel.

Roodle was overjoyed to learn that they were to set out at
last, but he was surprised at her decision to start first thing in
the morning. "We can't do it, ma'am. We ain't got no carriage.
If ye'll be wantin' me to 'ire one, I'll 'ave to go to Masham,
and it'll be noon, at least, afore I can be back with a rig."

"Oh, dear, I'd forgotten about the carriage. It's being repaired, isn't it? Well, at least we still have the horses. Will it
be difficult to hire a carriage, do you suppose?"

"No, ma'am, not with enough blunt it won't. But we ain't
got the 'orses neither, y' know. Lord Isham, he took 'em away
last night. Gave me a good jawin' as well when 'e caught sight
o' me."

"Did he?" She looked at him remorsefully. "Are you sorry
you agreed to throw in your lot with me, Roodle? Have I
selfishly uprooted you from your accustomed surroundings and
left you abandoned and friendless? Have I made you miserable?"

"'Oo, me? Why should ye think so, ma'am? You ain't
abandoned me, 'ave ye? Y're takin' me to London, just like
ye said. Just 'cause 'is lordship jawed at me ain't no reason
to turn twitty. Fact is, when he began t' kick up a dust, I tole
'im to stow 'is clapper in 'is ear! 'I ain't on yer staff no more,'
I tole 'im plain, 'an' I don't need to listen to yer blabber.' It
was worth a yellow boy to see 'is face!"

Reassured, Meg gave him all the cash she had left in her
reticule and instructed him to hire horses and a carriage in
Masham first thing in the morning. But the interview with the
groom left her with a new set of worries, for she had not a
groat left in her pockets. Could she embark on a two-day
journey in so impecunious a state?

But surely, she reasoned, any proper hostelry would extend
her credit when they learned her identity. She needn't concern
herself on that score. But it hurt her pride that she would have
to depart from Knight's Haven without being able to leave
Geoffrey the money for the repair to Isham's carriage. As host,
he would probably refuse to permit her to pay for anything
else, but *that* at least should be her responsibility. Oh, well,
it would have to wait until she'd returned home and instructed
her man of business to settle her debts.

She was surprised, the next morning, to be awakened early

by a neat young housemaid dressed in a cloak and carrying a small traveling bag. "I'm Brynne, your ladyship. I'm to 'company you to Lunnon. Roodle tole me to tell you the carriage is waitin' and that he's ready whenever you are."

"What?" Meg asked sleepily, trying to brush the hair from her eyes and the cobwebs from her mind. "Has he rented a rig *already?*"

"No, ma'am, I don't think so. It's Sir Geoffrey's phaeton that's waitin' at the door."

"Sir Geoffrey's!" Meg threw aside the bedclothes in agitation and jumped out of bed. "Now listen here, girl, you're to go at once to Sir Geoffrey and tell him that I've made my own arrangements, thank you, and that I've no need for his carriage or his servants. And then tell Roodle to get himself to Masham and hire a carriage as I instructed!"

She washed and dressed with lightning speed, a remarkable performance considering that her hands were trembling in rage. What right had that overbearing man to interfere with her plans? Was he determined to make even this, her last morning under his roof, a time of stress and argument?

She was tying on the second of her half-boots (the back of her dress still partially unbuttoned and her hair still tousled from sleep) when she heard a tap on the door. "Come in, Brynne. Has Roodle gone?" she queried.

"No, he has not," came Geoffrey's voice from the doorway. "You will ride in my carriage, and you will do so with good grace! I won't have you countermanding my orders and upsetting my household."

"Confound it, Geoffrey," she said furiously, jumping to her feet, "I'm not one of your family. I'm not under your jurisdiction. I don't have to obey your orders."

"It would help if you lowered your voice, ma'am. We needn't have the entire household privvy to our wrangles."

"Then you'd better come in and close the door, for if you intend to persist in your high-handed behavior, I'm very much afraid they'll hear me in Scotland!"

He closed the door and came up to her. "Turn around," he said curtly.

"What?" she asked suspiciously. "Why?"

"Must you question everything? Turn around."

With an impatient explosion of breath, she did what he asked and turned her back to him. Calmly, he began to hook up the buttons on the back of her dress as he spoke. "Now, ma'am," he said quietly, "please explain to me what possible objection you might have to my providing you with transportation home."

The homely intimacy of his doing up her buttons almost completely dissipated her fury. "Thank you," she said, embarrassingly chastened, "but I can do those for myself."

"Just hold up that mane of hair and answer my question! Why must you go to the trouble of renting a vehicle when I have a perfectly good carriage available for your use?"

She lifted her hair from the back of her neck with both hands and lowered her head. "I don't wish to be beholden to you for more than I am already."

"You needn't feel beholden to me at all. You were involved in an accident because of my coachman's carelessness, an accident which resulted in injury to you and illness for your aunt. Because the accident must be regarded as my responsibility, the indebtedness is all on my side. There—you may turn back now."

"Am I buttoned?"

"To the neck. Dash it, Meg, why do you wish to deny me the satisfaction of trying to make up to you for a fortnight of inconvenience and pain by seeing to it that you're delivered safely home?"

She turned around, much mollified, but stubbornly set on making her way back home without help from him. "You exaggerate your responsibilities, sir. There's no need to make anything up to me. After all, the results of the accident have not been so very disastrous."

He gave her a sharp look. "Haven't they?"

Her eyes flickered away from the intensity of his. "Well, my ankle is healed, and Isabel—have you heard that she's to be wed?"

He grinned his rare, surprisingly disturbing grin. "Yes, isn't it the most amazing pass? I guessed from the first that Fraser was taken with her, but I never dreamed that she had anything but the liveliest dislike of him."

"They both had me completely fooled. And now my aunt claims that it was love at first sight! Did you every hear anything so preposterous?"

"As Fraser himself would say (if it were anyone but he who was involved), it's entirely *withershins*. But then, almost anything you women tell me sounds upside-down to me."

Geoffrey had made the remark quite humorously, not intending it to cast any reflection on his relationship with Meg, but she made the connection at once. Her smile immediately faded, and he, seeing her changed expression, also drew back behind his protective reserve. "So you see," she said stiffly, hastily returning to her original argument, "there's no need at all for you to feel guilty about the blasted accident."

"Damn it, Meg don't be childish about this," he said curtly. "Do you seriously think I would permit you to leave this place in a rented hack, without servants, without funds and without proper escort?"

"You have no right to *permit* me anything!" she said angrily and turned away. "And how do you know *what* funds I have?"

"Twenty sovereigns were all you had at the Horse With Three Tails," he reminded her, "and I don't suppose you could have increased that sum since. With twenty sovereigns you may be able to rent a rig, but you'd not have enough left for a proper dinner."

"I shall manage. Good heavens, the way you speak, one would think you'd like to send me home in a coach-and-four, with footmen, coachmen, postillions and a pair of outriders! I am not the Queen Mother, you know!"

"But you are my responsibility, whether you like it or no, and until you've safely stepped over your own threshold, I intend to fulfill it. Therefore I shall send you home in my phaeton and pair, with my own groom riding the box with yours, and a maid to accompany you. Since, as you remind me, you are not the Queen Mother, I will forego the footmen, the postillions and the outriders. There, now, are we agreed? If you have the sense you were born with, you'll accept the offer as no more than your due, and stop this foolish argument."

She went to the window and stared out into a blur of sunlight through eyes that stung with tears she would not let herself shed. *Oh well,* she thought, *let him have his way.* She had insufficient strength with which to struggle. It would take what little stamina remained to make a departure with the proper dignity. "I didn't *mean* to have an argument with you," she muttered in glum surrender. "I didn't wish your last memory of me to be that of a stubborn shrew."

He gave an abrupt and bitter laugh. "There's no need to worry about *that*," he said, his voice husky with self-mockery.

"In any of your guises, even that of a stubborn shrew, my memory of you will be . . . will be too disturbing for my comfort."

When the import of his words struck her, she whirled about to face him. Their eyes locked, his clouded with unreadable emotions and hers plainly asking why—*why, if my effect on you is so strong, are you pushing us into this dismal separation?*

As if in response to her unspoken cry, and without taking his eyes from her face, he moved toward her. She felt a constriction in her chest, a surge of hope so strong it stopped the blood from coursing through her veins. But as if he saw a reflection of that hope leap up into her eyes, he froze in his tracks. With a shake of his head, he wheeled abruptly about and strode from the room.

He was gone. And she knew he would not appear at the carriage door with the others to say goodbye. Unless the Fates saw fit to intervene, she'd seen the last of Geoffrey Carrier.

Chapter Seventeen

January the first, 1814:

  My dearest Aunt Bel, your letter of December seventeenth has just reached me, probably delayed by the fog that has been hanging over us for the past four days, and I am hastening to answer it so that I can put your fears to rest. No, I am not in the least downhearted or glum. If you received that impression from my last, it was either because my phrasing was infelicitous or because your imagination is too vivid. I assure you that I am as active, cheerful, busy, lively and animated as ever and, except for missing you, of course, am enjoying life to the full . . .

Meg threw down the pen in disgust. How could she write a letter brimming with good cheer when she was deep in the doldrums?

The six weeks since she'd last seen Isabel had been the worst of her life, and having to pretend to her doting aunt that all was well was extremely difficult. Especially now that she'd sent Miss Dinsmore packing.

Miss Felicia Dinsmore, a maiden lady of indeterminate age, was a distant cousin whom Isabel had selected to fill her place in Meg's London household. From the moment the woman had arrived (with seven trunks, two abigails, and a fat lap-dog named Bo-Coo) Meg knew that not only the dog but Miss Dinsmore herself would be Too Much. The overly cheerful female chattered and giggled all day, and Meg (who only wanted to be alone, to be able to brood in silence and permit the wounds inflicted by her first rejection in love to heal) found her garrulous companion's constant presence almost too much to bear.

Last week, learning that a mutual relation was expecting a baby, Meg urged Miss Dinsmore to offer her services where they would be more greatly needed, and Miss Dinsmore cheerfully agreed. Meg sighed with relief as the seven trunks, the two abigails, the ugly Bo-Coo and her smiling cousin were loaded into a carriage and trundled off out of her life.

Meg knew that, sooner or later, she'd have to admit to Isabel that she'd sent her companion away, but for the time being she would avoid the subject in her letters. Before she would set about finding herself a new companion, she intended to enjoy a few days of peaceful solitude.

She leaned back against the graceful little Sheraton chair she kept at her writing desk and let her eye roam about the room. She'd always loved this room. It was square and high-ceilinged, and George Smith (one of the most talented interior designers in the world, who'd decorated it for her a few years earlier) had said that, with its tall, tall windows opposite the door and the way the bookshelves on the west wall balanced the marble mantelpiece of the east, it was perfectly proportioned. He'd placed her writing desk (a magnificent Harlequin trestle table of his own design, with inlaid woods, a leaf in the center that could be raised to prop up a book, and an elevated section at the back housing a dozen little cubby holes and drawers which kept her writing things in neat, well-organized symmetry) between the two windows, draped the windows with hangings of ornate grandeur, hung several of her favorite paintings on the wall over the mantel, designed a sofa and table to be placed before the bookshelves and two wing chairs before the fire, and—voila!—this beautiful room.

It had always given her pleasure to sit here, working on her correspondence or her accounts. In the bright daytime, she could lift her head and look out upon a small but elegantly landscaped courtyard. And when it was dark—or foggy, as now—the fire and the desk lamp gave the room a warm, golden glow that delighted her. The rose-colored, richly opulent orientals on the floor, the velvet-covered sofa at her left, the marble bust of a Greek boy on a pedestal in the corner had all added to her feeling of luxury, a feeling of being surrounded by comfort and beauty that had been a major source of her own sense of security and self-worth. Why was that feeling eluding her now?

At Knight's Haven, the furnishings and accoutrements had been so sparse and shabby that there had been no pleasure in looking around the rooms. In spite of their impressive proportions, the rooms could easily bring a depression of the spirit to anyone with aesthetic sensitivities. *Then why,* she asked herself impatiently, *do I so crave to be back in those surroundings again?*

She didn't deny to herself that her feelings for Geoffrey accounted for a large part of her yearnings for the neglected old castle. But there were other factors as well to account for them. For the first time in her life she'd been part of a real *family.* True, they were eccentric, foolish and spoiled, but, she realized with some surprise, she *enjoyed* them. She'd liked being asked her advice, she'd liked the younger girls' obvious admiration, she'd even developed a fondness for the garrulous, selfish, wasteful and silly Lady Carrier. If Geoffrey had been willing to marry her, she could have helped him to direct his mother's interests away from card games by setting her busy at redecorating the house (for if Meg married before her birthday, she would surely have the funds to do it), she could have used her influence with Trixie to help the girl mature, and she could have helped Sybil divert her mind from her imaginary symptoms to learning how to turn herself into an attractive young woman. Yes, she would have very much enjoyed being at the heart of a large, noisy, annoying, demanding family that needed her. Why couldn't Geoffrey have seen that?

Of course she couldn't really blame Geoffrey. To him she'd seemed just another of the troublesome females who'd saddled him with problems and who'd distracted him from the goals he'd set himself. He'd wanted to be a soldier, and his women had kept him from that; now he wanted to succeed at land management, and his women seemed bent on making *that* difficult for him. And what had *she* done to convince him that things could be otherwise? She'd come into his life during a wild, ill-planned escape from an ill-considered entanglement, behaved in a high-handed, lofty, lady-of-the-manor-greets-the-peasants style, jumped to false conclusions about his family and his problems, and ended by encouraging him to believe that she was a heartless, superficial London flirt to whom love was only a social game. That certainly was not a portrait of a marital partner on whom a hard-pressed, insecure, suspicious, thrice-burned, woman-shy male could pin his hopes.

Oh, well, it was too late now to dwell on it. *There is a tide in the affairs of men*, Shakespeare once said . . . and she'd missed hers. Her chance had gone, and the end was, as Shakespeare had predicted, *bound in shallows and in miseries*.

But she was not the sort to wallow in self-pity. Even on the journey back to London she'd hardly shed a tear. (Perhaps during the first hour or two she'd turned her face to the window and permitted some tears to fall, but it was so slight an emotional display that the little maid, Brynne, didn't even notice.) And in the weeks since, she'd hardly cried at all. Oh, sometimes late at night when she couldn't fall asleep . . .

However, this blasted letter was a different matter. It was hard to pretend in a letter that one's heart was ready to go skipping through the daisies when, in reality, one wanted to hide in the corner and lick one's wounds. How could she write to Isabel a spirited, carefree letter when her spirits were as heavy as lead? If only she'd forced herself to attend the D'Eresbys' ball last night, she might have been able to record some lively gossip that would convince Isabel that . . .

Her thoughts were interrupted by the butler's tap on the door. "Mr. Steele is calling, your ladyship," Maynard, the butler, informed her. And Arthur, for too many years a visitor to this house to stand on ceremony, promptly strolled in. "The fog is so thick out there, I couldn't take my curricle. Had to walk over," he remarked.

"Arthur, this *is* a surprise," Meg said, rising and extending her hand. "I thought this was the day you were to take tea with your sister and brother-in-law."

"So I was, but I cried off. I was too worried about *you*, you see." Having placed his hat and cane on a table, he bowed over her hand and began to pull off his gloves.

"Worried about me? Whatever for?"

"You never appeared at the D'Eresbys' ball last night!" he accused, permitting the butler to help him off with his greatcoat.

"Oh, that."

"Yes, that. Half the bachelors of London have fallen into flat despair. How could you have disappointed us so?"

"I shall explain in a moment. But first let me arrange to give you some tea, since you walked all the way in the fog and probably haven't had any. Maynard, will you see to it, please?"

The butler nodded, collected Arthur's things and bowed himself out.

"I was convinced you'd fallen ill," Arthur said, taking a seat beside her on the sofa.

"No, not ill. Just uninterested," she admitted with a guilty smile. "I somehow couldn't seem to dredge up the enthusiasm necessary to bother with having my hair done up, donning a ball gown, sending for Roodle to ready the carriage, and struggling through the fog and the traffic only to have to endure the dubious pleasures of standing up for a country dance with D'Eresby treading on my toes, of eating Lady D'Eresby's dreadfully parsimonious lobster cakes which everyone knows are made of halibut, and of coming home in the wee hours with a splitting headache. So, instead, I simply ate my dinner at home, read a few chapters of *The Absentee* and went to bed."

"You read a book?" He stared at her in genuine horror. "I don't know what's come over you of late, my dear. You're not the girl you were. Who would ever have thought that the celebrated Lady Meg Underwood, always at the forefront of the fashionable, would choose a book over a ball!"

"Well, it's quite a fascinating book, you see. Miss Edgeworth has written a somewhat satirical tale about an Irish landlord who tries to make his way in London society and—"

"Spare me, Meg, please!" He held up his hands as if to ward off an attack. "I find literary discussions to be the greatest bore. I hope you are not going to make a habit of this sort of thing. People might begin to say you're a bluestocking, and that will be the end of your reputation as the Reigning Belle of the *ton*."

"Will it?" She got up, wandered across the room and stared down into the fire, resting her forehead on the mantelpiece. "I suspect that my reputation has long since been superceded."

"What rubbish! There wasn't a single female in the ballroom last night who could have held a candle to you!"

She smiled wanly. "You needn't try to flummery me, Arthur. I shall soon be twenty-six. Twenty-six! By any method of measuring, that means I've been 'on the shelf' for a considerable length of time already."

"Oh, well, as to that, I don't deny that you've been devilishly adept at avoiding matrimony. The stakes at White's *are* getting lower each season on the chances that anyone will nab you. But that doesn't mean there aren't any number of eligibles who would jump at the chance. I, for one, am still ready at any time to take you off the Marriage Mart."

She shook her head. "What a complete hand you are, Arthur. I think you persist in making that offer only because you're certain I shan't accept you! Besides, if I'm turning into a bluestocking, as you claim, you'd find me a dead bore."

"But one book and one missed ball don't make you a bluestocking yet, ma'am. Let me save you from that fate. Marry me before the disease progresses any further."

She laughed. "Enough, Arthur. I thought we'd agreed to avoid this subject."

"Yes, we did. Forgot myself. Making you offers has become a habit with me. But you know, Meg, this bluestocking business is not as silly as you think. You've changed since you returned from Yorkshire. Is it because of that Carrier chap? Was there something between you that—"

He was interrupted by a tap at the door. "There's the tea," Meg said, relieved to be able to drop the subject. "Come in, Maynard."

The butler, however, was not carrying the tea things. His brow was creased with a slight suggestion of irritation. "There's a lady and gentleman at the door, your ladyship. I told them you were engaged, but they insist on seeing you at once."

"Do they indeed? What effrontery! Do you know them, Maynard?"

"No, your ladyship, I haven't seen them before. But the gentleman said that they'd come a long way. And the lady said that if I gave you her name she was certain you'd see her. She's a Miss Carrier. Miss Beatrix Carrier."

"Good heavens!" Meg gasped. "Trixie?" She darted past the astonished butler and ran down the hall. Standing just inside the front door, Trixie, bundled against the cold in a heavy cloak and carrying a large muff, looked red-eyed and miserable. "Trixie, my dear, what a complete surprise!" Meg cried excitedly. "How did you—? Why didn't you warn me that—? Good Lord . . . Mr. *Lazenby!*"

The man standing beside Trixie was indeed Mortimer Lazenby. "Good evening, your ladyship," he said, his voice suffused with relief at her obvious gladness at seeing Trixie. "Sorry we had no opportunity to—"

Meg looked from one to the other with a sinking heart. "Trixie, you haven't . . . ? You didn't . . . ?"

Trixie nodded, but it was not the happy gesture of a new bride. "Yes, Lady Meg, we did. We eloped. Day before y-yesterday."

"Do you mean you're married?"

Trixie's eyes filled, her underlip trembled and, instead of responding, she burst into tears.

Mortimer removed his hat and began to twist the brim with his fingers as he spoke. "Made all the arrangements with a J. P. in Ripon, everything proper and right as rain, and then, when we got there, he wouldn't do it!"

"The Justice of the Peace refused to *marry* you? Is that what you're saying?" Meg asked in a state of confused alarm. She didn't know which she feared more—the news that Trixie was wed or that she was not.

"Yes. Can't understand it. Everything all *arranged.*"

"It was wh-when he heard my n-name," Trixie sobbed. "He was afraid of G-Geoffrey . . ."

"Had dealings with Sir Geoffrey, it seems," Mortimer amplified. "Thinks highly of him, too. Wouldn't hear of doing anything to incur his wrath. Wanted a letter of *permission!*"

"He s-said the whole b-business looked havey-cavey to him. He suspected it was a runaway m-match!"

"Then why didn't you go back home at once?" Meg asked, her alarm increasing by the moment.

"No, I couldn't, don't you s-see?" Trixie lifted her head, her brimming eyes wide with anguish. "Geoffrey would have already f-found my note. He'd be furious with me!"

"She wouldn't hear of anything but that I take her to you," Mortimer explained, making certain that Meg should not find *him* at fault. *"Told* her the fog would make the driving tricky, but she *would* come. Said over and over that Lady Meg would find a way."

"Oh, Lady Meg," the girl sobbed, casting herself into Meg's arms, "it's been so dreadful! The J. P., the journey through this awful fog—*everything!* Please say you'll help us!"

Meg patted the girl's shoulder, biting her underlip worriedly. "Don't take on so, Trixie. Of course, I'll help you. But we must try to keep our heads. I *must* ask this of you, my dear—have you been traveling for two days ... er ... just the *two* of you?"

"No need to kick up a dust about *that,"* Mortimer said cavalierly. "She has her *maid* with her."

Trixie lifted her head and nodded solemnly. "It's Brynne. She's out in the carriage."

"Thank heaven for that!" Meg breathed in relief. "Go fetch her, Maynard, and see that she gets something hot to eat. And tell Roodle to see to the horses. Now, then, Trixie, wipe your eyes and come along to the sitting room. You, too, Mr. Lazenby. You must both be chilled through. We shall sit down near the fire and have some hot tea, and then, perhaps, we shall be better able to think about what to do."

Arthur, who had followed Meg out of the sitting room but had hung back for fear of seeming to intrude, now stepped forward. Meg introduced him to the miscreant couple and led them all down the hall. "I suppose you'll be wanting me out of the way," Arthur whispered, pulling Meg aside as the runaway pair divested themselves of their outer garments and went gratefully to the fire.

"No, Arthur, don't go," she answered in an undervoice. "You may be of great use to me. If you don't mind, after we've had our tea, I'd like you to take Mr. Lazenby away with you. Find a place for him to stay, can you? To have him here would be quite improper ... and would also set my teeth on edge."

Arthur nodded agreeably and set about making the red-eyed girl feel at home. Before the tea was brought, he'd already made her laugh. But it was the sight of the well-laden tea tray that really lifted Trixie's spirits. She explained that she'd been in such a state of agitation that she'd permitted Mortimer to make only the briefest stops during the almost two-day journey from Ripon, and they had scarcely had a bite to eat in all that time. Arthur watched with considerable amusement as the two young runaways devoured everything in front of them. Then, obedient to Meg's request, he suggested to Mortimer that it was time the two of them departed to find him a room in a hotel.

"Goodnight, Mortimer, dearest," Trixie said prettily, her good spirits restored. "Have a good night's sleep and come back first thing tomorrow. By then, I'm certain that Lady Meg will have found us a way out of our difficulties."

Meg groaned inwardly. The young girl's sanguine expectation that Meg could—and would—assist her to arrange a marriage was very disturbing. Meg didn't in the least wish to help her in that direction. While it was not in Meg's province to make decisions about Trixie's life, she couldn't help feeling that Trixie was embarking on a disastrous course. Mortimer was a vain, foolish, contemptible man, and Meg would be decidedly at fault to assist Trixie to wed him. Geoffrey would have every reason to despise Meg if she did. In fact, she would despise herself.

She glanced over at Trixie warily. The girl had pulled her chair close to the fire and was watching the play of the flames with dreamy eyes. *How easily,* Meg thought, expelling a troubled sigh, *the girl flits from the dismals to the heights.* No wonder Geoffrey had found it necessary to keep a firm guard over her. Well, whatever Trixie desired, Meg would not be so traitorous to Geoffrey as to help his sister leap into a foolish marriage without the brother's knowledge and consent.

In truth, if she had any character at all, Meg would do what Geoffrey himself would do if he were here—try to find a way to break the pair apart! Meg had once devised a plan to do just that. She'd thought of it weeks ago, when she and Geoffrey had discussed the matter. She'd even been about to divulge it to Geoffrey when Charles and Arthur had come upon the scene and driven the matter from her mind. If she could bring herself to interfere in this matter, she could execute that plan quite easily.

It didn't sit well with her conscience to interfere so drastically in the affair, but Trixie *did* choose of her own free will to drop the problem into Meg's lap. Meg was under no moral obligation to solve that problem in the manner Trixie wanted. *Yes,* Meg decided with a sense of firm conviction that it was the proper course. *I'll do it! I'll make the girl see just what sort of fellow she wants to marry.* She would earn herself

Trixie's everlasting enmity (and even Geoffrey, when he heard the story from Trixie's lips, would probably misunderstand Meg's motives as well), but Meg was not doing this to earn gratitude. She was doing it for the satisfaction (it was a pitifully small, insubstantial reward) of knowing that she'd be doing the right thing.

She got up with a deep breath and, crossing to her young guest, put a gentle hand on Trixie's shoulder. "Come along, Trix, and I'll show you the pretty bedroom where you'll sleep. I know it's a bit early, but you must be yearning to put down your head. And you'll *need* a good night's sleep, my dear, for tomorrow may prove to be a more difficult day than you expect."

Chapter Eighteen

The following day could hardly be said to have dawned at all, for the fog was so dense that day looked almost like night. The cold was so intense that Arthur and Mortimer, who appeared at Meg's door red-nosed and frozen in the middle of the afternoon rather than in the morning as they'd promised, swore that their walk was the most unpleasant they'd ever experienced. "You can't see anyone standing two feet away from you!" Arthur muttered in disgust as he warmed his hands over the sitting-room fire. "Passersby suddenly appear right on top of you, seeming to materialize out of nowhere. It's positively frightening!"

"And so cold one doesn't dare take one's horses out!" Mortimer added glumly. "Never known *Yorkshire* to be as cold as this!"

Arthur explained that they'd not even made it to Fenton's

Hotel the night before. The fog had been so thick that he'd decided to put the young man up in his spare bedroom rather than walk the added distance to St. James Street. "One daren't risk using horses in such fog—any slight mischance and the animal might be fatally lamed."

Meg cast her friend a look of gratitude. It must have been irksome to Arthur to be forced to endure the companionship of the foolish young braggart she'd foisted on him.

But poor Arthur was to endure much more. The next day, with the fog still persisting and the weather growing even colder, Arthur came to Meg's door to inform the ladies that Mr. Lazenby had come down with a case of the sniffles which he didn't wish to aggravate by taking himself out in the cold. He'd sent his good wishes to the ladies and begged to be excused until the weather had improved.

Meg had no opportunity to speak to Arthur alone during the visit, for Trixie, obviously untroubled by her betrothed's illness, sat all afternoon at Arthur's side, questioning him interminably about the various places of interest in London which she would soon be able to see. It was only when he rose to take his leave that Meg, accompanying him to the door, was able to exchange a private word with him. "I don't know how to thank you, Arthur, for inviting Lazenby to stay with you. It must not be very pleasant to have to endure his company."

Arthur shrugged. "It's not so very bad. Although the fellow has told me several times already about some sort of race on a high-perch phaeton which he won. One would think it was the only event in his life worth speaking of."

"Do you mean he hasn't yet bragged to you about his remarkable attraction for the ladies?"

"Oh, yes, and his rare ability to outstrip Londoners in matters of dress. The mushroom is convinced that he'd put Brummell in the shade."

"Oh, dear," Meg sympathized, "he seems to have put you through almost his entire repertoire. But don't despair, my dear. This fog can't last much longer. Once it passes, I promise I shall put things to rights."

But the fog lasted three more days. Even the intrepid Arthur gave up his attempts to inch his way along the streets to Meg's domicile. Meg and Trixie, trapped within the house with only each other for company, found the hours oppressively hard to fill. The thick, almost black mist pressed in on their windows, making it seem as if the house had been transported to a world made up of a strange, tangible nothingness which, if they stepped out the door, would swallow them whole.

They passed the mornings in sewing or reading, the afternoons playing endless games of Piquet and an unsatisfactory, two-handed version of Whist called Hearts, and the evenings in chatting, telling each other bits and pieces of their past lives and becoming almost as close as two sisters in the process. Meg admitted that she'd missed having sisters and brothers during her childhood years, while Trixie revealed a number of stories about her youth which often included sketches of Geoffrey which held Meg spellbound. Trixie didn't remember a great deal about her brother's early years (being sixteen years his junior) but she did recall how exciting it had been when he'd come home on holiday from Cambridge or how magnificent he'd looked when he'd had leave from the army and had come home wearing his regimentals. Meg put a strict rein on her tongue to keep herself from asking too many questions about him, but she couldn't keep herself from hanging upon Trixie's words every time Geoffrey's name came into the conversation. Fortunately, Trixie herself was so disenchanted with her brother since he'd opposed her attachment to Lazenby that it never occurred to her to suspect that the odd fascination Meg seemed to show for anything having to do with Geoffrey could possibly be a sign of affection.

One of the things that their hours of enforced solitude accomplished was to give Meg the opportunity to work out in her mind the details of the scheme she'd concocted to bring Trixie to her senses. Ever since the night at Lady Habish's party, it had been obvious to Meg that Mortimer Lazenby's heart was not so occupied with love for Trixie that he wouldn't be extremely susceptible to the charms of other females. He'd made it plain that he didn't consider himself so closely bound (either by affection or honor) to Trixie that he wouldn't, with an encouraging word from Meg, forget his earlier obligation "like that!" Therefore, Meg would *offer* him that encouragement. Then, when she'd managed to get him in a compromising position (preferably in an embrace), arrange to have Trixie discover them. Trixie couldn't fail to find the fellow a revolting specimen after coming upon such a scene.

By the evening of the third day of Trixie's stay, it began to seem as if they would be marooned forever in the sea of mist. But on the morning of the fourth, they drew aside the draperies to find that they could see the houses across the street. The fog had lifted! And although the day was grey and dreary, their moods brightened at the prospect of rejoining the rest of the world. The rejoining was not long in coming; before eleven in the morning the door knocker sounded and Arthur and Mortimer both presented themselves to the ladies, their faces beaming with eager good spirits. All four agreed that they'd been shut up indoors too long and that, despite the cold, a drive through the streets was the proper sort of activity for the day.

Bundled up warmly (the gentlemen with caped greatcoats and long mufflers wound several times round their necks and the ladies in heavy cloaks and huge fur muffs), they climbed into Arthur's carriage and set off for St. James Park. They were amazed to see the numbers of people thronging the streets. Disregarding the cold, the citizenry of London seemed all to have emerged at once. Trixie, her nose pressed against the window, kept exclaiming with surprise at the crowds, the colors, the noise and the infinite, seemingly patternless movement.

After circling the park and traversing the Mall, Arthur directed his coachman to proceed up the Strand. By that time, Meg had had enough of listening to Mortimer disparage the sights in irritating counterpoint to Trixie's effusions, and she suggested that they turn back. "Oh, no!" Trixie begged. "I could drive all day! May we not go on?"

"Why don't we drive across Blackfriar's Bridge and see the doings on the river?" Arthur suggested. "Then we can take Great Surry Street south of the river to Westminster and home."

The plan was accepted with varying degrees of enthusiasm, the coachman was so instructed, and they rode on. The ride through the City, with its crowded buildings and teeming streets was a sight completely new to Trixie who, although she'd lived in London during her earlier years, had never been brought to its business heart. Her eyes were wide with awe. "I didn't know there were so many people and so many edifices in the *world!*" she said breathlessly.

But the view from the bridge brought her most intense reaction. "My Lord! It's frozen over! The river's frozen over!"

The others were equally fascinated. "Good heavens," Meg exclaimed, "what are they doing out there?"

Stretching below them, all the way out to London Bridge,

people and carts were traversing the river right on the ice. They seemed to have established a passageway—an actual road—right down the middle of the river. Here and there along the route enterprising persons were setting up little booths made, tentlike, with nothing more than ropes and blankets, as if they were about to establish residence on the river and move right in.

"They can't mean to *live* out there, can they?" Mortimer asked.

"No, only to sell things, I expect," Arthur answered. "If the cold weather holds, I suspect there'll be a fair."

"A fair!" Trixie clapped her hands in excitement.

"Oh, yes," Arthur elaborated. "It's been done before, you know."

"A fair on the *Thames?* You're cutting a wheedle," Mortimer said.

"Not at all. My father told me about attending one back in eighty-nine. The frost lasted seven weeks, I'm told. Papa wanted to take me, but I was only an infant and Mama wouldn't permit it. But Papa told me later that the place was as good as Bartholomew's, with games and entertainments and all sorts of food and drink right on the ice. They made a fire, too, and roasted an ox whole."

"A fire on the ice?" Trixie didn't know whether to take him as his word or laugh the tale away.

"Oh, there were several fires. The ice was so thick, you see, that the heat from the fires made very little difference."

"Do you think," Trixie asked, her eyes shining, "that there will actually be a fair *this* year?"

"It certainly looks as if there will. There are the beginnings right before your eyes."

"Oh, Lady Meg, do you think we might come back and actually go out on the ice to see the fair for ourselves?"

Meg threw Arthur a troubled look. "I don't think it will be a place for delicately reared young ladies. Fairs, whether on the ice or on dry land, are certain to attract all sorts of ruffians, rowdies and rag-tag louts, you know."

Arthur looked at her with surprise. "I don't know what's come over you, my girl. You were always prime for a lark before you went up to—"

"Never mind!" Meg cut in sharply. "It's quite different when a young lady is in my charge. Besides, I see no reason to debate the subject now. A thaw may set in *tonight,* and the entire argument will have been to no purpose."

"Oh, I *wish* there'll be no thaw," Trixie sighed, pressing her nose against the window again to take her last glimpse as the carriage rolled off the bridge. "I would so love to see a fair on the ice!"

"That's a very selfish wish, Trix," Meg said rather sanctimoniously, "for a prolonged freeze is very hard on all the poor and those not fortunate enough to afford the increased cost of wood and coal. There's more to these extremes of weather than fun and fairs."

"Hmmph!" was Arthur's only comment.

Trixie made a face. "Well, then, I shan't *pray* for continued frost. But if it *should* continue—through no fault of mine—I intend to find a way to enjoy it!"

Meg's mood didn't lighten during the drive home. She found herself extremely annoyed by the conversation and her own part in it. She'd sounded strangely surly, more like a sour-faced old governess than a confident young woman. And Arthur had been quick to point it out to her. But she was irritated with *him*, too. Why did he persist in making the Frost Fair sound inviting to Trixie when Meg was plainly trying to tell him that it would not be appropriate for the girl to go? While Trixie lived in her house, Meg had responsibility for her safety. If she permitted the girl to go and do as she pleased, and an accident occurred, how could Meg forgive herself? She was being placed in the position of maiden aunt, and she didn't like the role.

If I don't settle this elopement business soon, she told herself, *I shall turn into a sour-faced fidget!* The sooner she put her plan into execution, the sooner Trixie would run weeping home to Yorkshire, and the sooner Meg would be able to return to the peace and quiet of her life. Perhaps, if she played her cards well, she could pull the deed off this very afternoon.

With that in mind, she began her machinations as soon as they returned to the house on Dover Street. "Arthur," she said in her most liltingly appealing voice, "don't take your things off yet. Be a dear and execute a little commission for me. Run down to Gunther's—in Berkeley Square, you know—and bring us a box of pastries for our tea. Cook told me this morning that the fog has brought the supplies in the larder embarrassingly low, and I don't suppose they've yet had time to replenish them."

If Arthur felt any annoyance at being asked to run a servant's errand, he was too gentlemanly to show it. With a bow of acquiescence he turned to the door. "Be back in a trice," he said good-naturedly over his shoulder.

"Oh, but you must be certain that you ask that the pastries be made up while you wait. Apricot tarts and sugar plums, I think. It wouldn't do at all to have them palm off a parcel of pastries that have been standing about on the shelves. They must make them up *freshly*. At the exhorbitant prices Mr. Gunther dares to charge, that is the *least* we should expect."

Meg watched him go with a mischievous feeling of satisfaction. If he followed her instructions he would be out of the way for the better part of an hour. Then, instructing Mortimer to go into the sitting room and warm himself at the fire, she turned to Trixie, who had removed her cloak and was primping before the mirror near the door. "What have you done to your hair, Trixie?" she asked, her voice carrying the slightest suggestion of disapproval.

Trixie turned. "Don't you like it? I suppose it *is* a bit hastily done. I was so eager to dress this morning that I didn't let Brynne take the usual pains."

"Well, there's plenty of time for it now. Arthur will be gone for a while, and we shan't have tea until he returns. Why don't you run upstairs and refresh yourself? I shall find Brynne and send her up to you. Oh, and while you're upstairs, ask my Nora to take out the lavender lustring for you to try. You haven't brought nearly enough gowns with you, you know, and if the lavender suits you, you may wear it *today,* if you like."

"Oh, Meg," the unsuspecting girl sighed with pleasure, "you're so good to me!" She planted a quick kiss on Meg's cheek and ran up the stairs.

Meg, rubbing her cheek with a twinge of remorse, went to find Trixie's maid. She instructed Brynne to give Trixie's hair a thorough combing. "It will not take you more than...let's say twenty minutes...will it?" she asked.

"No, ma'am, I don't think so," the abigail said.

"Good. It's now twenty minutes before three. When the large clock in the hall strikes three, I want you to send Miss Beatrix downstairs. You can hear the clock from her bedroom quite easily. This is very important, Brynne. You are to say nothing to her about this, for I have a surprise for her, but you must see to it that *at the stroke of three* she comes right downstairs. Can you do it?"

"Oh, yes, ma'am, I think I can. Sounds so funny, though. Like Cinderella on the stroke o' midnight."

"Yes," sighed Meg, turning to the sitting room, her heart full of nervous misgivings, "just like Cinderella."

Mortimer was sitting near the fire, his feet in their tasseled Hessians stretched out on the hearth. "I'm happy to see that you're making yourself at home," Meg said cheerfully.

He scrambled to his feet. "Yes, your ladyship," he said, suddenly ill-at-ease. "Very . . . er . . . comfortable room, this."

"Thank you. Do sit down, Mr. Lazenby. There's no need to stand on points with me. And why don't you call me Meg?"

"Didn't seem to want me to when we . . . that is, when I met you at Lady Habish's—"

"Nonsense, of course I wanted you to. And I'll call you Mortimer. Won't that make things easier between us?"

He smiled tentatively. "Should think so, yes. Been thinking, you know, that you don't like me much. Can't think why. Great favorite with ladies in Yorkshire, you know."

"Yes, so I've been told. But I can't think why you believe I don't like you."

He shrugged. "Just a way you have . . . a sort of look. Can't put my finger on it."

"Come now, Mortimer, you mustn't be overly sensitive." She gave him a wide smile and sat down on the sofa. "Do sit down, please." She patted the seat beside her. "I shan't be comfortable with you hulking over me that way."

With a flip of his coattails, he took the indicated seat. "Been hoping for an opportunity to talk to you."

"Have you?" she asked, looking up at him coyly.

"Yes. Never managed to find you alone. Wanted to explain about Trixie."

"What about Trixie?"

"The elopement, you know. All *her* idea. Wanted you to know that."

"You wanted *me* to know that? Why?"

"So that you'd understand that I meant what I said to you that night."

She blinked. "What you said to me—?"

"Yes. About being smitten with you. Still am, you know. Only ran off with Trixie because she was in a desperate case. Didn't think *you* liked me, anyway."

She felt her fingers curl angrily. Was the fellow merely callow, or was he a complete opportunist? Whichever the case, he made her itch to box his ears. "But I . . . I *do* like you, Mortimer," she forced herself to say.

He hitched closer to her, his stiff shirt-points making his movements ludicrously awkward. "You do? Even though Trixie and I are . . . are . . ."

"Promised? Betrothed? About to be wed? Is that what you find so difficult to say?" She couldn't help herself—the sarcastic response popped out before she could stop her tongue.

Completely oblivious to the acerbity in her tone, he nodded glumly. "Got myself hobbled pretty neatly this time. I'd have to anger her into breaking it off."

Meg clenched her hands, compelling herself to gaze limpidly up at him. "Would you . . . *consider* such a course, Mortimer?" she asked in a soft murmur. "For me?"

"Told you I would. Smitten, you know." He reached for her hand. "From the first."

There was a sound in the hall. Meg winced. Brynne had sent Trixie down too *early*. The clock hadn't yet struck three. This mere grasp that Mortimer had on her hand would not be enough to shock Trixie into drastic action. Mortimer could quickly drop the hand and the whole scene would look quite innocent. In hasty desperation, Meg threw her free hand round his neck. "Oh, *Mortimer!*" she sighed and lifted her face to his.

The young man hesitated only a moment. Convinced that women found him irresistible, he moved quickly from a feeling of surprise to the glow of self-satisfaction. As quickly as his high shirt-points and stiff demeanor permitted, he put his arm about her and pressed his lips to hers in a smothering embrace.

"Good *God,* Meggie!" came a voice from the doorway. "Have you lost your *mind?*"

Meg, recognizing the voice, pushed the young man away abruptly and wheeled about. In the doorway, looking absolutely horrified, stood her Aunt Isabel. And as the three gaped at each other, speechless and aghast, the clock in the hallway solemnly struck three.

Chapter Nineteen

The three of them stood staring at each other in shock, each of them having good reason to believe that at least *one* of the others in this room was badly out of place. For Mortimer, it was the aunt, who had arrived at precisely the worst moment and had spoiled what was becoming a very romantic adventure. For Meg, it was also Isabel, whom she'd believed to be idyllically fixed in her own happy world hundreds of miles away. But for Isabel, it was *Mortimer,* who had somehow cajoled her usually sensible niece into behaving in a most uncharacteristic way with the foppish creature whom she would normally have scorned to admit inside her home.

Before any of them uttered a sound, there was a rustle of silks on the stair and Trixie pranced in, resplendent in Meg's lavender gown. "Look, Meg," she clarioned, floating in prettily, "isn't it just perf—? Oh!" She'd been so absorbed by the enchantment of her own appearance that she hadn't noticed Isabel, standing just inside the door. Her attention was first caught by the shocked expressions on the faces of Meg and Mortimer, but as soon as she noticed Isabel, she understood their astonishment. As for herself, she saw nothing in this little tableau to disturb her. "Mrs. *Underwood,*" she exclaimed happily, "I didn't know you were coming."

Meg frowned, feeling puzzled and troubled. "It's Mrs. Fraser now, you know. Aunt Bel, what are you doing here?"

Isabel had not yet recovered from the shock of the scene she'd burst in upon. "I might ask the same of you," she muttered sourly.

Meg, too confused by these surprising circumstances to be able to ascertain how badly her scheme had been muddled, thought it best to silence her aunt on this subject until the two of them were alone. "I suppose you mean to ask what Trixie and Mr. Lazenby are doing here," she interjected quickly. "I shall explain everything to you in a moment. But first, Trixie dear, may I ask you and Mr. Lazenby to go to . . . to find Maynard and ask him to see that tea is set up for all of us in . . . in the drawing room?"

"Perhaps your guests had better look out the window," Isabel suggested caustically. "If they have far to go, they may not feel that they can take time for tea when they see—"

"Goodness," Trixie exclaimed, peering outside, "it's snowing!"

"Oh, dear," Meg muttered, rapidly coming to the end of her rope, "I hope we shan't be foreced to endure another *storm*. Well, Trixie is staying here, you know. And Mr. Lazenby hasn't very far to go. In any case, he will have to wait for Arthur. So do go along, you two, and see to the arrangements for tea. And Trixie, that dress is very lovely. Now that you are looking so very captivating, why don't you and Mr. Lazenby take the opportunity to have a little *tête-à-tête?* It's been days since you've been able to be private, and you both must be eager for the chance."

Trixie cast Meg a look of hesitation which Meg could not interpret, but the girl obediently left the room. Mortimer followed, but not without glancing at Meg with a look she had no problem at all in interpreting—it was as if he'd said aloud, "I know what you want me to say to her, and for your sake I'll find a way to break her heart and free myself for you."

Meg could only respond by lowering her eyes, but she would have very much liked to wring his neck!

As soon as they were alone, Isabel fixed her with a glaring eye. "Meg Underwood, what were you *thinking* of, permitting that . . . that countercoxcomb to molest you!"

"He was not molesting me. It would be more accurate to say that I was molesting *him*. But I won't be put off another second." She crossed quickly to her aunt and gave her an affectionate embrace. "What are you doing here? Is Dr. Fraser with you? Whatever possessed you to come to pay a visit in such dreadful weather?"

"I am not paying a visit," Isabel said, turning her face away. "And the doctor is not with me. I've left him!"

"*Left* him? Aunt Bel!"

"He's a stubborn, cantankerous, maddening old *wanwyt*, and I want no more to do with him! Here . . . help me off with this cloak, if you please, or I shall begin to feel that I haven't a place in the world where I'm welcome."

"But, dearest, I don't understand," Meg said in bewilderment, taking her aunt's cloak and leading the sad-eyed, tired, chilled woman to a chair near the fire. "You've been married little more than a month! You were so happy! Your letters were brimming with it."

"Yes, but that was before I found out his true nature. The man's a Bluebeard!"

"Oh, come now, Aunt Bel. Are you trying to make me believe that he has other wives hidden away?"

"Not other wives . . . other patients! Those patients mean more to him than his . . . his . . ." Her eyes began to fill. "His . . . own w-wife!"

Meg sat down on the hearth at her aunt's feet and took hold of Isabel's hand. "You poor dear. Has the man been neglecting you?"

"He's *shameless* about it. He promises faithfully that he'll return in time for dinner, and then he doesn't arrive till midnight! We dress to go out to a dinner party and half-way through he disappears and I find myself going home *alone!* The truth is that I saw more of the man at Knight's Haven than I did after we were wed. I've even considered contracting a severe case of *consumption* so that he'd pay some attention to me again."

"But Aunt Bel, aren't you being a bit unfair? If he's dedicated to his work, that's not such a despicable quality, is it?"

Isabel leaned back and shut her eyes wearily. "Meg, I've thought the matter through, and I think, in a way, it *is* a despicable quality. We are neither of us young. The years left to us are probably not many in number. If he chooses to shorten his life even further by overtaxing himself, I do not intend to stand by and watch him do it."

"But have you tried to reason with him? Have you talked it out?"

"I've tried. He only says, 'Woman, y're havin' a soor tirrivee owre naught.'"

Meg smiled at her aunt's newly acquired talent for mimicry. She could almost hear Dr. Fraser saying those words. But she couldn't encourage her aunt in this runaway solution to her problem. Isabel clearly cared very much for the man she'd left. "Perhaps if he took on an assistant . . ."

"I suggested that. But he doesn't trust anyone else to do his work. I even offered to go along with him on his calls, but he wouldn't hear of it. Didn't want me coming down with his patients' illnesses, he said. Though if *he* manages to stay healthy, I don't see why I would not."

The two of them fell silent, each one watching the flames and thinking her own thoughts. Meg felt less alarmed than she'd been when she first saw her aunt in the doorway. The problem was not insoluble. Meg was certain that she could in time convince her aunt to return to Yorkshire where she belonged. But first, Meg had to untangle the confusion of her *other* problem.

As if Isabel had read her mind, she brought up that very subject. "And now, my dear, tell me why you were kissing that dreadful popinjay. And where, pray tell, is our cousin, Felicia Dinsmore? One would think that in the midst of all this confusion she would—"

In as few words as possible, Meg explained what had happened to the ever-smiling Miss Dinsmore. And then, rapidly changing the subject, she went on to describe to her aunt the plan she'd concocted to make Trixie discover the shortcomings in her betrothed's character. But Isabel, instead of commending her for her cleverness and ingenuity, looked at her with scorn. "It's the most foolish scheme I've ever heard," the older woman declared. "It seems to me that you've only succeeded in making the fellow believe that you care for him, without in any way showing Trixie that he's false."

"But that's only because you arrived at just the wrong moment," Meg declared in her own defense.

"I'm sorry about that," Isabel said, rising from the chair in offended dignity and frowning at her niece, "but if I *hadn't* interrupted, I have no doubt that Trixie would have believed, when she burst in upon that scene, that the incident was entirely *your* fault. She would have blamed you for wanton flirtatiousness and would have promptly forgiven her beloved for having momentarily strayed."

Meg blinked up at her wonderingly. "Do you really think so? Is that what *you* would believe if you'd discovered Dr. Fraser in such a situation?"

"If I had discovered Dr. Fraser in such a situation," Isabel responded acerbically, "I'd merely assume that he was administering a *medical* procedure—some sort of resuscitation of the breath! And I'd undoubtedly be right!"

Meg burst into a peal of laughter, jumped up and ran to her aunt to plant a kiss on the older woman's cheek. "You know, my love, you sound more and more like the man you married. He must have spent more time with you than you're willing to admit, to judge by how much of his character seems to have rubbed off on you."

"If you mean to say, Meg Underwood, that I'm beginning to sound like an old curmudgeon, I do not take it as a compliment. And now, if you don't mind, I'm going to take myself off to bed, provided of course that you haven't given my room away some *other* stray runaway."

"Your room is, and always will be, waiting for you, my dearest. But must you retire so soon? I need your help in getting myself out of this fix I'm in."

"It's been a long trip, love," Isabel said with a wan sigh, "through fog and cold and snow. If I don't get some rest, I really *will* sound curmudgeonly. Besides, you got yourself into this fix without my help, and I have every confidence you'll get yourself out of it that way. I have troubles enough of my own."

The snow that Isabel brought with her fell thick and fast and lasted for three days. After only a few hours of relief following the fog, the entire city was again immobilized. The snow was so heavy and covered so wide an area that all traffic from the north and west was cut off. Meg, Trixie and Isabel, trapped in the house without prospect of company, tried to make the best of the situation, but the days seemed gloomy indeed. Each of them tried to show the others a cheerful face and to make hopeful conversation, but each had something troublesome on her mind. Isabel brooded over a neglectful husband; Meg struggled to find solutions for two knotty problems; and Trixie, Meg noticed, would lapse into silence or pace about the rooms chewing her fingernails. Meg had no idea what was worrying the girl, but she didn't pry—she'd taken on too many problems already.

But afer a few days the sun appeared, and although it was still frigidly cold, the digging-out began and the traffic began to move. No sooner was it possible to maneuver through the streets than Arthur and Mortimer appeared on the doorstep of the house on Dover Street. The ladies, who had taken to sleeping late during the inactivity of the past few days, were still at breakfast and invited the gentlemen to join them at the commodious round table in the morning room. The two men had risen early and had gone outdoors to investigate what was happening in the world. They were full of news about the fair that was burgeoning along the "roadway" they'd seen on the Thames. "Everyone is talking of it," Arthur reported, buttering a biscuit. "The roadway that we saw the other day has widened and lengthened. People are calling it Freezeland Street, although there are signs along the route reading 'City Road.' And there are hundreds of little tents being erected all along the entire length—right in the center of the river from Blackfriar's all the way to London Bridge."

"Saw a carriage cross the way this morning . . . with four horses!" Mortimer added, ceasing for a moment his voracious devouring of a large slice of York ham. "Word of honor, four! Most amazing sight I ever saw!"

Trixie was beside herself with excitement. "Oh, I can't *wait* to see it! Is it truly like a *fair* . . . with pie-men and puppeteers and strolling musicians?"

Arthur smiled at her like a fond father. "I don't doubt it. By tomorrow, everything will probably be in full swing. The crowds were enormous even this morning."

"Tomorrow! How absolutely thrilling! Oh, Meg, we *must* go tomorrow . . . very early, so that we may spend the entire day!"

"But, Trixie, I *told* you—" Meg began.

"I say, Isabel," Arthur interrupted impatiently, "have you noticed anything strange about your niece of late?"

"Strange? What do you mean, Arthur?"

"I mean that ever since she's returned from that disastrous sojourn in the north, she's not been herself. She seems to fall into odd humors, she avoids company, she doesn't go to parties, and she even reads *books!* And *now* she wants to spoil our sport at the Frost Fair!"

Isabel perceived that Arthur was speaking half in jest, but she wondered how much of what he said was earnest. "Is any of that true, Meg? Have you been in the dismals and avoiding society?"

"Of course not. Arthur, must you be so provoking? Just because I don't wish to subject myself—or Trixie—to the jostling, the indignities, the vulgarities that will certainly afflict visitors to a public spectacle like a Frost Fair—"

"But Meg, aren't you being over-cautious?" Isabel asked mildly. "You would not be without escort, after all. Even *I* am curious to attend the fair, for a little while at least. It will be quite exciting—"

Meg put down her teacup irritably. "I don't wish to hear any more about this matter. While Trixie resides under this roof, she must be considered in my care. How could I face her bro . . . her *family* . . . if I permitted her to come to grief? I'm sorry if my decision seems unkind or too severe, but I can't permit a situation to develop which I'll later regret. Now, if you please, let's speak of other things."

Meg had not often seen Trixie in resentful or rebellious moods (although Geoffrey had tried to warn her that the girl was quite capable of such displays). Therefore, she was startled to see Trixie rise slowly from her chair, her petulant lower lip trembling with hostility. "I'm sorry, Lady Meg, but I don't have to obey your orders. You are not my guardian! Even though I'm living under your roof, I intend to go where—and with whom—I choose. And if you try to oppose me, I shall . . . I shall go to live somewhere else!" And with a breathy sob and a great swish of skirts, she ran out of the room and slammed the door.

Meg was appalled. Had the girl no gratitude? Her behavior was that of a spoiled, thoughtless child. And she'd only made herself despicable in the eyes of everyone else at the table.

But the others at the table were not in complete agreement. "Now see what you've done!" Arthur muttered. "You've *upset* the poor chit."

"I?" Meg asked in amazement. She looked at each of the

faces staring across at her. "Do you *all* think that I'm at fault in this?"

"Well, the girl should not have spoken to you in that way," Isabel said, "but Geoffrey Carrier had told me that his sister had been spoiled by her parents, so one can't expect conduct that's always beyond reproach. But as for the Fair, one can't expect a lively young girl who's been imprisoned indoors for so many days not to wish to have a little enjoyment—"

"Exactly!" said Arthur with vehemence. "I *told* you, Meg, that you're turning sour. There's no good reason for you to be so hard on the girl in this matter."

Meg glared at him furiously. "So *that's* what you think of me, is it? And what about *you*, Mortimer? You haven't given *your* opinion yet. Do *you* agree that I'm too sour?"

Mortimer grinned at her in a self-satisfied, completely fatuous attempt to signal their secret intimacy. "Wouldn't say you're sour. Wouldn't say you're wrong, either. Would only say that if you were to go to the fair in *my* escort, you'd have nothing to worry about. No one would dare to molest you in my presence. Assure you of that!"

This piece of conceit was the last straw. "I want to thank you all," she said disdainfully, getting to her feet, "for your loyal support in this matter. But with or without your support, I intend to hold fast to my decision. Neither Trixie nor I will indulge in such a . . . a *raffish* outing while she remains in my care!"

Meg spoke only in the most necessary monosyllables for the rest of the day, and, observing how all the others maintained a determinedly cheerful demeanor and joked and laughed among themselves all through dinner (to which Isabel had spitefully invited the gentlemen without even asking Meg's approval), she left them to their own devices and retired early.

However, she found herself unable to sleep. Arthur's accusations rang in her ears. Was she truly turning sour? In her attempt to conquer the depression of her spirits because of Geoffrey's rejection of her love, was she becoming an embittered, irascible old maid?

A vision of her future loomed up before her, its aspect as forboding and fearful as a Greek tragedy. In a little more than two months her fortune would be taken from her, her aunt would have returned to Yorkshire and she would be alone.

With only a small competency, she would be forced to leave her lovely home and move to some squalid little place in an unfashionable part of town. She would grow more sour and irascible as the days passed. Her friends would drop her, and she'd have to take in a pair of cats for company. She would grow old, crotchety and eccentric and would die in her bed unloved and unmourned.

It was a grim prospect. Perhaps, in order to avoid it, she ought to consider marrying Arthur. He had been very critical of her in the past several weeks, and it was quite possible she'd already lost him, but if she made herself recapture her former vitality, she could probably win him back.

But she didn't *want* Arthur. She didn't want anyone but Geoffrey. She wasn't the sort who could live a life of falsity, pretending to a husband an affection she didn't feel. She couldn't marry anyone while this love for Geoffrey clouded her mind and ate at her heart.

As she tossed about on the pillows sleeplessly, and the hours ticked away, she tried to devise other plans for her future. She needn't necessarily become an eccentric old maid. She could find employment . . . as a governess, perhaps, or a teacher in a school for young ladies. She could open up such a school herself! If she could convince enough of her friends to send their daughters, she might well be able to keep the house. She would turn it into a school and keep the sitting room as her office. It wouldn't be so very bad . . . she would have at least one room in which she could surround herself with the remnants of her past . . .

With thoughts of this nature tumbling about in her head, she eventually drifted off to sleep. It must have been just before dawn when sleep finally came, for a moment later—or so it seemed—she was awakened by a tapping at her door and opened her eyes to bright sunshine. "Come in," she muttered groggily, snuggling deeper into the pillows and covering her face with her comforter in an effort to keep hold of whatever dream had been engrossing her.

"It's I, Meg," said Isabel from the doorway. "I don't wish to disturb you, my dear . . ."

"Mmmmfff" was the sound that came from the pillows.

". . . but I can't wait much longer to say adieu. We're going now."

"Going?" Meg muttered.

"Yes. To the fair. See you later." And the door closed.

Meg dug deeper into the pillows in relief, expecting sleep to overtake her at once. But a word her aunt had said kept whirling about in her brain. Was it something important? Something disturbing... like fair? *Fair?* She sat bolt upright and stared at the closed door. "Aunt Bel!" she shouted. "Wait!"

She leaped out of bed, shivering with the icy cold. "Aunt Bel!" she cried again and snatched up the comforter. Wrapping it about her she ran barefooted to the door. "Isabel Underwood Fraser, you *can't* go off to that wild circus all by yourself!" She pattered down the hall to the top of the stairs, but there was no one to be seen. Isabel had gone.

With feelings which swung from extreme chagrin to extreme worry, she ran back to her room. Shouting for her abigail, she threw off her nightgown and began hurriedly to dress. Nora, the abigail, scurried in to lend assistance, but when she was questioned about Mrs. Fraser's departure, she could give no information. She hadn't heard Mrs. Fraser leave and didn't know if she'd been alone.

Meg had no choice but to follow her aunt. If she was unable to catch up with her before arriving at the fair, she would probably be out of luck—for there was little doubt that the area would be thronged with people. But she had to try.

As soon as she was dressed, with her fly-away hair carelessly tied back and a cloak thrown over her shoulders, she ordered Nora to tell Roodle to bring the curricle to the door and ran out into the hallway. There she came face-to-face with Brynne who was on her way to the back stairs. "Where's Miss Beatrix?" Meg asked her.

Brynne made a little curtsey. "Still asleep, it seems, ma'am. I jest knocked."

"Good. Let her sleep. But, Brynne, when she wakes, tell her that she's not to leave this house until I return."

She flew down the stairs, hoping that Roodle was making haste with the horses. Impatiently she pulled on her gloves, but her nervousness made her incompetent, and she struggled with the little buttons in vain. With a shrug, she left them unfastened and ran to the door. Just as she was about to open it, a loud knocking sounded. She pulled it open, preparing herself to dismiss whatever caller had chanced by with the most cursory excuses. But standing on her doorstep, his expression as dour and forbidding as she'd ever seen it, was Dr. Fraser.

"Donald!" Meg cried, her agitation fading away. "I don't think I've been as glad to see anybody in my *life!"*

"Good day to ye, lass," he said, only the slightest twitch of his lips indicating acknowledgement of her effusive greeting. "I take it I've come t' the right abode?"

"If you mean to ask if this is where your wife has chosen to hide herself, yes, this is the right place."

"Aye, I thought so. Like as no, she'll ha'e instructed ye not t' admit me, but ye downa wish fer us both t' be standin' here chitterin' in the cold, do ye?"

"No, of course not. Do come in." She stood aside to let him enter and closed the door. "As for not admitting you, Donald, she gave me no such instructions. I don't think Isabel expected you to follow her."

"She *dinna?* Then the woman's a greater gowk than I thought. She could nae ha'e expected me t' merely let her *be!"*

"I expect she thought you'd be too busy with your patients to notice she'd gone."

The doctor grimaced. "Dinna *you* start t' fall out wi' me. Where *is* the woman? Still abed?"

"I wish you will stop calling her 'the woman.' She has a name, you know. You can even call her 'dearie.'"

"I'll call her what I please, the flicherin' female. Will ye call her doon, or shall I seek her out mysel'?"

"She's gone out, I'm afraid. I was just on my way to find her when you arrived."

"Find her? Why?"

Meg made a little, helpless gesture with her arm. "I don't know how I permitted matters to get so out-of-hand. I didn't think she'd even consider doing such a thing without at least discussing it properly—"

"Michty me, lass, what's amiss? Has my wife done something *else* throughthither and witless?"

"I don't know. Perhaps I'm foolish to be concerned. She's gone to the fair they've set up on the river."

"Fair? Do ye mean that curriebunction I noticed frae the bridge? Good God!" He stared at Meg a moment, shook his head and turned abruptly to the door.

"Donald," Meg objected, putting a hand on his arm, "where are you going?"

"T' find her, o' course."

"But in all that crowd...you'll never—"

"Set yer mind easy, lass. I'll find her."

"Then I'm going with you," Meg insisted, running out the door after him.

"Nae, lass, you wait here. I'll do better by mysel'." He ran down the steps and jumped up on the carriage he'd left waiting down below. "If, by some mishanter, I should miss her," he shouted as he picked up the reins, "you, lass, keep her here 'til I come back even if ye must strap her doon!"

Chapter Twenty

Meg paced about the sitting room, beset with unaccustomed anxiety. While one part of her mind told her that it was unlikely that the day's adventure would bring harm to her aunt, another part concocted frightening visions of robberies, accidents and other shadowy misfortunes. *Mishanters,* Dr. Fraser had called them. Dr. Fraser, too, could fall victim to some such disaster in the midst of the mayhem and confusion that were characteristic of public gatherings. And, worse, the ice could crack and . . . but it didn't bear thinking of. How would she endure the suspense until they returned?

When in the early afternoon the door knocker sounded again, Meg flew to open it, not waiting for Maynard to make his way up from below. It might be Isabel returning, perhaps even holding her Donald by the arm. A reconciliation between them would do much to raise Meg's long-depressed spirits. But it was not Isabel at the door. It was Mortimer.

He walked in with all the aplomb of a lifelong intimate. "Knew I'd find you alone," he said with a smirk, strolling into the sitting room and throwing his greatcoat over a chair.

"Really, Mortimer, I must ask you not to make yourself at home today. I am in no condition to entertain visitors." She took a stance in the doorway to make it clear that she wanted him to leave at once.

"Daresay," he agreed, grinning at her like the proverbial cat digesting a very delicious canary. "Worrying about our situation, no doubt. No need for it, assure you. Not any more." With these cryptic words scarcely out of his mouth, he came up to her, lifted her high against his chest and whirled her around the room in a spirit of elated exhuberance.

"*Mortimer,*" she gasped, "have you lost your *mind?* Put me down!"

"No reason to put up a fuss, my dear. No reason in the world. Needn't feel the least twinge of shame, even if the butler sees us. Or your aunt. Or *anyone.*"

"Mortimer, I don't wish to make a scene, but if you don't put me down I shall *scream!*"

With a shrug of reluctant acquiescence, he set her on her feet. "Hang it, Meg, no need to kick up a dust. Perfectly respectable now, you see. The thing's *done.*"

She pressed a hand to her breast and tried to calm herself. "You do have the most *incoherent* way of speaking, Mortimer. *What* thing is done?"

"The betrothal. Mine and Trixie's. All over with!"

Meg turned pale. "What are you talking about? It *couldn't* be!"

He chortled at her patent disbelief. "Knew it'd surprise you. Came right over soon as the news was out."

"But you're not making any sense. Sometimes, Mortimer, I get the oddest feeling that you and I speak in different languages. *What* news is out?"

"About Trixie. Released me from my pledge, as easy as *that.*" He snapped his fingers.

"But when? How? She's been up in her room all . . . I think I'd better sit down and let you explain everything to me from the beginning."

"Yes, but first . . ." He pulled her into his arms with a grip of iron and leered down at her. "Been waiting for the chance to do this ever since your aunt interrupted us," he said, gloating.

"Mortimer, no!" But she was unable to stop him. He locked his mouth on hers so tightly that she could scarcely breathe. She pushed against his chest with all her strength, but it had no effect. He was like an ox. So intent was he in his purpose that he even forgot to worry about his shirt-points. If she weren't so completely furious with him, she would have found it amusing to realize that she'd had so strong an effect on him that he was willing to bend the points in this heedless way. But this drawn-out and presumptuous embrace was not amusing, and she could hardly wait for him to release her so that she could smash the nearest vase over his head.

There was a cough from the doorway. Mortimer lifted his head but didn't release his hold. Meg, feeling helplessly humiliated by being caught in this hideous embrace, hoped desperately that the person in the doorway would be the finally awakened Trixie. But the cough had been deep and masculine, and when she glanced, wincing, over her shoulder at the doorway, she was not really surprised to see an embarrassed Maynard standing there staring at her. The real jolt came a fraction of a second later, when she caught a glimpse of a man standing *behind* Maynard. But no . . . it couldn't be!

"I'm sorry, my lady," Maynard mumbled awkwardly, "but this gentleman insisted—"

"I had no *idea*, of course," the gentleman said in icy disdain, crossing the threshold of the room, "that I would be interrupting so intimate a scene."

"Geoffrey!" Meg gasped, wishing the floor would open and swallow her up.

His eyes were blazing, and his lips were set in a tight line. "I would, in ordinary circumstance, make an immediate withdrawal and leave you to your . . . er . . . *activities*, but unless I'm mistaken, the fellow so awkwardly embracing you is *my sister's husband.*"

"I am *not!*" Mortimer exclaimed sullenly, dropping his hold on Meg and taking an instinctive step backward.

Geoffrey (who did indeed look threatening with his greatcoat flapping open, his hair tousled, his boots muddied and a riding crop held carelessly in his left hand) grew pale at Mortimer's words. "You . . . haven't *married* her?" he asked, aghast. "Why, you repulsive whelp, I'll—"

"Don't, Geoffrey," Meg said, stepping between them. "There's no need to look so stricken. Trixie has been staying with *me* all this time. There's been no impropriety, I promise you, either before or during her stay with me."

Confused, Geoffrey glanced from Meg to Mortimer and back again. "Do you mean she's been here from . . . from the *first?*"

Meg nodded. "As soon as she learned that the Justice of the Peace would not permit the marriage, she came straight here . . . with her abigail."

Geoffrey shut his eyes and took a breath of intense relief. "Thank God," he muttered, turning away and wandering absently across the room, his instinct leading him to the fire. "I've been so distraught," he said quietly, leaning exhaustedly against the mantelpiece. "I'd searched everywhere . . . every inn and hostelry in Yorkshire . . . then all the way to Gretna without finding a trace. At times, I wanted that fellow's neck in my bare hands with such . . . !" He shook his head, smiling bitterly at the memory of his own useless rage. "At other times . . . well, I would have been grateful just to learn that she was alive. Finally, when it occurred to me that they might have come to you, I couldn't wait to . . . But the snow came, and it was days before I could get through. And then to find you in—"

He stopped himself and looked up. Meg met his eyes, for a moment ready to launch into a tearful explanation of her behavior. But there was something in his look, something so cold and disdainful, that she wanted to slap him. *Let him believe what he pleases*, she said to herself furiously. *And to think that I'm in this fix for his sake!*

For a frozen moment neither of them moved. Mortimer, still apprehensive of Geoffrey's temper, stayed quietly in the background. At last Geoffrey spoke. "May I see my sister now?"

"Of course," Meg said, making her voice as cold as his. "I'll tell Maynard to inform her that you're here." She went to the bellpull. "I don't know why she hasn't risen yet. It's not like her to stay abed so late."

Mortimer was making strange motions and hand-signals at her. The gestures were so ludicrously broad that Geoffrey's attention was caught at once. "I think your . . . er . . . Mr. Lazenby is trying to tell you something, ma'am," he said drily.

"He is not *my* Mr. Lazenby," Meg muttered savagely. "What is it, Mortimer? What are you trying to say?"

"Not sleeping, you know. Not in her room."

"What?"

"Trixie. Not up in her room," Mortimer declared firmly.

"What do you mean? Of course she's—"

Maynard reappeared in the doorway. "Did you ring, my lady?"

After throwing Lazenby a last, puzzled look, Meg turned to the butler. "Will you ask Miss Beatrix to come downstairs, please, Maynard."

"But Miss Beatrix has gone out."

"Gone out? How could she—? When?"

"Early this morning, my lady. With your aunt and Mr. Steele. Mr. Lazenby was with them also, I believe."

Meg, astounded and angry, nodded to Maynard that she had no further need of him and turned to Mortimer. "Do you mean to say you took her to the *fair?* After all that I *said* on the subject?"

Mortimer shrugged. "Said she was a free adult. Not my place to argue."

Meg, with real effort, smothered her chagrin. "It seems, Geoffrey, that I've been laboring all day under a misapprehension," she said, her mouth tight with suppressed indignation. "Your sister has gone to a fair. The Frost Fair. It's being held on the ice, right on the Thames."

"I see." Geoffrey eyes her shrewdly. "I take it she went without your approval?"

Meg would have liked to kick at the walls in frustration. She'd tried so hard to behave in a way that would earn his approval, and not one of her efforts had turned out well. Her eyes flickered to the ground. "I didn't think you'd wish her to attend such a gathering," she admitted.

"So you, too, have been finding her difficult to manage," he said with a touch of wry amusement. "I suppose this means I had better take myself over there and attempt to rescue her from whatever scrape she may have tumbled into." He turned to the door, but before he reached it, he stopped and turned back. "I hope you don't mind my asking, but I find myself confused by the romantic little scene I witnessed on my arrival. Is my sister still expecting to marry you, Lazenby? Do you consider yourselves betrothed?"

"No," Mortimer said with obvious satisfaction. "Released me, Trixie did. Betrothed to Meg now."

"Mortimer, I *never*—" Meg cried, outraged.

"Are you indeed? To *Meg?*" His tone was icy with revulsion and scorn. "What an astounding turnabout, my dear. Once you thought of him as a foolish coxcomb, and now you're betrothed. What miracles love can inspire!"

She flashed him a searing glance. "Don't be a clunch! You can't seriously believe that I intend to—"

"I believe that you women are capable of all sorts of idiotic behavior."

"I say!" Mortimer interjected in offense, "you can't speak to my Meg that way!"

"Dash it all, Mortimer, I am *not your Meg!* And please stay out of this!"

Geoffrey eyed Mortimer with teeth clenched and fists curling. "Forgive me, ma'am, for indulging in fisticuffs in your charming sitting room, but this fellow has had this coming to him for a long time."

He pulled off his gloves and cast them, with his riding crip, into Meg's hands. Then, in two quick strides, he came up to Mortimer and grasped the bewildered fellow's neckcloth with his left hand. Holding him firmly at arm's length, he swung his right fist—in a motion so swift that Meg's eyes were not able to see the movement—and smashed it against Mortimer's chin.

Meg screamed. Mortimer staggered backward, stumbled, pushed over a chair and crashed to the ground. He lay in an awkward sprawl, completely unmoving, a small trickle of blood beginning to seep from a cut in his lip.

"Oh, my God, you've killed him!" Meg muttered in agony.

"No, I haven't. A little splash of cold water to the face should bring him round. If he *is* your betrothed, my dear, I'm truly sorry. But it was something I couldn't resist."

"He is *not* my betrothed," she declared tearfully, kneeling down beside the fallen Mortimer and looking at him worriedly for signs of life, "but that doesn't mean I wish to see him *mauled.*"

"If he's not your betrothed, then why was he kissing you?" Geoffrey demanded, reaching down and taking his gloves— which she'd forgotten she still clutched in her hand—from her grasp.

"It's none of your affair," she said in angry pride.

"No, it's not. But I wager, ma'am," he smiled grimly as he went to the door, "that it'll be at least a month before he'll be able to do it again."

She listened to his step retreating down the hall and to the slam of the door behind him. He was gone from her life *again*. Why hadn't she considered the possibility that he would come to search for his sister? If she'd had the sense to anticipate the possibility, she might have been better prepared for him. She might have been ready to receive him like a confident, sensible, serene lady-of-the-house, the sort of person she'd always believed she was. Why was it that whenever he was around to observe her, she behaved like a bubble-headed, blundering, graceless, indiscriminate wet-goose?

Two fat tears dribbled down her cheeks and splashed into her lap. She lifted her hand and brushed away the dampness from her cheeks, but she felt her eyes fill up again. It wasn't at all kind of the Fates to have compelled her to endure that scene. Her heart had been broken by Geoffrey Carrier once before . . . did she have to go through it twice?

"Are you all right, your ladyship?" Maynard asked from the doorway. "Shall I try to restore Mr. Lazenby to his senses?"

Meg wiped her eyes with the back of her hand and squared her shoulders. "Yes, thank you, Maynard. Bring me some wet cloths, if you please. And . . . do you think perhaps a sip of brandy might be efficacious?"

Maynard came into the room, righting the furniture as he approached. He looked down at the prostrate Mortimer thoughtfully. "Brandy will be just the thing," he said impassively. "I'll get a glass at once."

He turned to go, but not before Meg noticed a slight twitch of his lips. "It seems that Mr. Lazenby," the butler remarked with what she suspected was a touch of glee, "is not very handy with his fives."

Whatever the butler's private feelings toward Mortimer might have been, he did not reveal them again. Within five minutes, he'd brought the fellow round and helped him to stretch out on the sofa. After leaving Meg with a supply of wet cloths to be applied to the gentleman's chin, he bowed himself out. Meg took a seat beside Mortimer on the sofa and carefully pressed one of the cloths to the area on his face which was already discolored and swelling. "There . . . is that better?" she asked soothingly.

"Shan't be able to eat for weeks," poor Mortimer mumbled. "Damned bruiser!"

"Well, you did abscond with his sister, you know. You

can't blame him for wishing to wreak a measure of revenge."

"If he hadn't taken me by surprise, I'd have shown him! If I'd have known what he was about, I'd have planted *him* a facer he'd not soon forget."

"Yes, yes, don't take on so," Meg said, patting his shoulder. "There's no use getting upset about it now."

"Don't believe me, do you? But I've done a round with Robert Gregson, and he, you know, was the Lancashire Giant."

"Mortimer, let's not talk about fighting any more. I'd rather hear about what occurred between you and Trixie. Are you feeling well enough to talk about it?"

"Nothing to talk about. She released me from the betrothal, that's all."

"Today? At the fair?"

"Yes."

"But wasn't it a bit sudden? Didn't you ask her why?"

"Didn't need to. Plain as pikestaff why."

"Is it? It's not at all plain to me."

"Intends to wed someone else, that's why."

"Someone else?" Meg rose to her feet and gaped down at him. "But . . . whom? She hasn't been able to meet anyone since she arri—Oh, good God! Don't tell me she's already become enamoured of someone she met on the *ice!*"

"No, of course not. It's Steele."

"Arthur?" Meg sank down upon the sofa again, feeling her knees give way under her. "You don't mean it!"

"Happy as grigs, the two of em. Word of honor!"

Meg could only stare at Mortimer in complete stupefaction. Trixie and Arthur! It was a pairing that had never occurred to her. Arthur was at least ten years Trixie's senior and had never seemed to be taken with girlishness. And as for Trixie, one would have thought she would prefer a handsome boy . . . like Mortimer. Why, with Arthur, Trixie would find herself being watched over as closely as she'd been by her brother!

But the more she thought about it, the sounder the match seemed. Arthur was, at bottom, a perfectly sensible man. His income was substantial and his character firm. And Trixie was probably attracted to him for the very reason that she resisted her brother—he would look after her and protect her. The difference would be, of course, that when she really wanted her own way, she would be able to twist poor Arthur round her little finger.

She smiled gleefully. What a marvelous solution to the problem! Even Geoffrey would have to agree that it was a wonderful match. And even though she hadn't suspected that the romance was brewing, the match *had* come to pass under her own roof, and she intended to take full credit for it. Now Geoffrey did have cause to be grateful to her!

Unless he found Trixie at the fair, snatched her away and dragged her home. Good Lord, that mustn't happen! She turned to Mortimer, grasped his hand and pulled him abruptly to a sitting position. "Mortimer, are you feeling well enough to get up?"

"Right now?"

"Yes. Right at this moment."

He touched his jaw gingerly. "I suppose so. Why?"

"Because, you see, I want you to take me to the fair."

Chapter Twenty-One

Geoffrey climbed out of his carriage at the north end of Black-friar's Bridge and gave his tiger instructions to stable the horses for two hours. He then turned and took a place among the numbers of people who lined the bridge from one end to the other to watch the scene below. It was an oddly colorfully sight that in some strange way moved him. The Frost Fair seemed to him a rather inelegant but eloquent testimony to man's ingenuity. Nature had provided, with little warning, this temporarily habitable surface, and Man had promptly climbed upon it and put it to use.

Below him, a roadway had been marked out leading down the center of the river all the way to London Bridge. Rough tents had been erected all along this Grand Mall on the ice, made of light materials that could be easily and cheaply assembled and just as easily dismantled when the thaw came.

Business was booming. Thousands of people thronged the road, stopping at the booths to eat, drink, dance and play. He could read some of the gaudy signs that identified the rickety structures: HORN'S TAVERN BOOTH; LOTTERY; SKITTLE ALLEY; OYSTERS HERE; THOMAS THAMES, PRINTING.

Men, women and children in all manner of dress and condition cavorted together in apparent harmony, sending up a din that seemed to tinkle with merriment in the icy air. Trumpets blared, and various stringed and horned instruments mixed with the human voices, the music evidently providing encouragement for many enterprising, irrepressible couples to dance. The sounds, the color, the movement were joyously festive, as if the merrymakers were telling a cruel Father Frost that the human spirit would not be crushed.

Two men in rough clothing, with ragged mufflers tied round their heads to protect their ears, jostled for a place beside Geoffrey on the balustrade. "Wut do ye think, guv?" asked one cheerfully. "When the tide rises, do the 'ole bloomin' ice shelf rise wi' it? Or did it freeze at the 'igh point?"

"I tell ye, Jeddie, it *couldn't* freeze at the 'igh point," the other argued, "'cause then at *low* tide, there'd be a *space* underneath, wouldn't there? Do ye think the ice would 'old all that weight if there wuz nuthin' but space underneath?"

"But the ice's pretty thick, ain't it? Wut do ye think, guv?"

Geoffrey smiled in appreciation of the complexity and logic of the problem they'd put to him in such simple terms. "It's a very good question," he said, "but I have no idea of the answer. I'm not a man of science, you see."

They discussed the question at length, but Geoffrey eventually excused himself, saying that he wanted to walk on the ice but that if he listened to them much longer he'd be too terrified to venture out.

Down below, milling about among the crowds, he found the noise more deafening and less pleasant. But the smells were delicious now. There at his right, someone had built a fire and was roasting a lamb whole. He walked up to watch.

"Ye can 'ave a slice fer a shillin', guv. It's right tasty."

"No, thank you," Geoffrey said.

"Then it'll be sixpence fer watchin'," the meatseller insisted. "Watchin' ain't fer free."

Geoffrey grinned, shrugged and threw the fellow a coin

before walking on. To his left was a baker's booth, and the smell of gingerbread tantalized his nose. A woman walked by shouting "Brandy balls . . . hot! Brandy balls!"

The crowd pressed in on him and milled around him in such numbers that he began to lose hope of discovering his sister in the crush. There were all sorts in the crowd—dandies with elegant ladies on their arms, lightskirts, beggars, a few uniformed soldiers, sporting men, working men, and women with youngsters in their arms or hanging onto their skirts. Over to his left, an enterprising person had set up a swing on which laughing ladies could ride up in the air and dangle their legs over the people below for ten pence for two minutes.

He walked along enjoying the sight of the barber-in-the-ice, the bookseller-on-the-ice and the tavern-on-the-ice. It was wonderful how city tradesmen whose businesses had probably been sluggish had simply packed up their wares or the tools of their trades and brought them to where people had gathered. It bouyed up one's spirit to see their enterprise. They'd managed to pull out a few days of prosperity from the misfortune of the cold.

Too soon he realized that more than an hour had passed since he'd dismissed his tiger, and still he'd had no glimpse of a familiar face in all the throng. He would have to turn back before long. But not before he paid a visit to the Printing booth.

The sign THOMAS THAMES, PRINTING had intrigued him from his first glimpse of it. Had a printer really dragged his press upon the ice? Apparently he had, for Geoffrey had noticed a number of people carrying slips of paper bearing their names printed in large letters, with the words PRINTED ON THE ICE THIS NINTH DAY OF JANUARY, 1814 engraved below. The fellow calling himself by the temporary but appropriate name "Thomas Thames" was probably taking a great risk by hauling the press out here, but it was likely that his earnings in the few days of the fair's existence would be more than he'd see for the rest of the year.

Geoffrey's surmises proved to be true, for the Printing booth was one of the busiest of all, with a line of potential customers waiting patiently for their turn to see their names printed on paper to take home with them as substantial evidence that they'd been present at this noteworthy event. He was just about to take a peep inside, curious to see the size of the press that was noisily working away, when someone familiar emerged from the booth.

"Dr. *Fraser!* And *Isabel!*" he shouted.

"Michty me, it's Geoffrey!" the doctor chortled.

"Geoffrey!" Isabel squealed in delight. "Isn't this wonderful? What are you doing here? This has been the most amazing day. First I came upon *this* great gowk, and now *you!*"

"I don't understand," Geoffrey said, puzzled. "Do you mean that Fraser was not with you at the *start* of this expedition?"

"Oh, dear, no." Isabel's eyes twinkled with excitement. "When we started out this morning, I thought Donald was sulking all alone in Yorkshire."

"Aye," the doctor nodded and glared down at the little lady clinging to his arm, "this pernickity woman ran off days ago."

"Ran off? Isabel, I don't believe it of you!" Geoffrey chided.

"Well, it's all ended well," Isabel said, beaming. "I can't wait to tell Meg that my mulish husband has hired himself an *assistant* . . . and all for my sake!"

"But, Geoffrey, lad, ye'll no ha'e a mind fer this chatterin'. Tell us what brings *you* here."

"I'm looking for my sister. Wasn't she supposed to be with you, Isabel?"

"Yes, she was . . . and *is*. She and Arthur are right there behind you, in the printer's booth. I wonder what's taking them so long."

Geoffrey turned round just in time to see Trixie and Arthur emerge from the tent. Trixie was absorbed in studying the newly printed paper in her hand, but Arthur caught sight of Geoffrey at once and stopped short. "I say," he muttered in an undervoice, "isn't that your brother?"

Trixie looked up, gasped and turned quite pale. A wave of guilt (for her elopement had begun to seem, in the past few days, more and more foolish) swept over her. Geoffrey was probably furious with her, and the fact that she was ready at last to agree with him did not make it easier to face him. She wanted very much to flee.

But Arthur was holding her firmly by the arm. "Don't be frightened, my love," he muttered. "He won't dare to scold you . . . not while I'm here."

Geoffrey, however, didn't look very forbidding. He was smiling at his sister with surprising warmth. "Don't look like a frightened little rabbit, Trix," he said heartily. "I've looked for you for too long not to feel anything but relief at seeing you at last."

With those reassuring words, he opened his arms, and she threw herself into his embrace like a lost child who'd found its mother. "Oh, Geoffrey," she murmured tearfully, "I am *so* glad to see you!"

Then everybody began to speak at once, trying to tell him all the exciting news which had transpired since Trixie's arrival in London. It was all a jumble in Geoffrey's ears, but he did grasp enough of their chatter to discover that, although she'd freed herself from her entanglement with Lazenby, she had already become involved with someone else. With, of all people, Meg's Arthur Steele.

As the five of them walked along with the milling crowds, Geoffrey studied Steele carefully. He remembered the man quite well from their earlier encounter, but at that time, believing Steele was romantically connected with Meg, Geoffrey had viewed him with eyes of extravagant jealousy. Now, however, the man gave a very different impression. He was older than any of Trixie's previous flirts and seemed a great deal more substantial. And he was not particularly handsome, a fact which Geoffrey found very encouraging. If Trixie cared for the fellow, at least it was not for so superficial a reason as appearance. He would reserve judgment for a while, of course, but there was every reason to hope that Trixie had made a good choice at last.

Asking the others to excuse them for a few minutes, Geoffrey took his sister's arm and walked ahead of the rest of the party. "Steele seems a solid sort, Trix," Geoffrey said bluntly, "but I can't feel comfortable about the suddenness with which you flit from one love to the next. Are you sure you're not making another hasty decision?"

"Perhaps I am," she answered thoughtfully, taking his arm in companionable intimacy. It was the first time she and Geoffrey had embarked on a discussion of her affairs which was amicable rather than argumentative. It gave the girl a very pleasant feeling. "I know I've been acquainted with him for only a short time. But it seems as if I've known him forever. We are so *comfortable* together, and he has a way of making me feel merry all the time. Do *you* think I'm being hasty?"

"Well, you've known him less than a fortnight. That certainly seems hasty to me. How long did it take from the time you met until he offered for you—one hour?"

She giggled. "He made the offer *today!* It was the *sweetest* thing. Arthur had bought me a pie from a pieman, and it was hot and very syrupy, and when I'd taken a bite of it, some of the syrup seeped out and dropped upon Mortimer's boot. Oh, did I forget to tell you Mortimer was with us? Well, he was, and when the syrup dripped on his boot, he was furious with me! You'd have thought I'd stained his *breeches*—which would have been very much worse, of course, and one couldn't have blamed him *then* if he'd carried on and sulked like a baby—but it was only his boot, and anyone could see that the syrup could be wiped away without a bit of trouble. But Mortimer grumbled and complained and said that I'd ruined his shine and kept on and *on* about it until I was on the edge of tears. Well, Arthur took me aside and tried to comfort me and asked how I could wish to marry such a foppish jackstraw. And I said I didn't know, and that I'd probably made a terrible mistake, as my brother had been warning me for ever and ever, but that a girl has to marry *somebody.* And he said, then why not marry *me,* and he explained that he'd been completely taken with me from the first night when I'd arrived at Meg's, and then I said that I'd been taken with *him,* too, and... well... he kissed me and here we are!"

Geoffrey shook his head, both amused and appalled. *Are all the important decisions of one's life,* he wondered inwardly, *determined by such trivial turns?* But aloud he only laughed and said, "That is undoubtedly one of the great love stories of our time."

They walked on for a while in friendly silence. "But tell me, my dear," he asked after a time, "how did Lazenby react when you informed him of your change of heart?"

Trixie halted in surprise. "How did you know I had told him?"

"Well, you see, I...er...ran into him earlier this afternoon. He informed me that you were no longer betrothed. He seemed rather unaffected by your blow, I thought."

"Yes, that's the most amazing thing. I hope you won't repeat this to anyone else, Geoffrey, for it is quite a comedown for me, I can tell you. There I was, in a tizzy of fear about telling him, but Arthur, you know, insisted that I must do it at once, and so I did. But Mortimer . . . well, he seemed *glad* that I cried off. Isn't it astounding?"

"Perhaps not so astounding," Geoffrey said, keeping his eyes fixed on her face, "for when I saw him, he told me he was betrothed to Meg."

Trixie's mouth dropped open. "To Meg? But . . . that's impossible!"

"Why impossible?"

"Well, for one thing, I only cried off a few *hours* ago . . ."

"Perhaps our Mortimer moves quickly."

"I tell you, Geoffrey, it's utterly impossible! You couldn't have understood him correctly."

Geoffrey was not quite ready to believe her. "It seems to me, my dear, that with females—especially in matters of the heart—nothing is impossible."

"But Meg doesn't even *like* him. Arthur told me that Mortimer sets Meg's *teeth* on edge."

Geoffrey felt as if a weight he'd been carrying inside his chest had suddenly lightened. "I see. Well, then, I must have been mistaken."

"Of *course* you were. Meg would *never* marry a twiddle-poop like Mortimer. When she marries, it will be someone like . . . like . . ."

Geoffrey watched his sister's face with fascination. "Like whom?"

Trixie knit her brow and pursed her lips in deep concentration, trying to conjure up a picture of a man admirable enough and suitable enough for Lady Meg. "Like a . . . a . . . King's minister . . . or a duke . . ."

Geoffrey smiled wryly. "Is *that* what you think . . . that only a minister or a duke will do for her?"

"Well, at least it would have to be somebody for whom she has a high regard . . . like *you*."

"Me? Aren't you pouring the butter sauce a bit thickly, my girl?"

"Oh, I didn't mean that she'd consider you *specifically* as a husband—although now I come to think of it, I don't know why she shouldn't, for you're quite good looking when you don't glower, you know—but I meant you merely as an *example*, you see, of someone for whom she has particular esteem."

Geoffrey knew perfectly well that this sort of conversation was quite beneath him, but he couldn't for the life of him resist going on with it. "What makes you think that she holds me in particular esteem?" he asked with the elaborate casualness of a twelve-year-old boy trying to prove to the pretty girl-next-door that he doesn't care for her a whit.

"It's obvious," Trixie said earnestly. "She's forever saying things to me like, 'I don't think Geoffrey would like that,' or 'Are you sure that your brother would approve?' Why, even yesterday she refused to permit me to come to the fair because she said she'd be afraid to face you if I should come to grief."

"Yes, but none of that sounds as if I'm a pattern card of estimable manhood, just somebody who inspires fear. However, I think it's time to turn the subject. I'd like to know, girl, why you are here if Meg refused to permit you to come?"

Trixie glanced at him askance and then hung her head. "I ran off. I was very rude to Meg, too. Do you think she'll be very angry with me?"

"I'm sure I couldn't say. But I hope, Trixie, that you'll tell her that you're very sorry and, for whatever time you remain under her roof, that you'll respect her wishes. She's a person of considerable good sense, and you'd do well to heed her."

They rejoined the others, and Geoffrey offered to take them up in his carriage and deposit them all at Dover Street. "Oh, no, Geoffrey," Trixie cried. "We haven't yet seen all the booths!"

"She's right, you know," Isabel agreed. "There's so much to see."

"But aren't you all frozen? Your noses are all red and your eyes are tearing."

"Aye, but we can warm oursel's at the fire owre yont," Fraser pointed out, eager as a child to enjoy this unexpected outing.

Geoffrey shrugged. "Very well, then, I'll say goodbye. I expect that we'll meet again before I return to Yorkshire. I'm staying at the Fenton, if you should have need of me, Trixie."

He walked back toward Blackfriar's Bridge through the crowd without taking any note of the colorful surroundings that had so fascinated him a short while before. His mind was troubling him with a peculiar sort of unease. The feeling was completely unwarranted, for the problem which had brought him so far from home seemed to have been very satisfactorily solved. But the sense of having left some important business unfinished was very strong.

He couldn't fool himself. It was Meg on his mind. She'd been lodged there making him uncomfortable ever since his carriage had taken her out of his life two months before. All through the dreariest November he'd ever experienced, all through the weeks of searching for his sister, Meg's face had haunted his dreams and her memory had clouded his days. He had to see her again. He had no idea of what could come of the meeting, but he knew that *something* between them had to be resolved.

It was foolish to hope that the resolution would be pleasant. She was an unpredictable female whose relationships with men were beyond his understanding. But he couldn't deny the strength of his feelings for her. And at Knight's Haven he'd believed that she'd seemed to care for him with a rather noticeable intensity. If he could somehow revive that feeling . . . if he could convince her, as he'd lately convinced himself, that they belonged together . . .

He raised the collar of his coat against the icy blast of the wind and trudged on through the crowd, letting himself dream of the happy possibilities. If he could convince her to accept him, they could be married by special license in three days, and he might be able to bear her off with him to Yorkshire before the week was out! The prospect made his heart pound with a kind of delirious excitement. But he was being unbelievably foolish. She would probably not have him at all.

Nevertheless, he would try. He'd drive back to her house at once. And he would tell her, without roundaboutation, that he loved her to distraction. Even if she laughed at him . . . even if she told him *again* that what had passed between them at Knight's Haven had only been a game (and he fully expected such a response), he would at least feel the satisfaction of having declared himself, of having mustered the courage (which he'd not been able to do before) to face defeat.

With the blood racing in his veins, he quickened his pace. In less than an hour he would see her again. Even if it turned out to be a last look, he wanted once more to see those taunting brown eyes, that freckled nose, her unruly hair . . .

Suddenly he stopped in his tracks, squinting in amazed distraction at a woman standing directly in his line of vision. It was as if the creature had materialized out of his thoughts,

for although her back was to him, the hood of her dark cloak
had fallen back to reveal a tousled head of magnificent hair,
the same hair he'd just been dreaming of. Even from the back,
the identity of the woman was unmistakable. No one else carried herself with quite the same proud set of the shoulders; no
one else cocked her head at quite the same angle; no one else
had hair of quite that magic fire. It was Meg, right here at the
fair . . . and standing not twenty yards away from him.

Chapter Twenty-Two

The sparkle of the late afternoon sunshine, bouncing off the ice and dazzling her eyes, was just one of the delights that set Meg's blood tingling as she stepped out on the frozen river and mingled with the roistering crowds. There was the nip of the cold, the sounds of excited revelry, the color of flags and scarves and mufflers and skirts and headgear. And there was music, and the smell of gingerbread, and the piercing gaiety of women's laughter.

But there was also Mortimer, whose escort had been required but whose presence was enough to drain the joy from the atmosphere. He had been persisting, ever since they'd set out, to challenge her refusal to admit her affection for him. "But I *don't* love you, Mortimer," she'd declared repeatedly. "I know I said I like you, but even *that* was an exaggeration, and even if I'd meant it, *liking* is far from *loving*."

But Mortimer, despite the various setbacks he'd suffered in the last few hours (setbacks which would have sent lesser mortals into paroxysms of self-castigation), had not seemed to sustain any injury to his remarkable self-confidence. He simply attributed Meg's disclaimers to the tendency of London ladies to be coy. "Aware it's much too soon for a lady like yourself to admit her feelings, my dear," he said, doggedly perservering, "but at least tell me that you'll accept me in due course."

She groaned in irritation. "I've told you too many times already that I will *never*, under any possible circumstances, accept an offer from you. Now, *please*, let's concentrate on looking for anyone in our party. You look to the right and I'll watch the left."

"Seems to me to be the outside of enough to have been battered and bruised today," he muttered, feeling his jaw gingerly to see if the swelling had gone down, "without having you play these coquettish games with me."

"Confound it, Mortimer, you are being deucedly exasperating! I am not being coquettish. I mean what I say. Now, either talk about something else or be silent!"

They walked on, Mortimer in petulant silence and Meg watching the activities about her with wide-eyed pleasure. "Oh, look!" she exclaimed. "There's a puppet theater! I do so love a puppet play, don't you? Too bad we haven't time to stop and watch. But perhaps later . . ."

She began to realize she'd been much too missish with Trixie when she'd denied her permission to go to the fair, for it seemed, now, to be safe enough. The ice felt solidly thick beneath her feet, the amusements neither corrupting nor overly vulgar, and the people not in the least menacing. She smiled at a little boy standing before a cook-tent, greedily licking his fingers after having devoured some favorite treat like chopped anchovies mixed with bacon grease and spread on bread, or a bit of liver sausage. If the fair was suitable for children, surely she'd been overly solicitous to ban Trixie.

After a quarter-hour of searching the faces of the passersby, Meg began to feel discouraged. "Do you think we'll ever find them in this crush?" she asked Mortimer, her excitement beginning to dim.

"Might find 'em at the skittle alley. Your aunt said this morning that she wanted a chance to knock down the ninepins before the day was out."

Meg brightened at once. "Let's go there, then. Perhaps we'll be in luck."

But Mortimer hung back stubbornly. "Not yet. Won't budge until I've had a proper word from you."

"If you've returned to the subject of a match between us, Mortimer Lazenby, I shall explode! You've heard my answer, and I don't intend to change it by so much as a syllable!"

"Won't move from this spot until you do," he said petulantly, crossing his arms over his chest and looking mulish.

She wanted to give him a shaking. Not only was he conceited and overbearing, but he hadn't any manners. "Very well, sir, if that's your intention, I shall go off without you. And if I come to harm, you'll have only yourself to blame." And she started off toward the distant booth which bore the sign reading SKITTLE ALLEY.

Mortimer was not so uncouth that he would forget his obligations as escort. He ran after her, caught her by the arms and swung her around to face him. "Dash it all, Meg," he muttered, holding her arms tightly and shaking her so roughly that the hood of her cloak fell back and her loosely pinned hair tumbled down, "don't push me too far. Dangerous fellow if I'm enraged. Ask anyone in Yorkshire."

"Mortimer, release your grip on my arms at once," she said icily.

"Warn you, Meg. *Dangerous!*"

"If you don't let me go, and *at once*, I'll . . . I'll . . ."

"You'll send for some assistance," came a calm voice behind her. Geoffrey's voice.

Oh, no, she said to herself, wincing. Why was it that he never seemed to come upon her when she was in a position of dignity? She had been searching for him ever since her arrival at the fair, eagerly seeking his eye and feeling perfectly adequate to stand up to his most critical scrutiny. Only *this instant,* when the nauseating Mortimer had taken her in his grip and disturbed her equilibrium, her temper and her hair, was the *one moment* when she was not prepared, and, of course, he had to appear. Some God was laughing at her; some mischievous Fate was using her for his entertainment. "Geoffrey," she said in an effort to exhibit breeding in the midst of embarrassment, "how fortunate that you happened along."

"Yes, I see it is," Geoffrey said, looking at Mortimer so threateningly that the fellow dropped his hold on Meg, stepped backward and put up a hand to protect his bruised chin.

"No," Meg said quickly, "I don't mean as a defender. I can take care of myself, you know. I mean that I've been looking for you."

Geoffrey raised an eyebrow. "Have you? Then it's doubly fortunate that I happened along."

"Fortunate for *you*," Mortimer muttered sulkily, kicking at the ice in his frustration at having been interrupted.

"Oh, it's fortunate for you, too, Lazenby, I assure you. For I was sorely tempted to plant you a facer on the *other* side of your chin, but I restrained myself."

"Needn't sound so smug, you know," Mortimer said defiantly. "If I weren't bruised, I'd square up to you and tip you a settler."

"Would you indeed?" Geoffrey asked mildly.

"Handy with my fives, don't think I'm not. Been in the ring countless times. Stood up with Gregson!"

"The Lancashire Giant? Well, good for you! Then I suppose I'm fortunate that you're out of commission. But we're being rude, you know. The lady can't be enjoying sporting talk. You *did* say, Meg, that you were looking for me, didn't you? Is there any particular reason?"

Something in the gallant friendliness of his manner and a new, warm smile in his eyes as he looked at her set her pulse hammering. Nervously, she put a hand to her tumbled hair and tried to brush it back out of the way. "Yes, there *is* a reason but it's rather...er...private. Mortimer, would you very much mind if I spoke to Sir Geoffrey alone for a moment or two?"

A chill gust of wind brushed by them at that moment, and Geoffrey, not really aware of what he was doing, reached out and lifted Meg's fallen hood back in its proper place. Meg's eyes flew from Mortimer's to his in questioning gratitude.

Mortimer looked from one to the other with dawning suspicion. "Ah, so *that's* the way of things, is it? Set your sights on Carrier now, eh? That's why you've played cat-and-mouse with me!"

Meg expelled a furious breath. "Really, Mortimer, *must* you make these embarrassing outbursts? I'm completely losing my patience with you!"

"Losing *mine*, too," Mortimer countered angrily. "No need for you to say any more, Meg. Don't need to be told twice, not I! You've a new escort now, so I'll take my leave. Good day to you both."

He turned and walked stiffly away. Meg looked after him with a sigh of misgiving. "Mortimer, wait! Are you going to look for Arthur and the others?"

Mortimer stopped, turned and frowned at her in severe reproach. "No!" he shouted over the wind and the noise. "Going back to *Yorkshire*. In Yorkshire, a fellow knows where he stands!"

"Coo!" laughed a woman in the crowd, "I kin show ye where t' stand, dearie!"

There was a hoot of laughter. "We'll miss ye, chum," a man chortled. "Don' stay away too long!"

Red faced, Mortimer turned away and, while the derisive jeering rose around him, he ran off and disappeared into the crowd.

"Poor fellow," Geoffrey murmured, taking Meg's arm. "I quite feel for him."

Meg looked up at him with sardonic disdain. "Oh, you do, do you? I suppose that bruise on his face is a sign of your *sympathy?*"

"But, ma'am," he responded in injured innocence, "if I'd have known then that the boy was a victim of your—how did he put it?—cat-and-mouse games, I might never have done it. Having been one of your victims myself, you see—"

"See here, Geoffrey Carrier," she exclaimed, snatching her arm from his hold, "I've told you before that I do *not* play the sort of flirtatious games you are hinting at!"

"Never, ma'am?"

"Never!"

"I seem to remember a time not so long ago when you fluttered your eyes and made provocative remarks and used all sorts of tricks—in very expert style, I might add—to make a victim of *me.*"

Her eyes dropped down in guilty recollection. "Well, perhaps I did, but only because you deserved it."

"Yes, I probably did," he said placidly, taking her arm again and falling into step beside her. "But aren't we forgetting that you have something particular and private that you wish to discuss with me?"

"Yes, of course. I *was* forgetting, and it's the reason I came! Mortimer gave me the most astounding news, and I wanted to speak to you before you hear it from Trixie. Now, Geoffrey, I know you'll think I'm interfering in matters that are out of my province, and that the suddenness of the arrangement is only another sign of Trixie's lack of particularity, but I'm convinced that *this* time the match shows the most *promising*—"

"Are you speaking of Trixie's attachment to Arthur Steele?"

"Yes! Good heavens, how did you—Have you seen them?"

"Just a moment ago."

She stopped her strolling and looked up at him in concern. "Oh, Geoffrey, you didn't storm in and spoil things, did you?"

"When, ma'am, have I *ever* stormed in and spoiled things? Isn't it possible that I have as good an instinct as you for recognizing a man of solid worth?"

Meg blinked. If one thought about it, one might realize that *that* was a very pleasing sentence. Not only did it mean that Geoffrey approved of the match, but there was an implied compliment to herself hidden in all those words. "Oh, I'm *so* glad!" she sighed, relieved.

"Are you, Meg?" he asked, watching her closely. "I had a notion that Steele and *you* might make a match of it."

She smiled, took his arm and began to walk on. "Because of the scene that night he came to see you with Charles Isham? I'll admit that I considered the possibility briefly. But I believe that Arthur and I are both relieved at the way things have worked out, Arthur in particular. He thinks I've become a sour old maid since . . ."

"Since?" Geoffrey probed gently.

She cast a quick look at his face and then dropped her eyes. "Oh, since . . . the winter set in."

"I see. And *have* you been a sour old maid since the winter set in?"

She looked at him challengingly. "I suppose *you* would think so. All you men seem to enjoy maligning our characters when we women see fit to disagree with you."

"You are referring to me in particular, aren't you, Meg?"

"If the shoe fits . . ."

"I'm no longer certain it does fit, my dear. It's been a very long time since I really believed that your character is seriously flawed. And certainly after the very generous and thoughtful care you've taken of my sister, I would be a fool not to recognize the depth of feeling of which you're capable. Don't think that I'm not fully aware of my enormous debt to you."

"There's no need to feel indebted. I've enjoyed having Trixie with me. I never before realized how much I . . . I miss having a family of my own."

They strolled on silently, neither of them sure how to go on. Meg, on her part, wondered if she'd revealed too much. Her mention of the change in her mood since "the winter set in," and her need for a family . . . was it all too obvious? But she'd said it, and it was too late for retraction. She would simply hold her tongue and wait for a reaction from him. Meanwhile, she could walk beside him quite happily, enjoying the amber glow of the setting sun which was making a golden firmament of the ice. It suddenly occurred to her that for the past few minutes she hadn't been aware of the surroundings, of the people, the noise or the sights. Here in the midst of this extravagant, boisterous, unlikely thoroughfare, she'd been aware only of the two of them. Was that what love was—two people feeling themselves alone in a crowded world?

Geoffrey was wondering uneasily why he couldn't seem to bring himself to speak aloud the words he'd promised himself to say. There hadn't seemed to be a right time, the right words, a proper opening. For a soldier, he wasn't planning the attack with very commendable strategy. And even if the strategy had been more promising, he was enough of a soldier to know that it wouldn't work if it weren't carried out with courage. He squared his shoulder for another foray.

But before he could begin, Meg spoke. "Oh, I almost forgot. You must have seen my Aunt Bel when you found Trixie. Was Dr. Fraser with her?"

"Yes, he was, and they seem to have had a most satisfying reconciliation."

"They have? How wonderful! How did it come about? Tell me everything!"

He sighed in frustration. "I don't *know* everything, my dear. And I'd rather not talk about your aunt and the doctor right now, if you don't mind."

"Oh? Well, we needn't, then. As long as I know they're reunited, I can learn the details later. And I'd rather hear about how you think Arthur and Trixie will suit."

Geoffrey was beginning to feel dismayed. Was she hemming him in with irrelevancies because she didn't want to reopen the door he'd once closed? But he was a soldier. When hemmed in, a soldier took advantage of whatever tactical openings the situation provided and fought his way out. "Speaking of Arthur and Trixie," he said with a sudden smile, "I must admit that I'm glad *you* and he didn't make a match of it."

"Well, of course you are. If we had, Trixie might still be betrothed to Mortimer. Of course, I was hatching a plot to scotch the affair, but my scheme wasn't working very well. I was trying to prove to Trixie that the fellow was a treacherous opportunist, but—"

"Good Lord, was that why you were kissing him today?"

"Yes, of course. What did you *think* I'd been doing?"

"I was trying not to think of it at all," he admitted, telling himself that this little diversion would not seriously deflect the direction of his attack. "But to return to the subject of—"

"Of Trixie and Arthur—"

"Of why I'm glad you didn't marry him," he insisted firmly. "It's because the fellow, solid though he may be, is not good enough for you. Trixie says that only a duke or a King's minister will do for you."

"Does she really?" Meg laughed. "Then it's no *wonder* I'm still on the shelf."

There it was—the perfect opening. Geoffrey had, with artful cunning, rock-like persistence, skillful adroitness and Machiavellian guile, maneuvered the conversation to just where he wanted it. All he had to do now was make the charge. "The men of London must be idiots," he said, mustering all his courage, "to have let a woman of your attributes languish on the shelf. We Yorkshiremen, on the other hand—"

"Look, Geoffrey!" she cried, looking down the river's street with eyes that shone with excitement, at a small, crowded, colorful booth. "There's the puppet theater!"

"Wh-what?" he croaked in frustration.

"The puppet theater! Don't you love puppet plays? I wonder . . . do you think we could—?"

"But Meg, I was telling you—!"

"Yes, I know . . . some nonsense about Yorkshiremen not letting a girl of my attributes lie on the shelf. Really, Geoffrey, for a man who claims to despise flirtatious games, that is the most *blatant* sort of cajolery. If I were you, I'd go back to my old, glowering ways. These sorts of blandishments don't suit you. Now, please, would it be too much trouble to take me to see the puppets?"

While he stood gaping at her, trying to restore his shattered defenses, she laughed, slipped her arm out of his and ran toward the puppet tent. With a cry of outrage, he dashed after her and, catching up, whirled her around. "Damn you, woman," he muttered furiously, grasping her shoulders roughly, "how can you keep chattering on about puppets when I'm trying to tell you that I love you!"

"Wh . . . what?" she asked, blinking up at him open-mouthed.

"I love you! Now please pay attention, for this isn't at all easy for me to say. I probably should have waited to say this in the privacy of your sitting room, but I've launched into it now, so there's no retreat. I love you, do you understand? I've loved you since that first night in the Horse With Three Tails Inn, when I looked up at you from my table and saw that red hair of yours all lit by lamplight. Oh, good God, I sound as idiotic as my sister with her story of syrupy *pies!* Well, are you just going to stand there gaping at me, or are you going to acknowledge in some way that you've heard what I said?"

"Oh, Geoffrey!" she breathed, her eyes wide and her expression awestruck.

"Yes, that *is* my name. Is that *all* you can manage?"

"Oh, I didn't expect . . . I never dreamed . . ."

"Meg, my dear girl," he said in an agony of suspense, "I know I didn't say it at all well, but surely you've understood enough to realize that you've got to say something more!"

"Oh, Geoffrey!" Her eyes filled with tears, and with a little shiver, she threw herself into his arms. The act drew the eyes of a number of passersby, but Geoffrey, completely unheeding, tightened his hold on her and put his lips against her forehead.

"Does this mean," he asked, choked, "that you in some manner return my sentiments?"

"Oh, y-yes! Very much! More than I c-can *tell* you!"

In spite of the audience that was growing into a crowd, he bent his head and kissed her fervently. The watchers laughed and applauded, but neither of them paid any attention. It was only when a boisterous little fellow tapped Geoffrey on the shoulder and asked if he might be next in line that Geoffrey recovered his wits, took Meg by the hand and drew her away from the teasing, cheering throng.

They walked along hand in hand, using this moment of silence to permit themselves to grasp the significance of what they'd just experienced. "I suppose you realize, my dear," he said after a while, "that I've made you an offer."

"Yes," she said.

"Then you will marry me?"

"Yes."

"And . . . you're really willing to . . . give up all your London luxuries . . . the balls, the modistes, the shops, the theaters, the flirts . . . and come to live with me in Yorkshire?"

"Oh, my dear . . . yes!"

He looked down at her with a kind of startled joy. "You know, my love," he said when he could trust his voice, "I really *must* kiss you again."

The warmth of his words and his smile made her blush. "Geoffrey, you can't! We'll only attract another crowd."

"Then let's go somewhere where I can."

"But . . . I haven't yet seen the fair!" she objected.

"That's true. We mustn't miss the puppets."

"Or the gingerbread booth . . ."

"And the Prick-the-Garter," he agreed. "It would be a shame to miss that."

"And there's the Wheel of Fortune . . ."

"And the oysters . . . only sixpence the dozen . . ."

"And the skittle alley! Even Aunt Bel says one shouldn't miss the skittle alley."

He grinned down at her. "Of course one shouldn't. And the woman selling Brandy-balls, *hot* . . ."

She leaned her head on his shoulder, smiling only slightly, and pressed his hand. "It all sounds *wonderful*, Geoffrey. Let's go home!"